"SPEAK, KATRINA, SPEAK TO ME FROM BEYOND YOUR GRAVE!"

"Charlie, there's so much I want to tell you." I jumped. It was Katrina's voice. I'd recognize her anywhere, even on a poor recording.

The tape started hissing louder and louder until her words were lost. The first voice, the channeler, came back and said, "Today is the third of March. Katrina died less than twenty-four hours ago." The recording stopped and Charlie looked at me, tightly clutching the lump of gold that had been his wife's wedding ring.

"This might be a hoax," he said, sounding like a distant, hollow echo. "And then again, it might not. This woman might be able to put me in touch with Katrina just one more time. Come with me to the channeling, Peter. Please."

I should have left when I had the chance. Now I found myself agreeing to help him contact the dead.

More Peter Thorne Mysteries by
Robert E. Vardeman
from Avon Books

THE RESONANCE OF BLOOD
THE SCREAMING KNIFE

ROBERT E. VARDEMAN

AVON BOOKS ◆ NEW YORK

DEATH CHANNELS is an original publication of Avon Books. This work has never before appeared in book form. This work is a novel. Any similarity to actual persons or events is purely coincidental.

AVON BOOKS
A division of
The Hearst Corporation
1350 Avenue of the Americas
New York, New York 10019

Copyright © 1992 by Robert E. Vardeman
Published by arrangement with the author
Library of Congress Catalog Card Number: 92-90331
ISBN: 0-380-76725-2

First Avon Books Printing: December 1992

AVON TRADEMARK REG. U.S. PAT. OFF. AND IN OTHER COUNTRIES, MARCA REGISTRADA, HECHO EN U.S.A.

Printed in the U.S.A.

RA 10 9 8 7 6 5 4 3 2 1

For the Ace Moving Company:
Mike Montgomery
Sal DiMaria
Dan MacCallum

CHAPTER 1

The sharp glass fragment cut deep into my palm. I winced as blood began flowing down my wrist to my elbow and dripped to the littered pavement. Lights flashed in my eyes, but I ignored them the best I could. Dropping the shard and shaking my head, I tried to get away.

"Here," came the immediate command. A twisted length of chrome trim jabbed into my hands. More blood flowed, faster, thicker like an obscene river, until my clothing was covered with it, drenched to the point I started to drown. No matter where I turned, they were there, insistent, demanding more from me than I could ever give.

"What about it, Thorne? Can't do it? Or maybe you don't want to tell us." The sarcasm whipped at me more than the chill wind blowing off San Francisco Bay less than a mile away. A part of me wondered how my body could be so cold and yet burn white-hot within.

I heard Willie Worthington's voice in the distance telling Burnside to shut up. It hardly mattered, because my concentration was deepening and the exterior world was vanishing from around me. My temples pounded and the blood—it gushed over me until I wanted to gag. Holding my damaged hand before me did nothing to stanch the flow. If anything, the red fountain increased and splashed over my face, turning me into the victim. I closed my eyes but still saw. I *saw*.

The chrome burned as if someone had applied a blow torch to the other end. The heat grew until a part of me wondered how any metal could retain its shape under such an onslaught.

Sinking to the pavement and pulling my long legs under me, I sat on the cold, wet curb. Tides of anxiety washed against the desolate shores of my mind. Trying to hold them back proved futile, so I let them flow, inundating me, carrying me away on waves both blood-hot and arctic cold. Breath entered my lungs raggedly and flowed past points of power before slipping easily from my lungs. Veins pulsating with unwanted power, I sank deeper and deeper into my trance.

"Fraud," I heard from a million miles away. Worthington's voice snapped something, but I had entered another realm, far from such petty concerns.

I looked at my bloodstained hand. Like a thing alive, the blood sinuously flowed until it covered my hand, arm, body and became a shield against the dark rays slashing through space around me. Although seated, I rose and drifted above the mist covering the ground. The piece of chrome began to blaze like a torch in the night. Its fierce heat no longer burned my hand; the blood protected me like a second skin.

Looking around, I wondered where I was this time. Billows of cloud rose and obscured the source of the dark rays seeking my soul. I dodged to one side, narrowly avoiding contact as an ebon ray flashed past. The strip of chrome began to glow more brightly as I turned. Using it both as a compass and a light took me in strange directions. The surface I walked on was level, but it felt as if I were climbing a tall mountain. My breath came in regular, deep gusts now, but logic told me I was straining hard. I walked uphill through the mist, the dark beams probing for me and missing, for what must have been a week or longer. Or was it only a few seconds? Time had become jumbled and meaningless, as had distance and perspective.

A jolt of electricity passed through my body, causing legs and arms to twitch when a black ray struck me. I was coming close to my goal, whatever it might be. I fought down panic. To lose concentration now would mean failure. This perilous journey would have been meaningless.

Blood flowed faster from my wounded hand and thickened the protective layers already on my arms and body. The shadow rays reflected from me now that new armor had been provided.

I came to the top of the mountain—and I screamed.

Hate! You will pay! Torture! Hate!

I recoiled from the blast of emotion boiling up from below. The chrome seared my soul but the blood shield turned away the worst of the stark hatred. It took several seconds—or years—to realize the loathing was not directed at me. Blinking, I saw through goggles of blood.

On the plain before me, rampaging through the impenetrable mist, came a mechanical juggernaut of impossible size. No sound reached my ears as its treads chewed up the muddy ground and threw gouts of filth into the sky. Fingers of gray haze whipped past as it sped along faster than sound.

And it spun rapidly and came directly at me.

I screamed. The light from my chrome torch showed the intimate details all too well. Huge eyes of glass winked balefully. A snout wrapped in barbed wire dripped blood. And from its forehead grew a figure, mouth screaming and head on fire, the column of flame rising to the heavens. Green eyes glowed with an eerie intensity I recognized as the hatred experienced earlier. And that impossible anger was now directed toward me. I had intruded. I threatened its revenge.

Black beams erupted from the sides of the huge mechanical beast, and again the overwhelming outrage hit me like a bludgeon.

You can't know, Denise, you can't know what you've done to me. You'll pay!

Arms thicker than sequoia trunks reached from the tank-creature and slammed together above my head. The silence was broken only by shrieks of incoherent fury.

They're mine, not yours. You'll suffer for this. Then the others will, too! I hate you, I hate you, I hate!

The burning chrome spat sparks and deflected the grotesque arms grabbing for me. My entire body quivered as the dark rays of hatred bored and drilled and tried to infect me. The shield of my own blood prevented it, but the nearness of such malice rattled me and caused my concentration to falter for a moment.

I suffered for the brief lapse as the snout of the mechanical monster came to life, twisted, and snapped, its barbed whiskers raking my belly. The pain focused me again, and I stepped aside. The ground shook, but there was no sound as the brute thundered past. Curiously detached, I turned and stared at its hindquarters. Trapped in a small cage with icicle bars, soundlessly screaming, was a tiny child who grew to womanly stature as I watched. Long brown hair snapped in the harsh wind of the mist roiling around her. She vanished from sight as the beast spun on its treads and prepared for another attack. But a tiny plea lingered, almost drowned out by the torrents of hatred from the man with flame hair and glowing green eyes.

Afraid, so scared ...

Darkness converging on me, torrents of malevolence crushing me to my knees, I stared up at my approaching death with odd insouciance. The chrome torch began to flicker and fade, and huge scabs of bloody material peeled from my body as I became more vulnerable to attack. Mist washed up and engulfed me. Then my death mattered. Everything mattered.

I screamed and screamed and screamed.

"Are you all right, Peter?" came a distant voice.

"Hell no, he's not okay," came Burnside's sarcastic voice. "I'm beginning to think he really believes all this bullshit. What I don't understand is why you believe it, Sarge."

"Go to hell, Burnie." Worthington's voice was as much an anchor for me as his bulky arm around my shoulder. I rocked forward and would have fallen facedown in the street if he hadn't supported me.

"Huge, the eyes and hate and it was all there."

"Is she dead? The woman who got run over?"

"No," I said, slowly slipping out of my trance. "She's imprisoned. He ... he's torturing her."

"God," Worthington muttered.

I heard a clang and saw I'd finally dropped the strip of chrome from the hit-and-run vehicle. Almost in disbelief, I stared at my hand, the one that had been awash in blood.

"It's not hurt," I whispered.

"The only place you're hurting is in the head, Thorne," Worthington's partner said. I looked up and saw Detective Burnside glaring at me. We had never been mistaken for friends. The source of his extreme antipathy toward me and my talent—my curse—was something he'd kept well hidden. After almost a year of dealing with his snide comments, I had reached the end of my patience.

"He's got bright red hair, hair like flame, and green eyes. And he is an immense man with the arms of a weight lifter. The woman he knocked down is named Denise, and he hates her. God, how he hates her!" I tried to put the searing emotion into its own little niche where I could deal with it. Some leaked out and directed itself at Burnside.

Only my extreme weakness saved him from getting the chrome strip laid directly on the top of his head.

"It's all right, Peter, really," soothed Worthington as if I were a small child who had lost his teddy bear. He dropped beside me on the curb and fumbled in his jacket pocket to pull out a small black-and-white photograph.

I stared at it until my eyes focused. A cold chill swirled around my body as I recognized the man in the mechanical creature.

"That's him," I said. "Does he have red hair and green eyes?"

"He hangs out along the Embarcadero and gets part-time jobs as a dock worker. He's one huge mother, believe me," Worthington said.

"Bullshit, that's all it is, bullshit. We knew he done it," complained Burnside.

"She's alive," I said. "Denise is alive. He has her somewhere cold." The cage of ice and her silenced screams were as clear now as they had been in the trance. "Does he have a cold storage locker available to him at the Embarcadero?"

"Dunno," said Worthington, "but Burnside will find out. And don't screw it up, Burnie."

The detective grumbled and went off to do his job. Worthington stayed beside me on the curb, saying nothing for a long time. I was grateful for his silence. It gave me time to center myself and try to decide what was real around me and what were lingering effects of the trance world.

"I can't keep doing this, Willie," I said.

"I know you got a gig coming up in Vegas in a couple weeks. That foxy assistant of yours going with you?"

"Michelle?"

"That's the one. I couldn't care less what your act was. Just sitting and staring at her is worth the price of admission."

"That's the idea," I said. "Up to a point." Michelle Ferris had worked out well as my stage assistant and had picked up on cues and covering quickly. It had been necessary to give her a few weeks to get her head together after she was almost killed. The respite had been as good for me as it was for her since I was trying to put together a new escape act to dazzle them along the Las Vegas strip. I didn't like working Glitter Gulch, except for the pay. There aren't many places that will pay a stage magician fifteen thousand a week for a month's stint.

"Want something to eat?" Worthington asked, changing his tack.

"No. You'd buy me one of those god-awful hot dogs. I don't think I could stand any of your coffee, either."

"You look pale. Want me to take you to the hospital?"

"I just can't keep doing psychometric readings for you," I said. "It's taking too much out of me psychically." Ever since suffering severe brain damage during a botched water-filled milk can escape, I've had the power to touch an object and "read" it. The more intense the emotion, the more I can discern after going into a trance. Most materials retain only trace amounts of their owner's feelings and thoughts, but metallic ones seem to resonate strongly and capture details.

Hate you, Denise!

"You always say that, Peter. I know this was a tough one. We've been on this guy's case for some time, but he never really did anything."

"Ex-wife?"

"Denise Morton. She got the kids and an injunction because he beat up on her and them. The usual."

"Why are you on the case?"

"You won't believe that it's been slow down at homicide, will you? No." Worthington snorted and pulled his coat around his bulky shoulders against the increasing wind off the Bay. "We thought he'd killed her, but there wasn't anything to tie him directly. Nobody saw the car and there's enough blood around to make us think a pedestrian got run over and killed here tonight. Can't say it makes me all that glad he didn't kill her."

"What?" I asked, startled. "Why?"

"Kidnapping isn't going to put him away for long at all. Still, the kids will have their mother back, but she's something of a basket case anyway. A real flake. Not sure they wouldn't be better off in foster homes."

"No," I said, my head beginning to hurt.

"Want some aspirin?"

I stared at my hand again. There wasn't even a scratch where the blood had flowed out, drenching me from head to toe.

"It was bleeding," I said numbly, still in shock from my experiences on the astral plane. The chrome strip from the hit-and-run car had completely swaddled me in the charged emotions of its driver. Such irrational, insane hatred would linger to haunt me for weeks.

"You told me you don't get injured on the astral plane," Worthington said. "It's all just make-believe."

"Yeah, fantasy stuff," I said.

"You get home okay?"

I nodded.

"I want to get this scumbag off the streets before the end of my shift. I don't trust Burnside not to screw up the bust. Call me tomorrow. Maybe we can get you a citation

or something fancy like that to hang on your wall."
Worthington stared down at me for a moment, then turned
and went to his car. He fumbled inside and got a bag of
candy and started munching at it as if it would be taken
away from him at any instant. That meant Worthington
was thinking hard. The monster who had run down his ex-
wife and imprisoned her in a meat locker would be behind
bars before morning.

In that I took some solace. I had rescued a woman from
a prison not of her making and that made me feel good.
But the echoes of her husband's hatred still rattled me. I
kept staring at my palm, thinking of the pain I'd felt and
the blood I'd seen.

In the psychometric trance state, matter and time don't
exist as we usually know it. There wasn't any way I could
have been hurt physically.

My belly on fire, I opened my shirt and saw the ugly
red gouges left by the barbed mechanical snout as it had
rushed past like a bull taunting a novice matador.

I was losing touch with what was real and what wasn't.
The damage being done to me now extended beyond the
mental and emotional. I had been right telling Worthington
I couldn't continue with my psychometric detection. I was
right. I was, I was. Tears trickled down my cheeks and I
wrapped my arms around myself and shook hard long after
the last of the police cars had left.

CHAPTER 2

It took more than an hour to get back to my apartment on Bret Harte Circle. The elevator crept so slowly to the top floor that I considered getting off and walking, but my condition was too debilitated for that. Seldom have I felt this tired in body and soul.

I fumbled out my key as I heard the telephone ringing insistently inside. I considered hurrying, then decided to let the answering machine do its work. There are times when the mechanical servants perform their task too well, filtering out important calls you want to receive and forcing you to play tag, but the other side of the coin is that you seldom miss the truly important message.

I opened the door and heard a voice saying, "Sorry to have missed you, love. Will call back soon. I'm gone."

Barbara Chan had transferred to the University of Maryland to finish her Ph.D. work in physics. I hurried and tried to scoop up the phone in time to catch her. I missed and got the dial tone. Muttering at my bad luck, I sat and dialed her number in Maryland. The phone rang and rang and finally I got her answering machine.

"Barbara, this is Peter returning your call."

It occurred to me after a few seconds that she might not have been at home when she called. Probably wasn't or she would have picked up at hearing my voice.

I dropped the phone into the cradle and punched the replay on the answering machine. It was as I had guessed. The first part of her message told me everything.

"Peter, sorry to have missed you. I'm calling from Fred's place. He's having a party, and I decided to use his phone when he turned his back. He's so filthy rich he never even checks his phone bill. You remember him. I told you how his folks own that restaurant chain out on Long Island. Anyway, I was missing you and wanted to hear your voice. The answering machine message will have to do, I suppose. When are you going to change the message? I've heard it a half dozen times and it's getting old."

The message went into the segment I had heard as I came through the door. I leaned back and closed my eyes, again bone tired. Using my talents on the piece of chrome had drained me, and now I had missed a chance to talk with Barbara. She was wild and uncontrolled and yet somehow provided a balance for me I hadn't found in any other woman. She seemed to sense my moods and deal well with them, keeping me from getting too morbid. As I was doing now.

I shoved to my feet, made sure the door was locked and then went to the kitchen. I opened the refrigerator door and stared at the shelves. It took me a few seconds to remember I had come here hunting for food. Deciding that I wasn't hungry after all, I closed the door and just paced the apartment. Ending up on the balcony overlooking the Golden Gate Bridge, I stood and let the salt air slip past me in a continual, cooling flow. The sight usually calms me. Tonight I found myself thinking of a million disparate things, none of them important. Leaning forward, I got a look around the edge of the building in the direction of Berkeley. It took several seconds for me to find a pair of red lights with a green positioned just below them forming a small downward pointing arrow.

Barbara had lived in that neighborhood when she went to school across the Bay. She had continued to room there when she got her master's degree from the University of San Francisco, though she had come to spend almost as much time in my place as she did at her own.

I turned back toward the north with its cold wind, my longing for Barbara making me even gloomier. I tried to focus myself on the stunts I'd be doing in the Vegas show. I was even considering trying the water-filled milk can escape once more, in spite of the trouble I'd had with it almost eight years earlier. The secret to escaping the can is half rivets and an inner shell. From the outside it appears that the rivets go through the can to fasten the top securely. An inner sleeve slides past the fake rivets after a bayonet fitting is released. The fitting is necessary to keep the appearance of a solid can. When I had done the escape the last time, the bayonet release had jammed.

I touched my head as if trying to probe where the blood vessels had burst, giving me my psychometric powers. CAT scans, MRI, positron emission tomography, they had tried it all to pinpoint the source of my talent. The best had tried and failed, including Barbara Chan. She had thought to use me as her master's thesis subject, but her efforts to find the source of my ability had proven futile.

"Dammit," I muttered. Even trying to concentrate on my act brought me full circle to Barbara. I dropped heavily to the couch and stared at the posters on my walls. My collection had been destroyed, and locating old lobby posters of famous magic acts was a painstaking undertaking, even in a city like San Francisco. Dozens of small shops had failed me as I sought to replace a prized Houdini poster and several of Thurston.

"Thurston's spirit cabinet," I said aloud, savoring the taste. It was a compelling trick, and an easy one, though it used a half dozen assistants. A cabinet is shown to be empty, then opened to phosphorescent objects floating about in its darkened interior.

As I thought of how to arrange the illusion, my eyelids drooped. I tried to fight sleep, just a little, then drifted away in the realm of Hypnos.

I slipped quickly from the god of sleep's arms into nightmare.

The huge machine crashed and clanked and roared, spewing filth from its nostrils. I turned and looked over my shoulder as I ran from it. Blood dripped from sundered eye sockets, and teeth like concertina wire flashed wickedly. Straddling the living machine stood the man with hair of fire and eyes so green it hurt to look into them.

Mighty arms swung at me. I cried out, but there was no escaping his grasp.

Arms like bark-encrusted logs crashed into my head and shoulder. I cried out in fear and pain—and awoke, lying on the floor. I had rolled from the couch and landed half across a footstool. More frightened from the echo of the psychometry than angry at my fear, I pushed myself to a sitting position and simply closed my eyes. Fear sweat rolled down my forehead and my chest heaved. It took several minutes to control my racing heart and convince myself the specters weren't real. I had caught their reflection in the chrome strip from the hit-and-run car.

"Not real," I told myself over and over, but I lied. The images were as genuine as any car traveling along 101.

It was a long, tiring night.

CHAPTER 3

The ringing in my ears bothered me. I swatted at the invisible insect, then shook myself awake when I realized it was neither a flying bug nor a leftover dream. Sometime between falling off the couch and falling asleep I'd made it into my bedroom and undressed. Rolling over, I snatched at the phone, hoping to catch it before the answering machine kicked in.

"Barbara?"

For a long moment there was only silence on the other end of the line. Whoever had called wasn't Barbara Chan. So much for intuition and my wish of speaking to her for a while about my problems. She had tried to find a physical explanation for my psychometric power and had failed; she provided a far better sounding board for my problems than she did as an investigator of the psychic realms.

"Peter?"

I struggled to recognize the voice. It tantalized, dancing just at the outer limits of my mind.

"Peter Thorne speaking."

Again came a short silence, as if I'd offended him by not knowing instantly who he was. Then he vented a soft sigh. "This is Charles Hayes."

"Charlie," I said, relaxing. "Sorry I didn't recognize your voice. I was asleep, and you know how long it takes me to get moving in the morning."

"Morning?" he said, a slight catch in his voice. "Afternoon is always more like it. You're always worthless until noon." He fell silent again, and I knew something had happened. Hayes was a jovial sort, the one from whom you always heard the newest joke making the rounds. He had tried to make a joke of my late rising and had failed miserably.

"What's wrong?" I asked.

"It . . . it's Katrina. She's dead, Peter. She died the day before yesterday."

"I'm so sorry, Charlie. What happened? An accident?"

"A car wreck. I . . . she was driving up the coast and went off the road in the fog, just south of Mendocino. The sheriff said there've been several other wrecks here over the years. A bad corner, a hairpin turn, really, and—shit, Peter, why'd she have to die?"

"Where are you?" I swung around and sat up on the bed, fully awake now and aware that Charlie was calling long distance. This wasn't the kind of news anyone enjoys hearing just a few minutes before nine in the morning, especially when it comes from a good friend. I hadn't seen too much of Charlie and Katrina in the past six months. Hayes's mother had died about that time, and he'd had to devote a considerable amount of time to settling the estate and keeping his custom computer chip manufacturing business going through a deep recession.

My own work had taken some unexpected turns during those months, and time had slipped past, as silently as shadows drifting across shadows and yet moving faster than light.

"I'm in San Tomás. Just south of Mendocino, near that winery Katrina always liked."

"I know the place. Are you coming back to San Francisco?"

"I'm burying her here, Peter. It was something we'd talked about. She loved this country. We were going to find a place on the ocean and—" He broke down sobbing.

"When is the funeral?" I asked, wondering if Charlie even heard me. He was trying to control his emotion. My own voice was choked. I liked Charles Hayes, and at one time had been more than a little in love with Katrina before they had married. She was considerably younger than Charlie, twenty-seven to his late forties, but she had made a better match in him than she ever could have with me. I had envied Charlie his catch. Now all I could do was share some of his sorrow.

"This afternoon, this evening really. Six o'clock. I know it's short notice, but I hope you can make it. I know you and Katrina were good friends, and you're one of my best friends."

"I'll be there, Charlie." It was going to be quite a drive up 101 to Ukiah and then along a miserable gravel road to Mendocino. This would be faster, though, than winding up the coast on Highway 1, with all its switchbacks on a two-lane road. I had driven north a few years ago on 1 and had developed knots in my shoulder muscles from the constant shifting since no stretch of straight road was longer than a hundred yards. It was scenic but not the kind of drive to make on the way to a funeral.

I shook myself, got up, and took a quick shower. Somehow, I didn't feel like eating, though it was going to be a long day.

The drive had been worse just across the Golden Gate Bridge and north through Petaluma because of heavy traffic than it was along the gravel road cutting northwest toward the coast from Ukiah. Montgomery Woods looked enticing, and I wished I had the time to stop. The serenity of the area was what I needed to calm my inner turmoil, but my own needs were secondary to those of Charles Hayes. I found myself wondering how he was doing. After his mother had died, Katrina was all the family he had. He would be taking her death hard.

Old feelings I had thought long put to rest rose up within me. I had loved Katrina, though we had never been lovers. She was always on the go, seemingly too busy to stay long with any one man. Her vibrancy was what I remembered as much as her beauty and sparkling green eyes. When Charlie had announced their wedding plans, I was as jealous as I was happy for them.

I shook my head and wondered at the turns fate takes. I had introduced them at a party.

The last of the gravel road quit spitting sharp-pointed rocks at the paint job on my BMW, and I wheeled onto pavement once more to the west of Comptche. It was another fifteen miles before I came to the Mendocino Headlands. To the north lay Mendocino. To the south was the small town of Little River and just beyond it along Highway 1 before reaching Albion was San Tomás. I tried to remember if it had been Katrina who first mentioned the winery there or if it had been Charlie. They had enjoyed driving up the coast, not caring if they took an hour or a day to make the trip from San Francisco. They would spend a day sampling the cabernets at the San Tomás Winery, then continue up the coast sometimes as far as Eureka before returning. It was as if I had been with them, so vivid were my memories of their trips. Charlie had shown enough slides and home videos of their trip to make a lasting impression.

And in every frame there had been the smiling Katrina, so alive and in love with him.

The few minutes' drive south brought me to San Tomás. I slowed, not wanting to miss it completely. It was just off Highway 1 and had only a single stoplight where the village's two roads crossed. It had been a long time since I'd been in a place too rustic to attract even a single McDonald's. That was part of the charm.

Finding the town mortuary proved easier than I'd thought. It was just to the east of the intersection. Finding a parking place was easy, too, another benefit of living in a small town.

I entered the dimly lit lobby and paused for a moment to let my eyes adjust. I'd made good time on the 165-mile trip, in spite of heavy traffic and gravel roads. The funeral wouldn't be for several hours.

"May I help you?" came the unctuous voice common to all morticians—or condolence mechanics or whatever name they've chosen for themselves. "I am Ronald Zwinger, Director of Grief Services."

"Grief services," I muttered. I kept from making any comment about Mr. Zwinger not looking like a swinger.

He stood slightly taller than my six feet and sported an average build. The small paunch betrayed a sedentary life, but the yellowed hand thrust out for shaking was strong and dry. He was dressed in an almost threadbare black broadcloth coat that would have looked more at home in a western movie. The front of his crisp formal shirt had mismatched onyx studs, and his large black silk bow tie hung slightly askew around a thin neck. From his appearance, the mortuary business in this part of California wasn't very lucrative.

"Charles Hayes called me this morning. I came for his wife's funeral."

"Yes, of course. This way, sir. If you would care to register your regrets in the loved one's memory book." Zwinger paused and indicated a lined book opened to the first page. Katrina's name was written in stylish, bold calligraphy across the top. There were only two names entered, and I recognized both of them as Charlie's business associates. Zwinger noted my curiosity about the dearth of attendees at the funeral and said, "Mrs. Hayes's death was both untimely and . . . violent. She was badly burned in the wreck."

"Mr. Hayes wants a simple funeral?"

"That is his wish, as it usually is in instances of extreme . . . disfigurement. Only a few people have been notified. It is my understanding there will be a tribute service for Mrs. Hayes at a later date, in San Francisco." Zwinger kept from sniffing in disdain at the notion of big city ways.

A few quick squiggles was all I could summon up for the book. I doubted Charlie would ever open the "memory book" after this afternoon and might even throw it away. I knew I would do something similar, wanting to live with the more pleasant memories of the time when Katrina was alive.

"You came. I'm glad, Peter. I need you now more than ever."

I turned to face Charles Hayes. He stood in a curtained doorway leading into the mortuary chapel. The earlier emotion had passed, leaving him calm and curiously serene. This might pass after the funeral when he finally realized Katrina was gone and had to deal with her absence.

I embraced him, but Charlie pushed away. In situations like this I'm always at a loss for words. As I get older and more friends and family die, it ought to get easier if for no other reason than repetition. It doesn't. The words never seem adequate to push back grief, even for a moment, and always ring like false silver coins in my ear. Even meaning the words of condolence doesn't make them seem any more potent.

"The funeral will be a short one," he said, turning away. "Closed casket. She was badly burned in the crash."

"There's no question?"

He shook his head. He had control of himself now but he looked a dozen years older. His broad shoulders slumped and his iron-gray hair was in wild disarray, as if he had forgotten to comb it after getting up this morning. I expected wrinkled clothing and found it, but the man himself was in a similar state. If anyone I had ever seen looked like he was collapsing in on himself, it was Charlie Hayes.

"The local coroner confirmed it from dental records. He said there wasn't any way of identifying Katrina otherwise." Charlie fumbled in his pocket and pulled out a lump of melted gold. It might have been a nugget from Coloma over at South Fork on the American River that had started the '49 gold rush. "This was her wedding ring. Never found the stone."

"Would you like me to look for it?" I asked, knowing what penalty I would pay. I held out my hand for what remained of Katrina's wedding ring.

"No, Peter, there's something else I'll need your help on. Later. I've got to talk with people now."

I looked past him into the chapel and saw the closed casket on the bier. A few wreaths had been placed on either side. For all the life that had been Katrina Hayes, there was only a coldness remaining behind. I wanted to go to the windows and throw open the heavy drapes and let in the afternoon sun, to bathe the room in the warmth that she had brought with her whenever she entered.

"I'll be back at six for the funeral," I said. "I'll go get something to eat and find a place to stay for the night." Driving back, either along the coast or back through the Coast Range and that gravel road, didn't appeal to me.

"I'm glad you're planning on staying, Peter. There are several good inns up in Mendocino," Charlie said, almost distractedly. "But I will need you back here tonight. It is *very* important, Peter."

"Of course I'll be here."

"Good, good, since it might be our only chance of talking with Katrina again."

I stared at him as he hurried off, clutching her melted wedding ring in his hand so tightly his knuckles turned white.

CHAPTER 4

A half dozen people sat in the uncomfortable pews, scattered around the mortuary chapel. Some I recognized from parties Charlie and Katrina had given: business associates. One tearful couple sitting near the front was stricken with more grief than I thought possible from people not related to the deceased. They hurriedly got up and left the instant the service was over, pausing for only a moment to shake Charlie's hand.

Charlie sat motionless, staring straight ahead, as if fixation on some inanimate object away from the casket would bring back Katrina. More likely, he worried that he would shift slightly, see the coffin and begin to cry. I took a deep breath and got to my feet. His last words to me before I left to find a small café down the street still burned in my mind. Some people go off the deep end with a personal loss of this magnitude. I hadn't thought Charlie would succumb, but what did I know about psychology? My sole exposure to it was legerdemain, misdirection, the capturing of people's imagination and redirecting their attention for a split second. The deeper emotions, the lasting ones, were as much a mystery to me as they were to most people not trained clinically.

"Peter," he said, turning quickly. I saw how his eyes closed momentarily so he wouldn't look at Katrina's eternal prison of wood and metal. "Thank you again for coming."

"You know what Katrina meant to me. Paying my respects is hardly enough."

"I—" He clamped his mouth shut, wanting to say something more and not knowing how. Realizing that it was sometimes necessary to prime the pump, I carefully formed my offer.

"There's no need for me to go straight back to San Francisco. Let's talk for a while." I put enough query into my voice for him to be able to decline, if he wanted to be alone with his grief. From all I had seen, Charles Hayes was desperately in need of someone to talk with now. All the words in the world wouldn't bring Katrina back, but funerals were for the living. There has to be a closure before any of us can accept a loved one's passing.

"The grave site service will be short," Ronald Zwinger said in his oily tone. "Will you be accompanying Mr. Hayes to the cemetery?"

I wanted to push his face in. Holding back from hitting him, I realized I had some unresolved feelings of my own to work through. Katrina of the long, dark hair, the dancing emerald eyes, the quick smile, and the sudden turn in temperament was dead, and I couldn't do anything about it. On stage, I can wave a silk scarf and conjure a kicking rabbit from thin air. Real life is much different. Unfortunately.

"Charlie?"

"Come with me, Peter. There's something I want to talk over." Again, the sense of anticipation was mixed with his obvious sorrow. I put my hand on his shoulder and squeezed gently to let him know I'd do what I could for him. If he got through his grief, I could get through mine.

"Let's go."

The drive to the cemetery outside San Tomás took less than ten minutes, even with the three-car procession driving at five miles an hour. The wind whipped harsh and cold off the Pacific, and a storm threatened to drench us in a few minutes. All in all, it seemed a fitting day for a funeral. No one should ever be buried on a pleasant day. There are too few of them to spoil.

I stared into the open grave, my thoughts twisting and turning randomly. I wasn't thinking of Katrina or her death or even the brightness lost to the world. In truth, nothing coherent flowed through my head. I just stood and stared, bowed my head at appropriate times and looked into the dense stand of forest surrounding the cemetery. Imagined phantasms cavorted just beyond my vision and hearing, ghosts of those lost over the years. Turning toward the ocean, I saw the dark legs of a storm skipping toward land. It would arrive in less than twenty minutes. Already the front dropped lacy veils of cloud to the whitecapped ocean, causing a heavier tide than usual.

"God rest her soul," I heard the minister finish. Blinking hard, I tried to remember what had been said and done. I had simply zoned out on the ceremony, knowing nothing more than that it had been brief, as Zwinger had promised.

"If there's anything more I can do, sir," Zwinger said to Charlie, "please do not hesitate to call."

The funeral parlor owner walked slowly from the grave to wait beside the limousine that would take us back to the mortuary.

"What a ghoul," Charlie mumbled. "I hope never to see him again."

Flip answers roiled up from within, a denial that Charlie would one day be buried, as would I and everyone else at the funeral. It might not be Ronald Zwinger who buried us, but the name and appearance didn't matter. I took Charlie by the elbow and steered him away from the grave, where two men with shovels stood, looking significantly from us to the storm and down to the grave. They wanted to finish their job before the squall hit.

"Let's have that talk," I said. "We can go to my motel. You were right about Mendocino having some decent ones, and—"

"Do you have a tape recorder in your room?" he asked unexpectedly.

"No, but I have one in my car." This seemed an odd time to worry about listening to music, even though it was supposed to soothe the savage breast.

"Never mind. I have one in my motel room. Come back with me. I have something I want you to listen to."

"All right," I said, wondering what I was getting myself involved in.

"I need advice, Peter," Charlie said slowly. He stared straight ahead again, maybe seeing something that I couldn't through the smoked glass partition in the front of the limo. "You know that Katrina came up here often because we were involved in a land deal."

"I know you wanted to have a vacation home around here."

"Business is struggling," Charlie said, "but this was going to bail us out. It was more than a home, it was a sweet land deal. Katrina was checking it out for us."

Land deals, especially in California, tended to be speculative. Translated into ordinary language, speculative meant something not quite ethical and probably intended to bilk all the investors of their money, and with the tacit blessing of the tax laws.

"I didn't know you were interested in real estate," I said, keeping my tone as neutral as possible.

"I'm not, but Katrina thinks it is too good to pass up— thought," he said, a catch in his voice. "I don't have the time to pursue it."

"There's no money on the line?"

"We hadn't signed anything."

I heaved a sigh of relief. Katrina was sharp, but she didn't have the training to properly evaluate a real estate deal, especially if it was set up by a syndicate of astute land rights lawyers. There are too many stories of seemingly intelligent people who saw a fast buck and lost everything.

The limo pulled to a halt in front of the mortuary. Neither of us said anything as we got out, Zwinger standing like an ill-dressed zombie as he held the door open for us. I nodded in his direction, wanting nothing more than to be free of him. I wasn't sure if it was the man I disliked or his profession. His very presence kept reminding me of my own mortality—and the fact that Katrina was gone.

"Let's walk," Charlie said. "My motel is only a few hundred yards down the road." We strode along in silence. The cold wind whipped faster as the storm edged even closer to land. Spray from the ocean left salty spots on my

cheeks and hands. I was glad to reach the sanctuary of
Charlie's room and sorry I hadn't followed him in my car.
The trip back on foot to where I'd parked would be cold
and very, very wet.

"Sit down, Peter. I'd offer you a drink but I don't have
anything. I could get something sent up—"

"Don't bother. There was a Coke machine down the
hall. Get you anything?"

Charlie shook his head. I wasn't in the mood to drink
anything fizzy, but getting out of the room and his presence gave me a few seconds to collect my wits. The machine stole my first quarter and finally accepted the next
three. A dollar for a can of pop was outrageous, especially
when I wasn't thirsty. I had come back with Charlie to
comfort him, perhaps talk of the good times with Katrina,
to reminisce and help him—and me—come to grips with
the tragedy of loss. Something about him put me on edge,
though. It had nothing to do with psychometry or psychic
powers, but I wondered if I wouldn't be better off simply
abandoning my can of Coke and leaving San Tomás.

I went back to his room. He didn't look up from the table as I slipped in and closed the door behind me.

He hunched over a cassette player on the table, staring
intently at the tape inside as if it contained the secrets of
the universe.

"Do you believe in life after death, Peter?" he asked unexpectedly.

"Not really," I said.

"But your talent shows there is something more than
our usual senses."

I knew where this was heading. I'd had the same argu-
ment with dozens of people over the past eight years. Anything out of the ordinary had to be ascribed to supernatural
events, or so their line of illogic usually ran.

"Some people have better vision than others. Chuck
Yeager claimed he was able to see fighters coming on the
horizon as much as five minutes before anyone else in his
flight. There's nothing supernatural in that."

"But others can't just touch an object and feel something of its owner."

"I don't believe God gave me the ability any more than I do that it is satanically imbued. It's an anomaly, a disorder, an injury that gives me a talent something like the World War One Russian soldier who was hit in the head with the bullet and never slept a wink the rest of his life."

"But you can't explain it."

"Charlie, where is this leading?"

"I want you to come with me to a séance, or whatever they call them now."

"Channeling sessions," I said, hating myself. He wasn't giving up on Katrina as easily as I had hoped. Trying to reach his dead wife through a fake medium would only keep him from healing his emotional wounds.

"That's it, channeling," he said, a hint of eagerness in his voice. "I want to talk with Katrina again."

"They are frauds, Charlie, all of them. The popularity of New Age beliefs has given them an unearned respectability, but they're still con artists intent on bilking the gullible." I put as much emphasis on the final word as I could, hoping it would shake him into seeing how desperate and foolish he was being.

"Will you come with me to a channeling, if only to tell me how I'm being duped?"

"I suppose," I said, wishing I were on the far side of the moon.

"You debunk them all the time."

"I try. Some of them are accomplished stage magicians, almost as good as I am. It's not always easy to find how they do their tricks, though most are inept."

Charlie looked grim. His lips were drawn back into a thin line and his forehead wrinkled with the intensity of his emotion. "I'm trying to be hardheaded about this, as logical as Katrina would be. I don't want to accept it, yet . . ."

"All right, I'll go to a channeler with you, but even if there's no obvious trickery, that doesn't mean I will believe anyone can speak with the dead—and neither should you."

"I have hard proof channeling works." Charlie turned to the tape recorder, his shaking finger on the play button. He took a deep breath and, as if coming to a conclusion, steadied and jabbed downward. The tape began with scratchy static.

After a moment of white noise, a low voice intoned, "I am in touch with Katrina Hayes. Speak, Katrina, speak to me from beyond your grave!"

"Charlie!" came Katrina's voice. I jumped. I'd recognize her anywhere, even on a poor recording. "Charlie, there's so much I want to tell you."

The tape started hissing louder and louder until her words were lost. The first voice, the channeler, came back and said, "Today is the third of March. Katrina died less than twenty-four hours ago." The recording stopped and Charlie looked to me.

"I got it in the mail this morning. This was wrapped around the tape."

Taking the letter, I quickly scanned it. A time three days from now was listed. I almost laughed when I saw the time of the meeting was midnight. Such melodrama might work in dead teenager movies, but it gave a touch of the absurd to the request.

"The address is here in town. I went over there yesterday, hoping to find whoever sent it."

"A woman, from the handwriting. Maybe the same one whose voice is on the tape."

"That's what I thought," said Charlie, his enthusiasm growing. "The place is deserted and no one knows who the house belongs to. There are dozens of abandoned places around San Tomás. This is hardly the crossroads of the world."

"Charlie, think about it. I'm not arguing about that being Katrina's voice, but you have no idea when it was recorded or how. She might have called someone, and they took it off an answering machine. It doesn't *say* anything."

"Don't you think I've worried over that, Peter? I am not a gullible man."

"But you might be setting yourself up for a con. This has all the classic elements. A grieving husband, a mysterious message, a plea from the dead wife—it's all here, and Katrina is dead. She is dead, Charlie."

He took out the lump of gold that had been his wife's wedding ring and clutched it tightly.

"She's dead," he said sounding like a distant, hollow echo, "and this might be a hoax. And then again, it might not. This woman might be able to put me in touch with Katrina, just one more time. Come with me to the channeling, Peter. Please."

I should have left when I'd had the chance. Now I found myself agreeing to help him contact the dead.

CHAPTER 5

I tried to sneak past the squad room without Willie Worthington seeing me. I missed by a mile. He was standing in the door to his office as if waiting for me.

"Peter, hold up for a minute, will you? I've got some news for you."

"Afternoon, Willie," I said, hoping to keep this short. I had a report in my pocket from a friend in forensics. Bill Walden hadn't been in his office, but the department secretary had given me the report. It was a violation of department rules for him to do work for me since I wasn't connected with the police, but he owed me for theater tickets I had found for him.

"Don't go runnin' off, now. Come on in." He motioned one pudgy hand into the dim interior of his office. There wasn't any way in hell to avoid him. Like a schoolboy sent to the principal's office, I went in, wondering if he really knew I was using the police department's valuable resources for my own ends. The first words out of his mouth told the story.

"You could have come to me with it, Peter," he said.

"How's that, Willie?"

"Stop pretending," he snapped. "We're up for an audit again. Always cutbacks and layoffs and don't use the copy machine so much. Do you know how much paperwork is generated out there?" He motioned vaguely in the direction of the squad room.

"How much?"

"That's not the point," he said glumly. "I'm being called on the carpet for not holding costs down. If they'd pay me more, give me a decent partner and—" He continued grumbling to himself as he stalked around the battered wood desk, possibly surplus from the Spanish American War, dropped heavily to a chair and hoisted his feet to one well-worn corner. The way he took out the yellow pencil and began gnawing at it like a beaver told me I wasn't going to get away easily.

"You are part of the problem, Peter. You're making work for me."

"You don't say that when I tell you what happened at a murder scene." I fought to hold down a convulsive shiver as echoes from the hit-and-run rolled like cannonade through my mind.

"You did good on that one, I'll admit it. We collared the perp before he could snuff his wife. He crashed into her, knocked her down and broke a leg or two, then dumped her in his trunk and went off. Your call on the meat locker was on the money, too."

"Glad to hear it," I said rising.

"Sit."

"I'm not a trained dog, Willie." I couldn't tell if I was more tired physically or mentally. Doing the psychometry for Worthington gave me the shakes, but for the past two days I had been struggling with a new escape for my act. My shoulders were stiff and movement caused me some pain if I twisted the wrong way.

"Bill told me he was doing some extracurricular stuff for you. I hope it has something to do with closing an open murder on the books." The look in his eyes told me he wanted me to lie so he could forget it. A perverse stream began to flow through me. Lying would be easy. But nothing else had been simple for me in the past week, and I saw no reason not to keep struggling against the current.

"Walden ran some voice tests on a tape I gave him. It might be bunco involved, but not murder."

"Damn," Worthington whispered. Louder, he said, "Peter, you always were happiest when you were making life miserable. If I were the only one to know about this misappropriation, it'd be fine. Bill said he owed you for something—those damned tickets you got him, I'll wager—and heaven alone knows I owe you. But we're in the middle of an *audit*."

He spat out the word as if it burned his tongue.

"Walden did it on his lunch hour. That's what he told me." I sat again, wondering if there was something to the tests the forensics scientist had run. The letter turned heavier than lead in my pocket. The information inside must be interesting enough to involve Worthington.

"He used department equipment. That's misappropriation, a crime, maybe a felony, depending on how long he took."

"I understand it's a felony in Boston to have an overdue library book. And in Washington, if you're a sex offender who's served his time, you can be sent back to jail because you *might* commit another crime. What's worse? Those or Bill checking continuity on a cassette for me?"

"Nobody's going to toss you in the slammer," Worthington said, still looking glum and chewing harder on his pencil until tiny yellow paint chips flaked off onto his lips, "but both Bill and I might be reprimanded or even lose our jobs."

The undercurrent in the room was wrong. The years spent on stage reading an audience for likes and dislikes was paying off. Though everything Worthington said might be true, it wasn't the entire story. All I could do was sit and wait for the rest to come out.

"Even being seen with you might trigger an investigation, unless you were doing department work," Worthington went on. This was the payoff. He was maneuvering me into another psychometry for him.

"No, I won't do it."

"Do what? You're a suspicious cuss, Peter. Haven't asked anything from you, except maybe that you reciprocate for all the consideration shown you. It took Bill time to do that analysis on the tape."

I pulled the report from my pocket and ripped open the envelope. Scanning quickly, the gist of the report did nothing to confirm my suspicions, but then it did nothing to allay them, either. The tape had not been put together by snipping sections of existing tapes apart and gluing them together, but the background static was so bad Walden couldn't determine if it had been a recording of another recording, with the fake medium responding as if Katrina were present. Using my psychometric power on the plastic case was impossible. It wasn't imbued with enough residue or resonance or vibration or soul, call it what you will.

"We made a fair trade. What he did is his business, as it is how I got the tickets I gave him." Making it sound as if I had risked life and limb or called in heavy markers added to my position. The theater tickets had been given to me, and I couldn't use them because I had been performing that night. Worthington didn't need to know.

"See that pinhead out there? The one with the squint? He used to wear glasses so thick you could have used them in the Hobble."

"That's Hubble telescope," I corrected.

"More like Hobble, the way they built it. Anyway, he probably saw about as good. A real Mr. Magoo type. He got contacts a year or two back. Thinks he's God's gift to women now, he does. He's a lousy bean counter and nothing more."

"But you're telling me he doesn't miss a bean anywhere," I said, relenting. Worthington was wearing me down, although, for all I knew, the guy in the squad room might be nothing more than a citizen come to make a complaint about a barking dog. It didn't matter that this was the homicide division; people called the emergency numbers all the time over trivial matters.

"We've got to go, Peter. Now. And play along. I know you're not keen on doing your trick again—"

"It's not a trick." The ice from my soul carried to my voice, but the coldness only hid the fear. One day I would explore that peculiar astral plane and be killed there or find myself trapped and unable to return. It was more than a feeling; it was a premonition.

"Sorry, I know how you feel about it. Been around Burnie too long." Worthington cast a quick look around the squad room and didn't see his partner. He took my arm and steered me out a side exit, avoiding the squinting man who had hiked up his heavy briefcase onto an annoyed detective's orderly desk.

"You've got seniority. Why don't you get someone else?" I asked while he hustled me down a flight of stairs. The air was so close and odoriferous in the stairwell that I wondered if this wasn't a good place to train for my sealed box escape. I made it all the way down to the ground level before breathing again.

"Funding, it's always funding. No money for raises, they say. We can't hire new officers. Go on and retire, make the ones left in the department happy they're not getting laid off. The bureaucrats make life hell for us this time of year. But wait a month when the budget's approved and they'll forget all about us." He was still steering me toward a run-down car in the rear of the building.

"You got a new car," I said sarcastically. He didn't take it that way.

"Sure did. Best they had to offer, too. The paint's hardly missing in places, and there's a good year left in it before rust eats away the body." Worthington sounded pleased at his new automobile. Considering what he usually drove, this might be an improvement.

"I'll drive," I said, thinking about other things.

Worthington's prattling about department budgets and internal audits and the like didn't bother me unduly. This was just a springboard for some other request. What did worry me was that the inconclusive results on the tape left me with nothing to take to Charles Hayes to convince him he was dealing with a fraud. Mediums are clever people watchers, adjusting their spiel to what their mark wants to hear. Slight nervous gestures, hardly noticed by most people, give them guidance in their scam. One way I have of debunking their claims is to feed them bogus body language clues and lead them so far from the truth even the most gullible can see their methods.

"No, no, Peter, I will. I'll take you to lunch. I know this place just off Market, out by Pier One just across from the World Trade Center."

"A hot dog place?" I didn't think I could face another of Worthington's mystery meat delights.

"A real place." He stared at me, sizing me up. "Really. Come on. I want to show you how much get up and go this buggy has."

The engine roared to life, and once it had cleared its throat it proved as lively as Worthington had claimed. He wasn't going to chase down a Porsche on 101, but a homicide detective seldom needed to do more than arrive in one piece at the crime site.

He wheeled out onto Seventh, took a quick turn and got onto Bryant, driving toward the Embarcadero. At the first on ramp, Worthington wheeled onto 80 and floored it. Portions of the road were still under repair from the earthquake, and when he started toward the section of 480 that had totally collapsed I began to doubt this was a simple luncheon.

"Where are we going, Willie?" I asked. I settled back on the hard bench seat, trying not to stick to the vinyl upholstery. "You're not taking me to lunch, are you?"

"Just got a quick stop to make. Maybe you can help me with it."

I closed my eyes and forced away visions of powerful machines wrapped in razor wire trying to slice me to ribbons. I was glad to help in his murder investigations, but the cost was becoming too great for me emotionally, and becoming embroiled in the scam to bilk Charlie Hayes wore on me, too. I wasn't sure if letting the man get taken in by a fake medium bothered me as much as besmirching Katrina's memory did.

I had already called in all the markers I had with the SFPD. Bill Walden hadn't given me what I needed on the cassette, but maybe something rested in the bunco squad's files. If anything did, it was closed to me—

unless someone pulled a few strings or called in favors of his own.

Someone like Willie Worthington.

"What's this worth to you?" I asked, keeping my eyes closed as we weaved in and out of traffic. The screeching of tires and sudden deceleration told me we were getting off the freeway. Daring a small peek, I saw we were just off Steuart, near Maritime Park.

"There's no money to pay you a consultation fee. You know that. Hell, I haven't gotten a raise, other than a bonus here and there, in a couple years."

"Willie," I said in exasperation, "I'm shaking you down. This is a trade. I might need information later."

"For Hayes?"

Nothing went by Worthington. He had checked with Walden concerning my illicit request for forensics work.

"What's the case you're on now?"

Worthington coughed to clear his throat and took a moment to find a spot to park, illegally near a fire hydrant. I thought and then said, "Don't want to give you too many hints as to what I'm thinking. Might prejudice you since neither of us knows how your talent works."

"Lay on, Macduff, and give me the best you've got." I heaved myself out of his dilapidated car, peeling exposed flesh off the vinyl. A car like this would be hell in a hotter climate.

"There are a few hole-in-the-wall apartments here. A woman was snuffed. We've got the weapon, we've got witnesses, we've got a suspect."

"Open and shut," I said, knowing there had to be more to it or Worthington wouldn't have involved me.

"Yeah, right. Come on in, Peter. Here's the place." He slipped under the police barrier and got out a key to open a heavy padlock on the door. We went into the tiny room, what passed for a living room if you were gerbil-sized. Clear plastic evidence tarps covered much of the furniture, and a large stain on a floral print slipcover over the sofa protected the spot where the deceased had been found. I wandered around the room, touching nothing, settling my mind and trying to get a "feel" for the place. The resonances were muddled and indistinct, as if dozens of people had lived here.

"How many lived here?" I asked.

"Just the two," Worthington answered. He stood like a dinosaur in one corner, too large for the tiny room.

"Too many imprints, strong imprints and not your crew, either. These are more permanent."

Worthington said nothing but began scribbling notes in his spiral notebook with the stub of a pencil he had carried behind his right ear. I kept wandering around the room, curious feelings building. Passion, intense passion almost boiled out of the bedroom. I backed away. There was more here, but it was closer to an animal lust, a need that had to be sated.

I stopped and took several deep breaths to calm myself. These impressions meant nothing. For a real reading I had to touch an object, preferably metal, that had been in a person's possession for some time. Violent emotion might imprint an image in the object, but that wasn't always the case.

Sociopaths took little pleasure in killing or raping; neither did they feel hatred. In such cases my talent was ill-applied. But not here. Intensity marked all the people who came and went.

"Here," Worthington said, placing a bagged pistol into my hands. I began to shiver. This was the murder weapon. I forced myself to breathe evenly. The curious astral plane where I get my best information eluded me today—or perhaps I was reluctant to allow myself to become that committed to another murder.

"He shot her," I said in a low voice, still pacing the small room. "But the gun wasn't in his possession long. It might not even belong to the man."

"What's he look like? The killer?"

Try as I might, no clear picture came. It was as if the murderer had walked in, picked the pistol up off the table and used it, dropping it the instant he had finished the crime. I put the gun down on a table and continued to walk around, touching furniture, the sofa, the chairs, spots on the living room floor, the unmade bed in the other room.

"So many people came and went," I said. "Maybe one of them did it."

"Just the two lived here, a man and a woman, for well nigh ten years," Worthington said.

I came out of the light trance. "Sorry, Willie, but that's all I can tell you. I don't think the pistol belonged to the killer. The images are all fleeting, hesitant, as if he saw the gun and used it, then dropped it and fled."

"What if the pistol had been in a closet for years, never even touched?"

"That would explain the lack of distinct imprinting," I said, "but the murderer was frightened of something and didn't know how to use the pistol." For the first time I looked at it with my eyes rather than my psychometric sense. "I've never seen a model like that before."

"Not too surprising," Worthington said. "I had to get an expert in on it myself. It's Finnish, a Lahti Model L35, chambered for 9mm."

"It looks a little like a Luger, except there's no toggle."

"It's the husband's. He got it when he was stationed in Germany, who the hell knows why. Maybe it struck his fancy. Maybe he won it in a card game, like he claims."

"So much sexual passion," I said, becoming distracted.

"Like the lady was chipping on the sly? No sign outside or anything like that but a few regular customers?"

"Maybe," I answered. "That could explain it, unless the husband is something of a sexual athlete."

"Doubt it," Worthington said, scribbling furiously again.

I hadn't helped Worthington much, I didn't think. There was no distinct picture of the killer, but something about this crime bothered me.

"You look bushed, Peter. Let's get lunch out of the way and you can get on with what you have to do. Me, I've got reports to write and an auditor to pacify."

Worthington led the way out. The slight mental effort on my part had produced a physical exhaustion I had seldom felt. I followed him from the murder scene, wanting a nap more than I did lunch.

CHAPTER 6

I was tired but needed to follow the line of reasoning I had blundered across accidentally during the psychometric session for Worthington. Charlie Hayes was upset about Katrina's death—but not upset enough. He had never believed in channeling or any of the occult fads that swept back and forth the length of California with the predictability of the evening tide. If anything, he had always been just a little unsure that I wasn't somehow cheating when I touched objects and studied their resonant imprint. The engineer in him demanded more proof than I could ever offer. He never came out and called me a fake, but the expression on his face told me he believed I was a good stage magician.

Katrina hadn't believed in such nonsense, either, so why would Hayes be so willing to believe she had returned from the grave? It might have been an unworthy thought, but it struck me that he wasn't grieving enough and the cassette tape he had given me was too flimsy for a rational man to hang much hope on. But then what did I know about the way anyone—including myself—really thought deep down inside?

I took 35 south until I could pick up 82 to South San Francisco. The area is heavily industrialized, too much for my taste. The businesses here tend to be more basic—steel, equipment manufacturing and polluters like that, rather than the somewhat cleaner chip and computer industries farther south in San Jose's Silicon Valley. There was enough toxic waste generated from those companies, but it was liquid rather than gray and it didn't hang in the air until you choked on it. Charles Hayes had picked South San

Francisco for his chip manufacturing because it was near enough to Berkeley and Livermore to recruit top talent without having to compete with the bigger companies to the south, who monopolized Stanford University's attention. Engineers and scientists would work for Charlie at RadChipTech for a few months or perhaps a year on specialized projects, then return to teaching or defense work. He never mentioned it, but I guessed he got most of his basic research and development money from DARPA.

As with most companies sticking their corporate tongues into the public feeding trough, the flow was drying up as federal tax money was diverted into paying interest on the national debt. The Defense Advanced Research Projects Agency, for all the fine work applicable to civilian products, had never been highly funded. If Charlie had lost even a portion of the money from DARPA, he might be hurting financially.

He might be hurting so badly that a fat insurance policy on Katrina would save his business. I almost bit my lip as these unworthy thoughts flashed through my mind. I had never seen anything to even hint that Charlie and Katrina weren't devoted to one another, in love as much as any couple I'd ever seen. But something wasn't right, and in a peculiar way I couldn't put my finger on, the psychometric session for Willie Worthington had nudged me to take the time to find out.

I owed Katrina this much.

As with most high tech companies, there wasn't any fancy sign showing where the RadChipTech labs were located. I had a devil of a time even finding the small building housing the administrative offices. People didn't usually call without arranging a tour in advance of their arrival. I doubted Charlie would be in. He seemed intent on staying in San Tomás and waiting for more information about the seance. I got out of my car, took a deep breath and composed myself, going over and over what I would say once inside. Charlie and Katrina were the only ones I knew well here. Any information I got would have to be taken like a thief in the night.

The best method was to walk in boldly and ask for Charlie. And I did.

"Sorry, sir," said the dark, petite receptionist. She flipped through a set of index cards and said, "I don't know exactly how to reach him. There was a death in the family."

"Yes, I know. His wife." I found myself surprisingly unable to force Katrina's name from my lips. She had meant more to me than I was willing to admit. I'd have to come to grips with my own loss before I'd be able to help Charlie with his.

I remembered why I had come and said, "Is there a plant director or manager I might speak with? There's no real reason to bother Charlie right now."

"This is a bad time. Many of our managers are at COMDEX to interest other companies in our products. The CFO is in. I doubt if she will do, though, if you want to talk to someone in research."

The chief financial officer was perfect and I said so.

"Mrs. Keenan will be right with you, sir." The receptionist turned back to her stack of index cards. I had to ask.

She looked up and smiled. "I've got it all in a computer data base, but this is quicker. I can flip through the cards in a second. It takes longer than that for our file server to even notice me, and maybe ten more seconds for me to get to my files. I've been telling everyone I need a PC of my own, but there's never quite enough money."

"Thank you, Clarissa," came a frosty voice. I turned and saw a severely dressed woman in her mid-forties stalking out of a nearby corridor. She wore sensible shoes, her hair was pulled back into a bun so tight that it must have been screaming silently, and her tweed dress was neat if a trifle too conservative for a research company like RadChip-Tech. I knew by experience that it was almost impossible to tell the top researchers from the janitors in such places if clothing alone were the criterion. Ties were unknown and cheap sneakers were almost regulation attire.

But Mrs. Keenan stood far to the other side of the spectrum. The creases in her skirt were sharp enough to cut a finger. I wondered if she kept a steam iron in her office to take care of unsightly wrinkles that appeared during the day.

"How may I help you, Mr. Thorne?"

For all the receptionist's complaint about slow communication with her computer, none of the sluggishness existed when it came to passing along names.

"I'm a friend of Charlie and Katrina's," I said. "Charlie is up in San Tomás."

"Yes, we know." Mrs. Keenan stood with her arms staunchly folded, an impregnable defense against any assault.

"Could we talk in your office? Charlie sent me down here on a somewhat personal chore."

"Very well." She spun. I had thought she would execute a perfect Marine about-face, but her turn was just a bit too sloppy for that. She marched along the corridor, expecting me to follow at her quick pace. I had scant time to look into the offices, mostly empty, as we went to the far end of the hall. If we had gone any farther, we'd've left and gone into the next building.

Her office reflected her precision and Spartan tastes, with one exception. A picture of a basket filled with kittens sat on her desk, about where most executives carefully placed pictures of family. She spun her high-backed black leather chair around and deftly dropped into it, swinging toward me like a fighter pilot lining up his F-117 for a bombing run.

"We are very busy, Mr. Thorne. What is this mission from the boss?"

I cleared my throat, then launched into the story I had been working over in my mind. "Katrina was an officer of the company." I had no idea if this was true but it seemed likely.

"She was a director," Mrs. Keenan confirmed. She rocked back and steepled her fingers, examining me like a biologist studying a germ under a microscope.

"Charlie needs the policy numbers on her insurance policies. He's planning to stay in San Tomás for a week or longer and wants to take care of this long distance."

"Why didn't he call?"

"I'd gone to the funeral. I've known Katrina for years, and had introduced her to Charlie."

"A friend of the family, eh?" She rested her sharp chin on her fingertips and rocked to and fro gently. "I can't give you the policies. I can call him with the information—or fax it to him."

I kept from smiling. This was better than I'd hoped for.

"I understand. Charlie appreciates your devotion to duty and your strict adherence to rules."

Mrs. Keenan sniffed. "That's the first I ever heard of it. He's always riding me about being too rigid."

"You do a fine job, and that's why you are CFO," I said. In spite of her stern exterior, I saw that flattery worked its magic as surely as pulling a coin from behind his ear delights a small child. "I've got the fax number here." I pulled out a slip of paper, then hurriedly scribbled the number on it.

She studied it for a moment, then nodded. Mrs. Keenan spun in her chair and tapped furiously on her computer. As she worked, she said, "Clarissa is old-fashioned. If she'd learn to use her terminal properly, she'd be able to get all the information she needs faster than using those darned three-by-five cards. I've told her about that repeatedly. Time is money, you know."

"I know," I said, looking past the woman to a bank of file cabinets. Somewhere in that cavern of paper was information which would either confirm my suspicions or put to me to shame for thinking poorly of Charlie Hayes. Getting it might not be too hard. "And Charlie said he wanted to go over the balance sheet for the year, too."

"No problem." She tapped a key on the keyboard. "The report's sent. I can't find the data on any insurance policy, though."

"You can't?"

Working for a few seconds longer, she turned, perplexed. "Are you sure Mr. Hayes asked for his wife's insurance?"

"I thought so," I said, fishing for more information. "He might have wanted to review his own."

"We've got Key-Man Insurance, ten million dollars on Mr. Hayes. But the company didn't have a policy on Mrs. Hayes. There wasn't any reason. I mean, directors are important but not *that* important. In the computer chip business, you can find a dozen Nobel prize winners willing to serve on a board. And a thousand college professors willing to do it for a few shares of stock."

"I suppose Charlie's austerity program extended to his wife," I said, more to myself than to Mrs. Keenan.

She laughed harshly. "Not wanting to say anything bad about the dead, Mrs. Hayes didn't approve of anything Mr. Hayes did when it came to spending."

"He was too much of a spendthrift?"

My question had been coated with enough bait to set off the woman. She opened up like a file folder, her dislike for Katrina apparent. "I'm not saying she was a gold digger, but she complained all the time about the cutbacks here."

"And at home. Charlie mentioned this," I lied.

"They weren't starving by any means," Mrs. Keenan went on, "but they weren't eating caviar and champagne every night, either. None of us are. When the recession is over and the development costs for products in the pipeline are amortized, we'll be in the Fortune 500."

"Charlie had mentioned he was a month or two late on his mortgage payment." Again the lie came easily.

"Nonsense. I keep his checkbook balanced for him. Heck, I set up most of his accounts as automatic withdrawals from his bank. He was always forgetting to make payments. Trouble stopped when he let *me* handle that for him."

"I guess he meant Katrina's spending had gotten out of hand."

"Hardly." She almost smiled. The smugness had to come from Charlie keeping Katrina on a tight leash financially. "Mrs. Hayes had a budget and lived within it." She heaved a deep breath, turned back to the computer screen and shook her head. A single strand of gray-tinged brown hair slipped free. Mrs. Keenan tucked it back into place with an automatic gesture. "I don't understand there not being a record of an insurance policy. I don't remember the company ever taking one out, but why would Mr. Hayes ask for it if it wasn't here?"

"How long have you worked here?" I asked, trying to divert her attention.

"Almost two years."

"Charlie might have gotten confused with one he took out when he and Katrina were married—before you were hired."

"Possibly, but that's not like Mr. Hayes. He has a steel-trap mind for details."

"If you come across it, fax it to the same number, would you?"

"Certainly, Mr. Thorne." She paused and fixed me with her gaze again. She might have been driving needles into my naked flesh so intent was her stare.

"Is there something I can do for you?" I asked.

"Sorry. You remind me of my dead husband. Just a bit." Mrs. Keenan stared at the picture of the kittens, took another deep breath and began shuffling the stack of papers piled with incredible precision at the corner of her desk. I slipped out, intent on getting back to San Francisco and the fax machine in Willie Worthington's office.

CHAPTER 7

My shoulders ached, and I was exhausted from too much driving. The BMW is a great road car but the rough roads required constant attention. I felt a little peculiar returning to San Tomás to go with Charlie to the séance. After I had learned from his chief financial officer that there hadn't been an insurance policy on Katrina, my feelings had shifted again.

Maybe I was reading too much into Charlie's apparent lack of grief. I corrected that immediately. It wasn't that he hadn't shown grief over his wife's death, it was just that I didn't think he was showing enough. I knew him well enough, but to really know a person it's necessary to see how they handle great misfortune in their life. Everything I had heard told me he and Katrina had been happy. Mrs. Keenan wasn't the best source of information on Katrina's spending habits, though I had known she wasn't inclined to let money matter when she wanted to spend it.

Charlie's reaction might be his way of handling the loss. Some people hold everything inside, letting the emotion ooze out slowly over the years. I was something like that. But I had expected something else from Charlie. And when there hadn't been a volcanic eruption of sorrow, my faulty judgment had led me to spy on his personal life.

There hadn't been a big life insurance policy on Katrina. Charlie wouldn't gain from her death, and I hadn't bothered going to Worthington's office to retrieve the fax of the computer chip company's balance sheet. But I was returning to San Tomás for the damned séance. Charlie had called twice to be sure I was coming, and this told me he was coping with Katrina's death in a very sick way.

He wasn't letting go. Intellectually he might admit that she had died in the car wreck, but emotionally he wanted to believe she was still here. This is what galls me most about mediums. They prey on people who desperately need healing, who need to let loose emotionally. The promise of communication from beyond the grave makes the acceptance all the more difficult. Some victims I've met refused to believe their mediums were frauds, even after I'd shown how the fake channeling sessions were run. If half the effort and skill shown had gone into legitimate performance, most mediums could have been expert puppeteers rivaling Jim Henson.

Instead of emulating him, they'd pretend to contact him from beyond the grave.

I rented a room at the same motel in Mendocino, took a shower and got something to eat before driving south to San Tomás. As far as I could tell, Charlie hadn't left the small town after Katrina's funeral. On impulse, I drove by the cemetery. On her grave stood a vase with fresh flowers. I knew how Charlie must spend most of his day. He must sit beside the grave, just staring, wishing for a sign, some hint that his love would return to him.

"Cruel," I grumbled. "Leading a man on like this is so damned cruel." I touched the pocket where I carried the cassette. It was a shame forensics hadn't been able to tell me definitely that the tape was a fake. The evidence might not have convinced Charlie outright, but it would have planted a tiny seed of doubt. That might be enough to bring him into the channeling session with a more open mind.

Parking in the lot outside his motel room, I pulled my collar close. Wet spray from the ocean drenched everything. It might as well have been raining from the way the droplets worked their way down inside my shirt and soaked the cuffs of my pants. Hurrying, I got to Charlie's door and rapped twice. He must have been sitting nearby; the door almost flew open.

"Peter! Thanks for coming. I was afraid you wouldn't make it in time."

"The road's getting to be an old friend. It's as if I know every turn by now," I said. I shook the water from my coat and looked around for a place to hang it.

"We'll be going to Nyushka's in a couple of minutes," Charlie said.

Nyushka had to be the channeler's name, and I didn't ask how he had found out. All would be revealed, as the mediums say.

"There was another tape. Here, listen, Peter, and tell me what you think." Charlie turned on the cassette player. More static, but this tape was a little clearer.

"That's Katrina's voice. I'd know it anywhere," he said. "Nyushka is actually reaching her by channeling."

I listened to the inconsequential rambling so ineptly recorded, probably intentionally so. The medium—Nyushka—asked the standard general questions, and someone duplicating Katrina's voice answered. I wasn't convinced, but Charlie was. The rapt way he hung on every word told how deeply he had swallowed the baited hook.

"Charlie, we don't have to do this." I tossed the other tape onto the table. "I had a friend in the police department examine it."

"In forensics?"

"Yes," I said.

"And it's real, isn't it? I can tell you're disappointed, Peter. But I'm not. You're the very one who ought to believe such communication is possible."

"I'm the very one who ought to disbelieve it," I snapped, more harshly than I'd intended. "I almost died and there was brain damage. Look, Charlie, you *want* to believe Katrina is still able to talk to you. This Nyushka is using that. She'll ask for lots of money. Are you prepared to deliver it on the flimsiest of evidence?"

"I'm an engineer," Charlie said slowly. "I hope I'll get more proof than you think I will before paying a red cent to her."

"Take the money from Katrina's life insurance policy.

Go somewhere. Take a month or two or more, if you need," I said, suddenly realizing I was still on a fishing expedition of my own. His answer made me feel guilty.

"There wasn't a policy on her. What was the need? I have the business, and if I'd died, she would have inherited it all."

"Take a vacation. Let her memory find its proper place in your life."

"You don't have to come, Peter. I want you along, just in case this is a fraud. You've got the eye to detect it. But I don't want you to come if you refuse to acknowledge a real channeling session."

"I've never seen a real one—real bunco, yes, but never contact with the dead. Don't put yourself through this, Charlie." My plea might have been whispered into a hurricane. He was going to let Nyushka go through her dog and pony act.

I nodded grimly. He wanted me along to debunk, if I could. There must be mediums working with tricks I've never seen, but a stage magician looks at things in a different way. Some of my finest illusions come from using what I see in everyday life. People's attentions drift or focus on the wrong places because of differing misdirections. Finding new ones makes my work exciting.

"So?" Charlie demanded. "Are you with me or not?"

"Let's go."

We drove back to the deserted house we had scouted out two days earlier. A single candle burned in the front window, showing that someone had preceded us. I wanted to walk around the house to see where a truck with equipment might have been unloaded, but Charlie would have none of it. He wanted to start the channeling session and see his Katrina again. I didn't argue. The mist from the ocean had turned into a full-fledged rain squall now. Oregon mist, a friend of mine had always called it.

He hadn't wanted to admit it ever rained in San Francisco, just as Charlie didn't want to admit his wife was dead.

Charlie knocked hard on the door. When no one answered, Charlie twisted the knob. The door was unlocked, and we hurried inside. I was glad to be out of the rain, and Charlie was eager for a date with the netherworld. The house's interior was even darker than it had been before. I saw where blackout curtains had been hung. A small army could work behind them and never be seen. The ceiling had also been draped in heavy, muffling dark fabric. A single table dominated the middle of the otherwise empty room. I almost laughed when I saw a crystal ball. Those had gone out with the traveling carnivals and sideshows in the '30s.

"Nyushka?" Charlie called again.

She made a decently dramatic entrance, slipping through curtains to one side of the room. I'd heard the faint squeaking of old floorboards and had turned to face her. She seemed a little put out that I hadn't jumped like Charlie had when she intoned in a gravelly voice, "I hear and obey, Mr. Hayes."

"Katrina," he started. Charlie bit back his eagerness and tried to calm himself. I was beginning to feel sorry for him, and my guilt soared to hitherto unreached heights. He wasn't grieving for Katrina because he really accepted Nyushka's claims of reaching her.

"We will attempt to channel tonight," Nyushka said. Her voice grated on me. I doubted if she had cultivated such a rough voice. More likely, she had been struck in the throat and her voice box had never mended properly. "We must form a circle around the table. I have placed a focus for us. It does nothing but serve as a way of holding our thoughts."

She looked directly at me as she spoke, almost as if Charlie didn't exist. She must have guessed I was the one she had to convince with her mummery. Nyushka dressed conservatively for a medium. She wore a dark black skirt and a lighter blouse. It was difficult to guess the color in the dimness, but it might have been gray silk. The more I looked, the more I thought this was a good choice. Small pearl buttons fastened the front. I remembered having seen a similar blouse in the Emporium a few months ago with a two-hundred-dollar price tag on it. Nyushka didn't flaunt her jewelry as many did, but the bracelet on her left arm was expensive and had probably come from Tiffany's rather than the netherworld.

She leaned forward slightly, hands on the table. From the angle of her leaning, she had to be about five foot eight. Her weight was hidden, but the fleshy appearance of her cheeks and chin made an estimate of one-forty in the ballpark. Her dark hair was covered by a patterned scarf, her only concession to the usual raiment, though it did nothing to make her look like a Romany.

"Come closer. We must hurry. The storm disturbs the spirits this night."

"Do they have rheumatism?" I asked, not able to control my sarcasm.

"They have difficulty reaching us because of the electrical discharge. In life we are both chemical and electrical. In death, there is only the ethereal. I do not know why it is, but channeling is increasingly difficult during lightning storms." Nyushka bent forward and stared into the crystal ball. She didn't have to urge Charlie to do so. I followed, but more slowly. This was a clever ploy and one I hadn't seen before. By having her marks lean forward, the ceiling became a potential hot spot for unseen activity by Nyushka's accomplices.

Gripping my left ring finger with my right hand, I turned my ring. A mirrored surface gave me a perfect view of the ceiling. The ring is useful in seeing what cards are dealt from a deck. This evening I needed to look a bit beyond the top card if I wanted to see how Nyushka's scam worked. The woman closed her eyes and began rocking slightly. A quick glance at Charlie showed he was captivated by her performance.

Something other than her name hinted that Nyushka was of Russian ancestry. Her inflection was more of Jimmy Carter's Georgia rather than the other one, but she had worked to cover the drawl. She was fair complected and her skin was crisscrossed with a spider web of scars, as if someone had systematically cut her with a fine knife. No competent plastic surgeon would have left such obvious scars, unless the damage to her face had been extensive and the reconstruction necessary instead of some passing cosmetic vanity.

"There is . . . danger," Nyushka said, her gravelly voice putting my nerves on edge. Straining, I caught the faint hum of a speaker. Ever since the *Exorcist,* it's been a trick of horror movie directors to run a low frequency hum through their speakers, then pick up the tempo until it matches that of the human heart. The audience can't consciously hear it, but when the tempo accelerates, so does everyone's heart rate. I suspected Nyushka of using the same trick.

"What danger?" whispered Charlie. "Can you reach Katrina or not?"

"I can," Nyushka said, her eyes closed. She began swaying as if she were a tree in the squall outside.

"We would speak with her," I said, adding fuel to the fire. What was next? An accomplice banging on pots and moaning?

"Our ancestry ties us together for the channeling," Nyushka said. "Katrina was Russian. I am Russian." She began babbling something that sounded vaguely like a foreign language, but I know enough Russian to identify it when spoken. This was something else.

Checking my ring, I saw reflections of fabric rippling above us. Something was going to happen soon.

Wetness caused me to recoil. An assistant sprayed Charlie and me with water. As cold as it was in the unheated house, we'd had to have been dead not to notice. I shook my head when Charlie looked at me, startled.

"I am Petrushka, a serf. Czar Nicholas is passing through my village today on his way to the Muscovite Palace."

Nyushka was a good ventriloquist. Her mouth only partially open and her lips hardly moving, she produced a convincing Russian peasant. Charlie was taken in, but he didn't question why the peasant spoke English, nor did he see the muscles twitching in Nyushka's neck. I'd always admired ventriloquists their talent and had tried to learn the skill, thinking it would help me misdirect my audience. As a stage magician I am better than average. My attempts at ventriloquism always left me feeling like the dummy.

Nyushka jerked from side to side, but her hands never left the table. I almost called out in irritation that this was an old-fashioned séance, not a channeling. A bright star burst in the depths of the crystal ball. Momentarily blinded, it took my eyes several seconds to adjust to the dim light again. A skeletal hand passed near Nyushka, pausing to touch her shoulder before moving on and vanishing. Another of her assistants had moved through the heavy hangings, wearing a blackout suit and a single phosphorescent glove. The ghostly Michael Jackson suddenly vanished into thin air. Charlie gasped but I wasn't impressed. Thurston had done it better with his spirit cabinet illusion.

This was a clumsy stunt compared with the other subtle nuances Nyushka tossed in. All that had happened was the assistant turning his hand sideways so the blackened edge faced us. It would seem as if the entire hand had vanished. Once he had turned, the man could slip to the floor and slither out of the séance area unnoticed. I blinked as more water dribbled down from above.

"Why are the ghosts always in houses with leaky roofs?" I asked.

"Hush, Peter. She's still trying to find Katrina."

Again a star-point of light blazed in the crystal ball. There wasn't any way to figure out where the light came from; Nyushka might be using a laser. Mediums weren't above using high-tech equipment in their deceit.

"Please, no, no, do not send me to a gulag!" Nyushka launched into another routine of some poor citizen being shipped off to one of Stalin's prison camps. She tossed her head back and wind blew through the room, causing the water spray on my face to turn to ice. I wiped it off.

"Your hands, Peter, keep them on the table. You'll break her concentration."

For Charlie's sake, I did as he instructed. The desperation in his voice hinted at how much he needed to speak again to Katrina. I watched Nyushka's performance and didn't see anything extraordinary in it. For most people, the channeling experience would have been adequate, if they had come into the séance wanting to believe. A few skeptics might know tricks were being played for their benefit but not figure out how. I saw each of Nyushka's gimmicks and was unimpressed. How she had cobbled together the cassette with Katrina's voice was incidental. A sound technician could do wonders given the raw footage. Nyushka might have gotten the voice off an answering machine. Con artists have incredible sources for such items.

"Forward," Nyushka gasped out in her own voice. "I must go forward in time, near to Katrina's death throes. The ... the road. It turns! Can't stop. Can't stop!"

The subsonics were turned up enough to make me want to scream. My inner ear protested against such torture, and I almost cried out for them to turn off the damned amplifier.

Katrina's voice quelled the outbursts.

"Charlie, is it you? You've come!"

I looked around, trying to find the source of the voice. It came from Nyushka's direction, but the woman was slumped forward, supporting her weight on her stiffened arms. Her head hung to one side, as if she had passed out and yet had remained standing. Watching carefully, I saw none of the telltale muscle jerks in the woman's throat as Katrina's voice came again.

"Charlie, it is so cold here. I don't want to stay, but I must—for a time."

"Katrina," Charlie sobbed. Any thought I'd had about him murdering his wife for insurance money passed in that instant. Tears rolled down his cheeks. "I want you back. Please come back."

"There's no way, Charlie. I . . . am . . . dead." Her voice faded.

I knew Katrina's voice well, and this was it. But a recording cleverly queued up could duplicate the conversation. Charlie wasn't likely to ask probing questions. Any truly grieving widower would profess his love and ask for his lost love to return, and a tape could be cut to answer such demands. Even more sophisticated, a voice machine might have analyzed and captured her tones. The cadence was right, the inflection true and it might have been a trick. Simply reproducing a woman's voice wasn't beyond the limits of modern science.

"Do you recognize me, Katrina?" I asked quickly. I feared the fading of the voice signaled an end to the channeling.

"Peter? Is it you? Thank you for helping Charlie reach me. I love you so, too. You are such a good friend."

I hesitated. Nyushka might have done her homework and known Charlie had contacted me. The fake medium would have learned innumerable things about me for the channeled spirit to drop casually.

"How long have we been friends?" I demanded, motioning Charlie to silence. I felt sorry for him, but I had to get a handle on how the fakery was done. The voice seemed to drift back and forth behind Nyushka, still paralyzed in her trance. Whoever—or whatever—spoke came from behind the thick hangings.

"Four years, Peter. How could you forget?" The voice faded, like a car radio going beyond the range of an A.M. station. It wouldn't be long before the channeling ended and financial demands were made of Charlie—demands that he was likely to meet unquestioningly.

"What was I wearing when we met?"

The pause made me smile. The answer dumbfounded me.

"Not much." A tiny chuckle sounded that matched Katrina's perfectly. "We were at Zuma Beach and you had on red Speedo trunks. You couldn't keep your eyes off me. Perhaps it was the yellow string bikini."

"Or what was in it," I finished. Katrina and I had laughed about this years ago, and there was no way Nyushka could have known the dialogue or what I had worn, even if she had a complete picture file on Katrina.

"You are a dear friend, Peter, but it is you I love, Charlie. I—"

A crash of thunder cut off Katrina's words. Nyushka jerked awake, her eyes wide. She stared in horror at the crystal ball, then up at us.

"Did I make contact? I remember one or two channeled spirits, but not Katrina's."

"You did," Charlie said eagerly. "Get her back. I need to talk with her."

"She is distressed," Nyushka said. "There is unfinished business."

"What?" Charlie asked, moving around the table. I stood and watched, hardly able to stir.

"I do not know. It is just a . . . feeling about a, a winery. She wanted to buy it or wine. I cannot tell. You need to speak directly with her, but I cannot recall her spirit this evening. The storm, the lightning." Nyushka shook her head sadly.

"How much?" Charlie almost shook with need. "How much to get her back?"

"No money," Nyushka said, startling me even more. "I do not accept money for this. When the time is right again, I will call you." She turned dark eyes toward me and added, "Both of you."

Nyushka spun and pushed through the heavy curtains. By the time I had shaken off my shock enough to follow, she was gone. Wind whistled through the back door, which was now slightly ajar, showing where she and her accomplices had fled. I took out a small flashlight and examined the floor behind the curtains, the hangings themselves, the overhead where the cold water had been dripped on us. Above, the curtains were soaked, as if the water pistol had leaked. Electronic equipment might have stood on the floor behind the curtains, but I couldn't be certain.

I certainly couldn't be as sure of that as I was that I had talked with Katrina Hayes's immortal spirit.

CHAPTER 8

"Can't say I'm too surprised at this, Peter," said Willie Worthington. The detective rocked back in his chair, thought about putting his feet on his cluttered desk for a moment, then rocked back with a loud clomp, finding the only clear spot with unerring accuracy. "You scream all the time about not believing—and you *have* done good work for the boys and girls over in bunco—but deep down I knew you believed in that shit."

"I don't," I said, trying to put my thoughts in order. It had been two days since the channeling had produced Katrina's spirit. The time I'd spent working on my new act was less than half the time I'd taken calling various electronics companies in the Bay area. I put the same question to Worthington that I'd asked them.

"Is it possible to duplicate in real time a person's voice if you have an analysis of it?"

"Can a machine copy human speech?" Worthington scratched his stubbled chin and shook his head. "Can't say that I believe it's impossible. Ever call time and temperature?"

"That's different," I said. "They record certain phrases and put them together depending on the time you call. They know what they need ahead of time. A few hundred responses is it. I tell you, Willie, this was like talking to a living person. The responses weren't quick, but they sounded natural when they came."

"Not quick, huh? Ever call a voice messaging gizmo?"

"No, no," I protested. "This wasn't anything like that at all. It might have been a recording but the words came out smoothly, well-tempered."

"You make it sound like someone's forging a sword."

"They must be," I said, thinking hard. I hadn't told him my real concern. Knowledge is a valuable commodity these days. I know of an airline that went bankrupt and sold its planes and computers for less than the reservation system it used. The names within that system were important, more so than the old equipment it hadn't updated in years. "Knowledge is power," I muttered, hardly knowing I spoke aloud.

" *'Nam et ipsa scientia potestas est,'* " Worthington said.

"What?" I blinked in surprise. I didn't understand what he'd said.

"Francis Bacon," he said. *"Meditationes Sacrae. De Haeresibus,* somewhere around A.D. 1597."

"I didn't know you were a scholar." Worthington surprises me with the way his mind holds onto bits of trivia, but that's one of the qualities that makes him a good detective. For all his appearance, there was nothing slovenly about his brain or the way it worked.

"So who's a scholar? Me and the boys was sittin' around a week or two back arguing over who'd win in a one-on-one, this Bacon guy or Marcus Aurelius."

"I trust you bet on Bacon?"

"Peter," he said solemnly, "there's more than you're telling me about the channeling. I've known you too long to believe you'd be taken in by a simple scam. You went into the channeling looking for the wires and buzzers."

"I need more information. Nyushka was slick. She didn't even hit Charlie up for money, but the hook was sunk deep."

"Yeah, sunk real deep," Worthington said, his eyes fixed unblinkingly on me.

"I didn't mean to get into this as much as I have."

"There's something else."

"What?" He didn't seem to be talking about the séance.

"The fax you had sent into the department's machine. You aren't supposed to use it for personal messages. The auditor is raising holy hell about this. I tried to call Mary to see what was for supper and he caught me. 'Don't use department telephone lines for personal calls,' " Worthington mimicked in a shrill, squeaky voice. "I couldn't get through to her so I went home." He rubbed his protruding belly. "The heartburn I got from her meat loaf was awful. Kept me up for hours. I'd hoped she wouldn't fix dinner, but she did and the auditor kept me from finding out. It was a killer meal, Peter. Sheer hell."

I had to smile at Worthington and his continual battle with his wife's poor cooking. To consider the garbage he ate as better than a home-cooked meal ranked among the world's greatest heresies, but I had eaten a few times at the Worthington household and knew he wasn't exaggerating too much. Mary Worthington was a terrible cook. Jokes about buying frozen leftovers weren't far off the mark.

"I don't need it anymore," I said.

"You think I'm going to toss it into the wastebasket where that pencil neck can ferret it out? No sir, not me. My mama didn't raise no fools." Worthington slid two sheets of cheap ammonia-smelling thermofax paper from a coffee-stained folder and shoved them across the desk. I glanced at them. They were the current balance sheet and income statements for the chip manufacturing company, the ones Mrs. Keenan had thought she was sending to Charlie. I put them into my pocket, but they weren't going to tell me what I needed to know.

"I've been thinking," I started, not sure what I was going to say. Everything was jumbled together in my head. Nyushka, Charlie, Katrina, vague memories of the barbed-wire-covered beast on the astral plane, snippets from my last psychometry for Worthington—it all melted and flowed and shifted in my head.

One problem with psychometric reading is the way senses get jumbled during the reading. Smell and vision and hearing and touch change constantly, letting me hear odors and see sound and feel light. Sorting it out is difficult.

"We've been digging around," Worthington said. "You might be interested in what we've found."

"What?" My mind had wandered, and I didn't know exactly what he was talking about.

"The place downtown? You remember that murder? It didn't feel right to me."

"The people," I said, getting a frayed end of thought and trying to follow it. "There were so many."

"You were right about her chipping on the side. Regular customers. When the fleet was in, she paraded them through one after the other. I did some footwork and found a half dozen off one ship who called on her."

"One of them did it?" That hardly seemed right. So much hatred, but it was a confused anger, misdirected and diffuse.

"You sound skeptical. We've still got her old man jugged on suspicion. The D.A. is screaming for us to wrap up the investigation so he can get a court date for arraignment."

"No, don't," I said, not knowing why I spoke. "There's more to this."

"Want to try it again?"

This was the last thing in the world that I needed. My head hurt from too many problems. I wasn't working as I ought to be, and there was Charlie Hayes. The séance hadn't gone the way I had thought, and that bothered me more than anything else. Hearing Katrina again with her disturbing precision of memory about our first meeting might be explained away somehow. A diary, perhaps, though Katrina had never seemed the type to record what happened to her. She was a live-for-the-moment type.

"Carpe diem," Worthington said. "Seize the day, and time's a-wastin'." He craned his neck to peer past me through the slightly ajar door to his office. Turning, I saw the auditor working across the squad room like a poorly dressed tornado. He seemed to do nothing, but everything around him went flying as officers struggled to shove papers into their desk drawers and keep hard-to-explain details from the man's probing eyes.

"Maybe that should be 'seize the neck and wring,' " I said. It was becoming frightening how well Worthington was able to read my thoughts. Or was it simply synchronicity? That opened new frontiers I was loath to explore.

"There'd be a line around the block and halfway up Powell Street, and I'm not sure who would have clout enough to muscle to the front of the line. The watch commander got nailed good about his 'coffee fund.' " Worthington cast a dour look in the auditor's direction and jerked his head, indicating we should leave.

I said little as we drove back to the small apartment. There was something hidden in the apartment I had missed before—and this was the same feeling I had about the channeling. It couldn't happen, yet it had. I doubted Katrina had told Charlie about our first meeting, though she might have. I tried to figure out what kind of scam Charlie might be running on me, if the séance had been for my benefit. Answers skipped just beyond my mental grasp.

"Quit sweating so much, Peter," Worthington said. "You haven't even started working." He heaved himself out of the battered green car and went to the front door. It took several seconds for him to find the proper key and open the padlock. I simply stood on the sidewalk and stared at the house.

It hadn't been a home. Nothing inside told me of love, just unsated appetites. What had the woman done with the money she got from her whoring? It hadn't gone into furnishings or a large apartment. From my quick glance through the closet, she hadn't been a clothes horse—quite the opposite. Her taste in clothing had been cheap and tawdry. Jewelry? Had she been robbed? Or was a flashy car parked in some rented garage nearby?

None of it fit together as it should.

"Got it," Worthington said, twisting the key savagely. "I ought to get them to oil these damned locks once in a while."

"What kind of car did the woman drive?" I asked.

"Didn't have a car. Her old man drove a VW Bug.

Mostly rusted through, model in the late '60s. I can find out for sure, if it's important."

I wandered through the room and stopped at the spot where the body had been found. A footstool was pushed against the wall. Stooping, I laid my hand on the discoloration on the rug. Almost immediately I shivered with cold. A light trance was all I needed for the sense-jumbling flood of information.

I heard freezing and saw the acrid tang of cordite. Wobbling, I ran my hand back and forth over the rug.

"What is it, Peter?"

"Why is the rug wet?" I asked, not sure if I was speaking to Worthington or myself. "There is a reason. Ice. Hate. Resentment." I slipped and fell over, not even trying to break the fall. I crashed into a table and just sat on the floor, staring at nothing. The trance wasn't deep enough for me to go to the astral plane where misty objects appeared and formed tangible metaphors for what happened in this world, but the gnawing feeling at my mind that I was missing something important made up for it.

"Where did the money go?" I asked Worthington.

"She wasn't robbed. There was almost forty bucks in her purse. And another ten in her dresser."

"What of her jewelry?"

"It's not worth the time to steal. No self-respecting fence or pawnbroker would give you the time of day for it." Worthington stared at me; I was still sitting on the floor, motionless, completely lost in thought. "What are you getting at?"

"Where is the money she made from servicing all the men?"

"Don't rightly know," Worthington said, scribbling in his notebook. "I'd missed that point. This place is a real dump. She sure as hell didn't spend it here. And I see what you were getting at about the car. We can check to see if she had some XJ-6 parked in a garage somewhere, but I doubt it. She didn't look the sports car type." He snorted in contempt. "She hardly looked the type to have fare for BART."

"Blackmail? Drugs?"

"I doubt the former and the answer's no to the latter," Worthington said. "She was clean on the autopsy drug screen. What would be evil enough to let anyone blackmail her? She didn't have position or money or influence. Who'd gain?"

Other notions occurred to me. A caged tiger, I paced the small room, letting sensations tickle at my brain like feathers. Part of the puzzle had been overlooked by the officers on the scene, by Worthington, by me. Lust and unresolved anger hung over the small apartment like a rarefied cloud of dust, not bad enough to make anyone cough but still annoying.

"Tell me how you see the crime," I said, more to keep Worthington from his habit of writing frantically than to gather information. I had pieced together a considerable amount of detail, but hearing someone else's perspective might help me in finding what I overlooked again and again.

"The official line is that her husband came home and saw one of her johns leaving. He got himself worked up into a lather, entered, confronted her about her little sideline, then blew his cork and shot her. She was standing over there by the footstool, stumbled back and fell across the table onto the floor."

"And your theory?" I continued to pace, adding the kitchen to my route. Something about the kitchen drew me, as if it would provide an answer to my nagging doubts.

"A gut feeling that he was shocked enough about the whole matter not to have done it. I figure one of her johns offed her, who knows why. Since we've got a list that includes half the sailors who've ever ported in San Francisco, we need something more substantial to hang a case onto the real killer."

"Tell me about the body."

"You're supposed to be doing your, uh, thing," Worthington finished lamely. He had started to say "trick" and had hardly been able to change before insulting me. "I didn't want to clutter your head with physical evidence."

"The body," I insisted. Sitting in the uncomfortable, straight-backed wooden kitchen chair, I stared straight at the dingy refrigerator. A few nondescript magnets held a grease-stained shopping list to the door. I had no desire to read what was on the list. The refrigerator hummed and groaned in agony from a motor that hadn't been cleaned in too many years.

"Gunshot, distance about three feet or so from the powder residue on her dress. The bullet entered—"

"Powder burns," I said; something nudged me in that direction. "Any residue on her hands?"

"Nope. That's one of the things that makes me believe her old man. We ran an NAA and—"

"What's that?" So close. The answer danced just beyond my fingertips, darting away as I reached for it. What bothered me most, I wasn't sure if my nebulous feelings were about this murder or Katrina's channeling.

"Neutron activation analysis. We swabbed her hands with dilute nitric acid and checked for nitrates. The scanning electron microscope was being repaired, but the NAA works fine. Nothing shows she had the gun in her hand when it was fired."

"No sign of struggle, either," I said, knowing this without Worthington telling me. I stood and placed my hands on the refrigerator's cold white enamel front. An electrical surge passed through me. Déjà vu rattled me. The same energy came to me that had been on the rug in the front room. "No money, no powder burns."

"That's it," Worthington said, staring curiously at me.

"Was she a nymphomaniac?"

"You mean, did she screw all those guys and not get paid? Maybe so. I never asked any of them what they paid her." He was off filling another page in his spiral notebook. He broke a pencil point and had to fish in his pocket for another stub of yellow pencil. I planted my feet and allowed calm to wash over me. Going deeper into a trance was tricky since so much distracted me.

Pictures of Katrina and the miasma of her perfume, memories of Charlie and Mrs. Keenan and the auditor of SFPD flickered like an out-of-sync movie. Sounds and smells piled atop one another in a weird sensual chaos that made my head ache horribly. In the distance roared mechanical dragons armed and dangerous.

Cold, just like him. This'll show him, it will!

I shook with the power of the hatred, but it wasn't a focused emotion. It was inner-directed and against others at the same time. It required a supreme act of will to push hard and shove myself away from the slick white front of the refrigerator. I stood and stared at my hands as if they had frozen and turned blue. I flexed them and feeling returned slowly.

"So cold," I said. "She hated everyone, everything. It didn't matter. She hated her husband and her life and the men she saw here. She didn't get money from them. It was a form of punishment. She reinforced her own feelings of unworthiness by sleeping with as many men as she could. Always sailors because her father was a sailor."

"He was?" Worthington continued to make notes. I ignored him now. The crime was fully formed in my mind. All that was needed was to put it into words someone else could understand. That was a chore that might be beyond me. I had experienced her intense self-abhorrence, and *knew* what she had intended.

"What of her shoes and ankles?" I asked.

"Nothing special."

"What did the coroner report?"

"Nothing," Worthington repeated. "What should he have found?"

"Powder burns, maybe on her shoe soles, maybe on her ankles." I opened the refrigerator door. Hand shaking, I pulled open the small freezer compartment. A small cardboard tube lay to one side. Indentations in the frost showed where a second one had been recently.

"What's that?" Worthington peered over my shoulder, having to stand on tiptoe to see.

"A two-foot-long icicle," I said. "She needed only one. Did you find a similar cardboard tube in the trash?"

"Yeah, here it is. The tube was cut lengthwise, though. Nothing had been inside."

"Water," I said. The explanation came faster now. "She froze a bar of ice and took it out. She rested the pistol against the footstool, placed the ice through the trigger guard, against the trigger, then sat and pushed both ends of the icicle with her feet. She killed herself."

"The damp spot on the rug," Worthington said. "That's what remained of the ice. But why'd she want to pin it on her husband?"

There wasn't any answer for that. She had hated herself and wanted to end her miserable life, but her love-starved ego wouldn't stand for that. She had to have one final bit of revenge on him.

One final bit of revenge on him. One final bit of revenge. The words rang in my skull like a clarion. One final bit.

CHAPTER 9

I sat on my small balcony staring at the Golden Gate Bridge. The great span never seemed to change, though paint crews worked constantly on it to keep it in repair. I thought I saw tiny black dots swinging back and forth in the high wind on the northern support, but I couldn't be sure. My eyes worked lower, toward Sausalito, over to Tiburon, north through the drifting fog obscuring 101 until I reached San Tomás in my imagination.

Something about the psychometric solution I had gotten for Willie Worthington kept haunting me. The woman had killed herself as revenge. Katrina had been a loving, happy woman—she would never do that. I closed my eyes and tried to get my thoughts into logical order. Everything was too jumbled for that. If my brain had exploded and the jigsaw parts put back together by a blind schizophrenic, there couldn't have been any more confusion. No matter what I worked on, my mind wandered along strange and flustering paths.

The cold wind finally drove me in from the balcony. I stared at the phone, willing it to ring. I needed to talk with Barbara, but she was studying for her comprehensive—that was the message left while I'd been in San Tomás with Charlie. We never quite connected these days. I wanted to call her and tell her what had happened, but there was no point burdening her now. She had too much to worry about in her own life. I had seen students turn psychotic worrying over their Ph.D. examinations. They were truly a rite of passage into the academic world and couldn't be made easy.

Listless, I turned and stared at the table strewn with

crude sketches for my new act. Time was running out for me to build and perfect some of the escapes and stunts I wanted for Vegas. An effortless performance is won by hours of long, arduous practice. Worthington had pulled me away from that rehearsal, if only for a few hours at a time, with his investigations. The mental image of the juggernaut roaring down on me was fading slowly, as was the horror of the woman killing herself. But it took time and effort to completely expunge them.

I heaved a deep breath. I had to keep telling myself that erasure from my memory *was* possible. Living the hell promised by the twisted minds of would-be murderers and suicides wore at me like water dripping inexorably on a stone. Nothing appeared to vanish, but every day a slightly deeper hole was cut in the stone. Given enough time, even the hardest rock would become a torus. That was the way I had begun to feel. A part of me, an important inner part, was becoming fragile. The constant use of my psychometric talent cracked it a little more each time.

What would happen when it wore through completely wasn't something I wanted to consider.

I pushed the papers around on the table, made a few more notes and thought about the order of escapes and illusions in my act. Pacing is important to keep the audience on the edge of its seat—and misdirected.

That notion sent me off into other directions, far from the stage and my magician's fantasies.

"Why would Charlie want me at the channeling? Why would he feed information to Nyushka just for me?" There didn't seem to be a good answer to those questions. He had no reason to scam me. He was far richer than I ever would be. Almost as an afterthought I pulled the pages of his company's financial statement from my pocket and looked over them.

It might take an accountant to figure out the complete picture, but it seemed to me that his company had lost a considerable amount of revenue in the past year. That didn't mean Charlie would have to declare bankruptcy; at least, I doubted it. That he had experienced a financial crunch was indisputable, but he wasn't profiting from Katrina's death. There wasn't any insurance policy.

And duping me out of a few dollars wouldn't help his ailing firm. He didn't need tens of dollars, he needed hundreds of thousands. It made no sense for the channeling to be a swindle aimed at me.

The unpleasant possibility that this channeling was real kept returning to haunt me. I had made a vocation of exposing frauds. In more than five years there hadn't been a single medium who came close to really contacting the spirits of the dead. As much as people wanted to believe movies like *Ghost,* there was no afterlife.

That was a basic personal tenet, and it was being shaken severely.

How could Nyushka know what I had been wearing when Katrina and I had met for the first time? Or where? It had to be a diary. Or a close friend she had confided in. The more I thought, the less sure I was of what I had seen and heard at the channeling. My willingness to believe might have influenced me, as it did so many others. I might have talked myself into hearing details that hadn't existed. Charlie had certainly swallowed the bait.

And so had I. Shoving the papers around on my table wasn't getting me anywhere. I went to change clothes for the drive back to San Tomás.

The winery Katrina had raved about sat on a small rise with a fabulous view of the ocean. The vineyards behind sloped down and ran off into the dense gray fog. Neat rows of growing grapes seemed so tranquil I felt myself relaxing for the first time in almost a week. It was easy to understand the appeal of this small town.

Driving around wasn't the way to see San Tomás, though. It was smaller than small; it was hardly more than a widening in the road. Parking off the highway, I started down the street, noticing they hadn't bothered putting sidewalks everywhere. A block would be concreted and then a patch of gravel or mud would stretch for a few dozen yards before the next section of sidewalk started. I had to pick my way past the muddy parts as I studied the stores lining the main street.

The funeral parlor held no attraction for me. The mortician gave me the cold creeps. As I wandered by I saw a general store that looked as if it had ridden out of the Old West. It even had a pickle barrel on the boardwalk in front, the obvious congregating place for San Tomás residents.

A trio of older men sat in the rear playing cards. Two women chatted over yard goods and the clerk waited on a man intent on buying fishhooks.

As soon as the clerk had rung up his sale, he turned to me and asked, "What can I do for you today? Interest you in fishing gear?"

There might be a more boring sport than fishing, but I couldn't think of what it might be. Bowling came close but sitting with a line dropped into a placid stream waiting for a fish to bite on a worm-laden hook seemed both a time-waster and not worth the effort.

"Seems to be a lot of fishing around here," I said.

"Not so much, but you have the look of a city fellow. Thought you might want to fish."

"A friend of mine was here a week or so back and highly recommended the place. San Tomás is heaven on earth, she said. Peaceful, just the sort of town to buy property and retire."

"You don't look like the retiring kind," the man said, suddenly frosty. "If you're looking for land to grow dope, you can get the hell out of here."

I had heard the mountains in Northern California were filled with marijuana growers. The customer ahead of me had been buying fishhooks. Maybe he was setting traps for unwary DEA agents rather than angling for a trout in some meandering stream.

"Nothing is farther from my mind. Katrina Hayes was my friend. She was killed in a wreck not too far down the road from here."

"Did see you in town for the funeral. Shame about her. She came in here a time or two. Pretty lady. Real nice."

"She buy a lot?" I asked, not knowing what prompted the question.

"Always. She carried a wad of bills big enough to choke a cow. I told her this was a law-abiding town and not like San Francisco where you might get mugged for that kind of cash, but it wasn't smart showing it around here, either. The last bit crime we had was when old man Murdoch's pit bull savaged a horse from a riding academy well nigh two years ago. No, wait, I take that back. The Dairy Queen down the road was robbed last year, but the highway patrol caught the kids a couple hours later. Out for a joy ride. Two of 'em from Sacramento."

I listened to the garrulous spiel with half an ear. Small town gossip was boring unless you were involved or knew the people who were.

"Mrs. Hayes was thinking on buying some property here, you say?"

"What? Oh, yes, that's what Charlie said."

"That'd be Mr. Hayes." The clerk nodded sagely, as if he had the world in his pocket now. "He's still around town, not taking his wife's death too well from all I hear."

"He loved her a great deal," I said.

"Didn't see the two of them together in town much. Usually just her."

"She was the one who wanted to find a house here."

"Just like you, eh?" the clerk said, eyeing me closer. "Too bad about her death. Just a darned shame, such a pretty lady."

"Who was she dealing with? What realtor?"

"There's only a couple. Leastwise, in these parts. Up in Mendocino there are a whole pack of them." He bit his tongue to keep from adding "jackals" to the sentence. For all the added money expansion would bring to San Tomás, this was one resident who preferred his rural life-style be left alone.

"Won't take long checking them out, then," I said, "unless she'd brought someone in from up north."

"Doubt it," the clerk said. Seeing I wasn't likely to buy

anything, he turned his attention to the woman wrestling over a basket filled with yard goods.

Checking the thin phone book showed the clerk was right. Only two real estate agents, or brokers or whatever they fancied themselves this week, carried local listings. I considered calling them, then decided, since both offices were within a five-minute walk, that I could use the exercise.

Spray from the ocean formed an invigorating mist in the air. I let it wash my face and carry away even more of my concerns. I took life too seriously. Everything was too earnest. I needed to relax more. A place like San Tomás might be the ideal getaway for me. When I was in my apartment the phone never stopped ringing. It was as much an office as a home, and I needed somewhere I could kick back and not be bothered by Willie Worthington or booking agents or any of the dozen other time-robbers who always seemed to find me.

The notion of putting a cellular phone in my car had been rejected a long time ago. My only concession to such modernity lay in the answering machine in my apartment, but maybe a car phone wasn't such a bad idea for out here. I wouldn't need to have a phone in a vacation home at all, yet would have access when I wanted it.

I stopped in front of Ocean View Realty, peering in the rain-streaked window. Two women worked at a desk, struggling in front of a computer terminal. I went in. Both looked up as if they'd been caught with their hands in a cookie jar.

"May we help you, sir?" asked the older woman. She was more conservatively dressed than the other lady, preferring earth colors to the flashier neons that were the fashion in San Francisco. The expensive outfit looked as if she'd had it for a dozen years and had taken good care of it.

I explained that I was looking for the realtor handling Katrina's search for a winery.

"You want Quincy," the woman said, her face falling

slightly. The only prospect she was likely to see today or maybe this week wanted the town's other real estate agent.

"Where might I find Mr. Quincy?"

This brought smiles to both women's lips. "No, no, his name's Quincy Graham. Graham Realty is his. The office is just down Oak Street, not a hundred feet."

"Thanks." I flashed them my most sincere smile and left. They went back to their technological fight with the desktop computer. I wished them well but doubted they had a chance.

The only difference between Ocean View Realty and Quincy Graham's was the name. The same brick front, the same smeared window, the identical display told me business wasn't too exciting in town. I forced my way through the balky, swollen front door. A bell jangled and someone called out from the back room that he'd be out in a minute.

No computer weighed down Graham's desk. In fact, very little cluttered it. He didn't even have the usual knickknacks one expects of a realtor to show they are family-oriented just plain folks. A toilet flushed and a tall, well-built man in his early thirties came from the rear, still working on getting his zipper up.

"Can I help you? My name's Quincy Graham." He thrust out his hand to be shaken. I wondered if he'd had time to wash after using the toilet. I doubted it but shook anyway.

"Peter Thorne." He ushered me toward a chair beside his desk. I considered various ploys and decided to do a little fishing before mentioning Katrina.

"What brings you to San Tomás? You from San Francisco?" When I nodded, he said earnestly, "Great place, San Francisco. But busy, isn't it? Always on the go. A lot to do and see, but crowded. There's not even a good place for a cemetery."

The mention of a graveyard made me sit just a little straighter. Graham was just making conversation, and I understood his tack. He wanted to let me know this was a place where you could spend your declining years—and stay beyond. No one is buried in San Francisco because of the high water table and limited space. Mission Dolores and the Presidio with its San Francisco National Cemetery have been closed for years to the newly deceased.

He saw my reaction and smoothly changed the subject.

"Views, you want 'em, we got 'em. The best in Northern California. And quiet. The woods inland are wonderful for just walking through. Some original stand redwoods."

"I was thinking of something more productive, say, a winery." The subtle play of emotion across Graham's face told me nothing. He didn't appear pleased to have a sucker on the hook for a big deal, yet I couldn't say positively that greed wasn't present.

"We have—had—a land deal in the works, but it has probably fallen through. One of the principals was killed."

"One of them?"

"The Alsace Winery up on the hill has been vacant for almost a year. The vines are in good shape—the drought hasn't hit us too hard here, but I'd need to go through a considerable amount of paperwork to be able to get out of the offering."

"If one of your principals is deceased, perhaps the others wouldn't mind a new partner? I have a considerable amount of money to invest in the right property." Again I watched elusive emotions chase across his face. He could only mean Katrina when he said one partner had died. Graham ought to be jumping at the chance to reconstruct what ought to be a lucrative deal. The recession had caused a major credit crunch and finding buyers for large properties wouldn't be easy.

"That's possible," he said, edging around a real answer. "Is there a ballpark figure you're considering for this investment?"

"Substantial," I said, playing the same game. "I need to know that it won't be thrown away, however." Leaning back, I laced my fingers behind my head and looked off into the distance. "Being a partner in an operational winery appeals to me. What type of grapes are growing there?"

"Sauvignon blanc," he said. "Let me contact the other investors and see if they are still interested. It's been a week now and they might have decided the deal had fallen through."

"Any other properties available that might produce a little revenue in the two or three million range?" I asked. Even mention of such significant numbers did nothing to excite Quincy Graham. Business couldn't be that good in San Tomás. From the look of the two women in Ocean View Realty, it was the pits.

"One or two, but the prospects aren't as good as for the Alsace property."

"What's the asking price on the winery? If the others aren't interested in a partnership, perhaps I can swing it alone or find a friend or two to go in with me. Talking someone into taking a minority stake in property like that ought to be easy."

Graham looked uncomfortable at the suggestion but said nothing to give the impression he wasn't on top of a good deal. He opened a desk drawer and fumbled around inside until he found a few colorful folders. He pulled them out and handed them to me. "Look these over. There are a couple places you might like better. I'll be glad to show them to you when you've decided."

I thumbed through the properties, seeing plat numbers and county document references on the backs of the slick presentations. But Graham hadn't given me any information on the Alsace Winery. This made me wonder about his motives. Nyushka was pulling some kind of scam. Graham might be in it with her.

"No other wineries, eh," I said. Then to put his mind at rest, added, "That's not too important. I really don't know what I'm interested in but will know it when I see it."

"Fine, fine, Mr. Thorne. Give me a call when you've had time to think it over. Be glad to show you just about anything that's got a listing. We're MLS, you know."

Seeing my quizzical look, he added, "Multiple Listing Service. If there's a property you like that's listed with another company, the commission is split."

"Of course." I tucked the brochures into my side coat pocket, shook hands and wondered why I felt unclean. Back on the street in the ocean spray, I stood and let the uneasiness wash away. Graham hadn't said or done anything to annoy me, but I felt edgy around him. It was as if he had lied constantly, and yet there wasn't any good reason to do so. On impulse, I turned and went back to Ocean View Realty. The two women still struggled with their computer, though one had the look of someone getting an inkling of the problem.

"Sorry to bother you again. Do you handle MLS properties?"

"Of course. See something you're interested in?"

"The Alsace Winery, outside town, up on the hill. I understand it's for sale."

"It's not MLS," the woman at the computer said, looking prouder of herself by the second. She worked a few more seconds on the keyboard, peered myopically at the flickering amber screen and said, "Graham Realty has an exclusive on it for another six weeks."

"Do you know who the current owner is? I'd like to talk with him."

"No information on someone else's exclusive. Sorry. But if you want that particular property, try back in a month or so. Usually if a place hasn't sold on an exclusive, the owner will go MLS with it or even change listed agent."

"Thanks," I said, going back into the weather. Leaving Ocean View's office made me feel as if I had gone from a cheery fireplace and into the cold, just the reverse feeling I had with Quincy Graham. I wandered around San Tomás a while longer, then got into my car and drove north to Mendocino and the local land records office. It took only two inquiries to find the office building and a few minutes following arrows to the lower depths of the structure before I came to the huge property records books.

Using the numbers off the backs of Graham's brochures, I looked up the deeds to the property for sale. I wasn't sure what I wanted to find, but it would take more than a superficial check to find it. As far as I could tell, the properties were legitimate, for sale and had clear titles and clean tax records, except one. An inquiry and an excursion to another book showed that Graham was handling a bank foreclosure that required payment of considerable back taxes before the new owner got a new loan on the property. In this day of savings and loan failures, it surprised me there weren't more delinquencies, considering the rising number of bankruptcies statewide.

There remained just one more item to check. Taxes had been paid on Alsace Wineries, but little other information was available.

"Pardon me," I called to the bored clerk. "I need more information on Alsace Wineries. The property is for sale and—"

"Alsace? Oh yeah, that place down near San Tomás. Don't know about it. Let's look it up." The clerk went over the same pages I had, then shook his head. "Taxes are paid by a corporation down in San Francisco. All we've got is a post office box number for them. You say the place is up for sale?"

"Graham Realty down in San Tomás has it."

"He's a good man. Everything looks to be in order."

"Isn't it odd that there's not more information about the owners?" I asked.

The clerk almost laughed. "Mister, we don't make it a banner headline every night, but everybody knows it's a fact that most of the places on the books like this have a couple acres of marijuana growing on them. You might check with the DEA if you're really interested."

"You're saying drugs are grown there?"

"No, no, nothing of the sort. What I'm saying is, a lot of places with registrations similar to this one are fronts. You understand? I *never* said anything illegal's going on."

The clerk seemed more afraid of being sued for slander than anything else. He had made an off-the-cuff remark and nothing more. I noted the box number back in the city but didn't think it would net me any new information.

What was I to do, stand by the box all day waiting for someone to pick up the mail? If the winery had been empty as long as people said, there might not be much more than junk mail going through the mail drop.

Everything seemed on the up-and-up in San Tomás, including Quincy Graham and the exclusive on the winery. But I worried all the way back to San Francisco. Something wasn't quite right and I couldn't put it into words.

CHAPTER 10

I smashed into the floor, struggling to get the handcuffs unfastened. Twisting sharply, I dislocated my right shoulder. The pain shot through me like a shark swimming for blood. Closing my eyes and breathing deeply, I calmed myself and got the pain under control. This was the way Houdini escaped from straitjackets, and I found it worked well in other situations. But it was so damned painful.

Then the telephone began ringing. I considered letting the answering machine pick up, then remembered Barbara Chan had promised to call today. She was nearing her oral exam and needed someone sympathetic to talk with. She probably had any number of other doctoral students at the university who were better able to commiserate with her on the strain, but it gave me a chance to be useful across the entire continent—and she seemed to appreciate my need to help however I could.

Moving swiftly now, I got my arms moved to a spot where I could kick my feet through my manacled wrists. My shoulder returned to its socket with a dull pop and the pain began to recede. This was a hell of a way to make a living, but sometimes the effect is worth the hurt. When I did this trick on stage, I had to get free within ten seconds. There couldn't be any fumbling or I'd end up in a world of trouble from the rest of the escape, suspended upside down over a vat of burning alcohol.

A quick clap of my hands opened the cuffs. They fell to the floor, shining brightly in the sunlight pouring through my east-facing window. I blinked for a moment when I saw that butterscotch diamond on the floor. I must have

been working all night and hadn't noticed. I'd've bet that
it wasn't much past midnight.

The phone kept ringing. Diving for it, I scooped it from
the cradle.

"Hello, Barbara?"

"You've got the little lady on the mind, don't you, Peter?" asked Willie Worthington. "Not that I blame you.
She's got a lot on the ball."

"What is it, Willie? I'm working."

"Doesn't sound as if your mind's on it," he said. I pictured him lounging back in his swivel chair, chewing av-
idly at the end of a once-yellow pencil. Thoughts of
human-termite genetic accidents at some illicit laboratory
crossed my mind.

"I haven't practiced much, and this is the longest stretch
I've had in a week."

"That Katrina Hayes business?" he asked, knowing that
it had taken more of my time than I liked. So much about
Nyushka's channeling gnawed away at me.

"What is it, Willie?"

"Can you come on down to the Hall? I've got a couple
things to go over with you."

"Is it important? Really important?"

Worthington paused for a long moment, then said, "De-
pends on where you're coming from. The auditor's taken
a few days off and things are returning to normal in the
squad room. That means our sources of information are
again at your disposal, in way of thanks for the efforts
you've expended on the behalf of justice in the past."

I closed my eyes and tried not to snap at him. His silly
little speech was as close as he was likely to get to thanking me for the work I'd done recently. The two cases had
been difficult—for me.

"Katrina?" I asked.

"That's part of it. Got a stack of papers relating to that
case."

"Case?" I almost pounced on the word. "Is there an investigation in progress?"

"Nothing of the sort. Open and shut, but the pertinent

documents are here. Fax machines are great. Wonder how we ever got by without them."

"So fax me everything."

"You don't have a machine. You ought to talk to your accountant about that. It might be a tax deduction. Be seeing you, Peter." The detective let out a short laugh and hung up abruptly, leaving me with the phone in my hand and a loud dial tone in my ear. I sat and cursed him until I started repeating myself. That wasn't a good sign; it meant my creativity was taking a backseat to actually thinking about seeing Worthington.

I heaved to my feet and rubbed my wrists. My shoulder throbbed a bit but a couple of aspirin took care of it. I'd have to come up with another way of getting out of the restraints. Otherwise, I'd be a cripple by the end of the week. This was fine for the occasional grand finale but simply wouldn't do for a regular act.

I got across town without hitting anything. My mind kept wandering to other things, not the least of which being the veiled promise of information about Charles Hayes and his channeling whiz.

The squad room always made me pause. Such chaos belied the real efficiency of the SFPD. Most of the homicide cases are solved within ten days, and those that aren't tend to be committed by drifters moving from one jurisdiction to another as the breeze blows them. I saw Worthington's partner Burnside and tried to ignore him. He might be a bigot and not a little stupid, but he had a quick eye. He saw me the instant I came in and there was no avoiding him.

"Hey, guys, lookit that? We got the psychic Peeping Tom come to visit. Who you gonna psych out for us today, Thorne?"

"Someone with a soul," I said, pushing past him as he tried to block my way to Worthington's office. "That lets you out. You don't even have a mind."

The woman seated at the desk behind Burnside said something I didn't catch. Whatever it was it started a chain reaction of laughter that spread through the room. Burnside turned bright red and sputtered out a retort. I didn't care to take part in what must be some sort of tribal bonding behavior. They might tear each other apart in private but they'd die for one another out on the street. The thought that anyone would die saving Burnside saddened me. Some people shouldn't even be wading in the human gene pool.

"Hurry on in, Peter," Worthington called out. He stood with his hand on his doorknob as if expecting to find a door-to-door encyclopedia salesman. I hoped I was more welcome than that. "He's back. Damn him, he's back!"

"The Zodiac killer?" A chill went up my spine. I didn't want Worthington putting me into a situation like that. The echoes from my psychometric readings were dying down but they still haunted me when I let down my guard. Sleep wasn't impossible, but hit-and-runs and bullets and the stark hatred of people willing to take another's life dogged my dreams. To enter the mental field of a serial killer was too much for me, yet if it took him off the streets permanently . . .

I shivered. I couldn't say no to such a request on Worthington's part, and yet I didn't know if I could handle it mentally.

"What are you talking about?" he snapped. "The auditor. That sneaky little bean counter. He found some silly discrepancy in the squad books."

"How silly?" I asked. "In terms of beans? A hill?"

"More like a mountain," Worthington admitted. "But it's got to be a mistake. Somebody entered the wrong number somewhere, or Burnie dropped a decimal point and never picked it up again. Things happen."

"So my trip down here was a waste?"

"A waste of your precious time? I should say not. Here. Look at this and tell me if it's a waste to accept it."

I stared at the fancy embossed envelope in my hand. "From the mayor's office?"

"Go on, open it. I want to see if he spelled your name right." Worthington looked downright jovial. I ran my finger along the flap and pulled the letter out with a dexterous motion. The bond paper had a nice feel to it, like the feel of a new dollar bill. The mayor's seal was affixed to the bottom and the letterhead looked genuine. I scanned down the page and read the congratulations on helping solve the hit-and-run kidnapping.

"It would have been a bitch of a trial if it had turned into a murder trial," Worthington said. "The guy was planning on torturing her to death and leaving the parts all over town."

"So now he's just up on kidnapping charges," I said, not feeling as if I'd done that much. Even a hard sentence would let him get free on parole in five years. What would he do to his wife then? If she were smart, she'd leave San Francisco and simply vanish. Even five years gave a lot of time to build a new identity.

"The D.A. says he'll nail 'im solid on a dozen other charges all adding up to habitual criminal," Worthington said. "I tried to get you a commendation for the other case, too, the suicide one?"

"I remember," I said, wishing that I didn't. Of the echoes of hatred and fear and longing, always the worst remained. I shivered again though it was stifling hot inside.

"That was just as nasty, in its way. We'd've had to arrest the woman for lack of self-esteem. In California, that's a violation of your constitutional rights, you know." He saw his feeble joke didn't much impress me, even if we both thought it ridiculous that the state legislature had made it illegal not to have self-esteem.

"Since I couldn't," he went on, "I thought I might do you a favor. Seemed only right. Count your lucky stars that the pinhead accountant wasn't around asking what I was doing pawing through bunco's records. These any use to you?"

He shoved a pair of folders across his desk. I cleared a small space on the corner and opened the top one. I didn't read it immediately. I looked up to see if Worthington was leaving the room. If these were sensitive For Your Eyes Only files, he wouldn't stay. He'd need to answer a call of nature or go bawl out Burnside for some fancied or real infraction of department policy, but Worthington didn't budge. That meant what he was showing me was virtually public knowledge.

"There's the entire list of fake mediums operating in the Bay area. A half dozen answer to the general description of Nyushka you gave, but none of the MOs match."

"It's unusual for them to change. Once they get a patter down, they stick with it. It's just like working up a new stage act. It takes a lot of work, and if the audiences buy your performance . . ." The pictures in the files were all mug shots and, as such, were akin to drivers' license pictures. Any resemblance they might bear to reality was purely coincidental. Still, turning and twisting them, trying to imagine what Nyushka might look like in bright light helped. A quick survey of the fake mediums' heights also helped put to rest the idea Nyushka was among these con artists. She was several inches taller than any of them.

She might have worn high heels, but why bother trying to disguise her height? The bunco felons I'd come across always thought of themselves as method actors, fitting themselves into a role when the motivation came. For most of them the motive was simple: greed. The possibility that a pigeon might identify them from their height was not at the top of their list of worries.

"She's not here," I said, pushing the file back to Worthington. He closed it and ran his fingers around the other file. It had different markings on it, markings I had seen before and had grown to dislike.

"You want to see the medical report on Katrina?" he asked softly. "The pictures are, well, let's say they're about what you'd expect from someone burned in a car wreck. They're not pretty."

"You should have let Burnside give me the file. He enjoys doing things like springing gory pictures on people." In spite of what I knew to be in the file, I took it from him and opened the cover. The interior was on different paper.

"I had it faxed down from San Tomás," Worthington explained, seeing my interest. "Professional courtesy."

"Oh?"

"So I stretched the truth. I told them it was for examination in an insurance fraud case. And if the auditor finds this out, my ass will be grass."

"And he'll be the lawn mower, yeah," I said, having heard it before. Worthington's effort was still appreciated, though I felt as if I had truly earned much consideration for all I'd done. A letter, even one laser-printed on fancy stationery and signed by the mayor, was hardly adequate recompense for all I'd done recently.

The officer's report of the accident scene was terse and lacking in the usual police jargon. I made a mental note of the man's name, wondering why I bothered. Everything pointed to Katrina's death being accidental.

"He writes a lousy report. Not enough jargon," Worthington said, watching me closely. Sometimes I am sure he can read minds. If so, he took what I was thinking with greater equanimity than I ever could have. I kept reading.

I found myself fighting to hold back even the barest hint of a tear when I saw Katrina's picture on the third page. It was the "before." The "after" was a grisly, twisted mass of bone and burned flesh that bore no resemblance to her—or anything human.

"Got dental records to match. Even to a new filling put in a couple weeks earlier," Worthington said. "From all I can tell, that's about the only way she could have been identified."

"How fast was she driving?"

"Fast doesn't cut it. That stretch of road has a sharp switchback, almost a 110-degree turn. If you're doing more than twenty, you're out of control. She was bopping along, in the fog, on an unknown stretch of road, doing fifty or so. Leastwise that was the reporting officer's guess. She never had a chance."

"Did the gas tank explode when she went over the cliff?" I spoke just to keep Worthington occupied. I stared at the stats on the cliff. Two-hundred-foot drop to the ocean, jagged rocks, instant death. There wasn't any way her tank could have escaped rupturing. When the gasoline vapor rushed over hot metal, only one thing could have resulted. And it had. Katrina had left damned little for the mortician to work with.

"Like a star going nova," Worthington said.

"Where's the coroner's report?" I flipped through the rest of the sparse file and didn't find the page where the county ME had signed off that the body had been examined.

"Didn't see one. There's just the coroner's signature on the death certificate. No detailed report. What are you thinking, Peter? That she was drugged and someone pushed her over the cliff? Who? It wasn't likely to be her husband, now was it?"

"No, not Charlie. He loved her." I wondered how much I still did. It's so damned hard to find anyone in this world to truly love, even platonically. To lose them in a senseless accident makes it even harder to let go of the memories.

"No insurance. We checked to see where copies of her certified death certificate had been filed. It hasn't come across the desk of any of the major life insurance companies."

It took several minutes for me to detail all I had discovered about Charles Hayes and his company and the lack of insurance on Katrina. What Worthington said next rocked me because it had never occurred to me.

"She had signed a prenuptial agreement with him, you know. You don't know," he said, reading my face. "Pretty standard these days when a young woman marries an old geezer."

"Charlie's not that old," I muttered. "Nor is he that rich. The company is just stumbling along."

"When they got married it was flying high. Even the *Wall Street Journal* thought it would be the next Intel. Hayes might have been a millionaire a hundred times over if things had gone his way."

"He's had a few setbacks."

"More than a few. Two of his biggest products were snatched out from under him. Another company beat him to market with one gizmo, and he lost a patent case on another. What's made him a profit the past year or so has been the nickel and dime stuff, not the home run that's needed in high tech."

"I don't think Charlie killed her. Why would he fake a channeling session like that if he had?"

"Maybe he was afraid you'd find out this Nyushka had approached him. Hell, maybe he was afraid she'd succeed and his wife'd come back to finger him."

"Charlie didn't believe in this before, and that's pretty lame, Willie. I expect better of you. If Nyushka *did* reach Katrina and Charlie found out she was that one-in-a-million medium, he'd want to keep anyone else from finding out."

"Spirits are tricky devils. He might have wanted to plead with her not to bedazzle him with ectoplasm."

I shook my head. It made no sense for Charlie to have killed his wife and then arranged for the séance. He didn't seem to benefit financially, and the people I had talked with never mentioned Charlie and Katrina fighting. If anything, he seemed to find an anchor in her—and she gave it.

"There's no insurance, she didn't have a big estate, and since there was a prenuptial, he could have just divorced her if he wanted. There's no need to kill her."

"Maybe the settlement was more than he could scrape together. Things haven't been going his way." Worthington leaned back and clasped his hands behind his head. He was enjoying this as an intellectual pursuit. By playing the devil's advocate he was just doing his job. I didn't think he considered Charlie a suspect and Katrina's death anything more than a tragic accident. For Worthington, though, such thinking was reflexive.

"What were the terms of the prenup?"

Worthington shook his head. He didn't know, and I wasn't sure there was any way of getting the terms.

"You can find out what Charlie's gotten as an inheritance, can't you?"

"I'm working on it, even as we sit here. It takes time for

probate, but when it hits the court it becomes public record. You ought to know that, Peter. Really."

Chiding me for missing the obvious was his way of telling me he had gone as far as he could in this. I couldn't let it drop, and I didn't know why. Something bothered me, and it was more than the channeling experience.

I scanned the file again, concentrating on names and details, using memory association tricks I've picked up over the years as part of a mentalist act, though in this case I wasn't sure I could forget any of the details if I'd tried to. They were seared into my brain by love for Katrina.

CHAPTER 11

I varied what had become a routine by driving up the winding coast highway. It took only an hour to remember why I had chosen the less scenic inner route the other times I had gone north to San Tomás. I keep in good shape but after an hour my shoulder began to throb with the strain of constant gear shifts. Still, the slower drive on paved road and the clean air blowing across my face from the lowered seaward window gave me a chance to purge everything from my mind. I drove along in a fugue state. It might have been dangerous if there had been heavy traffic, but I saw only a few cars during the three hours it took me to corkscrew back and forth along the road until I reached a straight stretch just south of San Tomás.

Katrina had died somewhere around here. I worried that I might not be able to find the precise spot. Going to the sheriff or having someone else show me the spot wasn't to my liking. There wasn't any reason for me to be so curious. The woman was dead, her husband grieving, and that was it.

Except I had spoken to her. And Charlie wasn't reacting the way I expected. I worried over this point as I took a gradual curve and began climbing up toward the top of a cliff. How much was too much grieving? And how much was too little? Charlie might not show his sorrow the way I would have. Was that all there was to it?

Another point might be Charlie hanging onto Katrina's memory due to the successful channeling. He might refuse to believe she was gone and thus be unable to show what otherwise would be eating him up inside. I just didn't know him well enough, I decided. And he had heard Katrina at the channeling. And so had I.

My mind turned to the séance repeatedly, probing for tiny points where trickery would come into play. The assistant crawling around spraying cold water in our faces had been pretty standard, but how the hell had Nyushka prepared for the questions I'd asked Katrina?

Good answers refused to come. Charlie wasn't shaking me down for money, and stranger still, Nyushka didn't seem to be getting anything from Charlie Hayes for her work. Con artists don't do these things for love of humanity; their scams are cruel deceits.

If it was a deception.

Braking hard, I skidded slightly when a hairpin curve loomed unexpectedly. I blinked as I stared at it. The weather was as perfect as anyone could wish for, the sun bright and the road dry. And I had almost slid off the road making the turn. Getting out, I walked back and forth along the stretch of the road, trying to figure out what had happened. If this was the spot where Katrina had gone off, she would have been going north to San Tomás, just as I was.

Kneeling and sighting along the road gave the solution to the engineering problem. Most roads bank slightly to give traction for the curve. This turn was perfectly flat, either from sloppy design or bad road laying. If the road had been damp from fog or light rain, it would have been incredibly treacherous. Walking to the sturdy guardrail, I followed it for several yards. Spots had been rebuilt recently—three from my inexpert view.

Behind the guard rail stretched a grassy shoulder cut up by deep ruts. I climbed over and followed the ruts less than five feet to an abrupt drop-off. A moment's vertigo came and passed when I saw how far down the cliff ran. If Katrina had gone over here, little wonder they'd held a closed-casket funeral. The fall was better than a hundred feet onto sharp rocks. Very scenic, incredibly lovely in fair weather or foul, but deadly because of the flatness of the road.

No path went down the face of the cliff. Looking around, I finally saw what might have been a trail down that began a quarter mile up the road. Returning to my BMW, I got in and drove the short distance, found a spot off the road to park and then locked the car. I doubted anyone would be along to steal the stereo, but old habits die hard. I'd had two ripped off in San Francisco in the past year, and I wasn't inclined to fight with the insurance company over a third.

Thinking twice about my descent caused me to perch on the edge of the narrow trail like a bird sitting on a wire. My toes were dangling in thin air and my heels were crushing juicy stems of grass and weeds. What would I really accomplish by studying the spot where Katrina must have driven off the cliff? I had no idea, and that tortured me as much as the uselessness of her death. My feet found the trail and carried me down before I had reached a conscious decision to continue.

There was a tidy white beach tucked up next to the base of the cliff, a sandy blanket that kept the rock insulated and safe from the cold of the ocean. The pristine area revealed more than a few traces of humanity's presence when I got closer. Glass from headlights and windshields littered the beach where the ocean was slowly turning the shards back to minute silica grains indistinguishable from the natural sand. Larger parts of autos had been dragged back against the face of the cliff, making them impossible to see from above. Standing at the base of the cliff and looking up, I saw a slight outjutting. This accounted for the lack of trail down this part of the rock. Deep grooves had been cut into bare rock, showing where a steel cable had been dropped over the side. Careful examination of the cliff face showed several bright scars, all recent vintage, where something heavy had banged against the front.

Katrina's car, I thought glumly. That was the only way a heavy vehicle could be hoisted. Closing my eyes I pictured the process. The winch lowering the hook and cable, a crew of bored men fastening it and giving the signal for the hoisting to begin. The car would lift off the ground, turning slowly once it was free. Any sea breeze would carry it into the cliff, banging loudly, drowning out even the whine of the winch and the cursing of the operator.

Walking back and forth across the beach, I closed my eyes and began my breathing exercise to get into a light trance. The world shifted and swayed eerily under my feet, but I didn't open my eyes. Pacing the distance of the secluded beach, I made an about-face and retraced my steps.

The cool wind from the ocean turned cold, but I was sweating. Segments of the psychometric readings I'd done for Worthington returned to haunt me. The juggernaut with its coiled razor wire threatened to roar through my mind and slice me to ribbons—and the horrible loneliness and self-hatred of the woman who had killed herself in a vain attempt to frame her husband. That hit me with the force of a battering ram to my knotted stomach.

I stopped and knelt, bent over as if a real blow had hit me. Somehow, I slipped deeper into the trance and began a staggering walk across the mist-shrouded astral surface where psychometry often takes me.

It was all here, somehow mixed up and twisted and denying my confused senses any real message. Katrina walked here, but she didn't. And the smell of the huge mechanical beast charging me was scented with blood. Worst was the burden of hatred. So much, so much I could hardly bear it.

Weeping, I fell to hands and knees, coming up from the jumble of my vision but not quite returning to the world where my body lived. My eyes opened. It took me several seconds to realize I saw with them rather than other senses. The brooch was real and not an image.

My hand shaking, I reached out and touched it, recoiling when my finger was pricked. The cheap piece of jewelry had been covered with sand, only a portion of its clasp poking up. Carefully scooping it from the beach, I dusted it off and just let it lay in the palm of my hand.

"Katrina," I said. This was hers. I didn't remember seeing her wear it, but the imprint was unmistakable. There was a tension imprinted on the object that defied me. It wasn't fear and it wasn't the catastrophic knowledge of imminent death. The best I could put to it was anticipation. She had been expecting something important.

"And then she went off the road," I said, in a low, choked voice on the verge of breaking, finishing a life in one quick sentence. She had skidded on wet pavement, gone through a flimsy guardrail and tumbled a hundred feet to this beach.

Staring at the brooch, I slid back into my trance, knowing the other specters I'd find and daring them to harm me while I was once more in touch with Katrina's vibrancy.

Bewilderment assailed me from all directions, worrying its way up for the bottom of the plane, dropping from above, swooping and soaring and coming at me as I tried to bat it away like an annoying insect. I fought a ghost and nothing more. My hand turned and the brooch fell back to the sandy beach.

I got my legs under me and just sat, staring at the piece of costume jewelry. Impressions from Worthington's two cases kept me from getting a good reading. The burning anger of the woman who had killed herself and the stark savagery of the hit-and-run driver mixed into a sickening stew that kept Katrina's soul from speaking more to me.

I heaved a deep sigh and got off the damp beach. There was more, of course. The brooch was pot metal and she might not have worn it much. There was her feel to it, but it wasn't strong enough to give a good psychometric reading. Dropping the brooch into my pocket, I brushed myself off and began walking aimlessly over the beach. I wondered how thorough the sheriff had been in his search after the crash.

A quick touch of the bulge in my coat pocket told me he had missed enough to make my continued search worth another few minutes. This time I found the partly buried object, but it was with simple vision and not with any psychometric talent.

Gold foil wrapping caught a glint of sunlight and reflected strongly in the early afternoon light. I blew off the damp sand and held up the box, turning it over and over to check it out. I shook it gently and heard a faint shifting inside. From the weight, there couldn't be too much inside. A card was stuck under the decorative string on the small box.

"With love," was all it said. I recognized Katrina's precise hand in the lettering. She always printed rather than wrote. I never knew why except that her lettering might have been done by a machine, perfectly formed, always legible and with just enough flourish to make it distinctive.

I kept up my search for another twenty minutes but found nothing more. The two items I had unearthed, though, told me the sheriff's team hadn't been very good at their job. They might have cleaned up the wreck, but they had done little to examine the area around it. The brooch and gift had been obvious enough to even a casual searcher.

I fumed at the two items laying in the sand for over a week as I made my way back up the narrow trail to the top of the cliff. By the time I reached my car, I'd simmered down a little. Why should the sheriff scour the area? All he had been interested in was getting the eyesore of a wreck off a fine little beach. The driver was dead, there hadn't been any sign of tampering with the car and, in any event, this was a deadly stretch of road. Katrina Hayes wasn't the first to die here.

My hand went to the brooch and box once more before I buckled my seat belt. They were such a small legacy, but they could be added to the other memories she had left behind. I put the car in gear and drove to San Tomás to find Charlie Hayes.

CHAPTER 12

Blood. Hate you, hate you!

I wrenched violently and almost drove off the road. In a cold sweat, I pulled the car to the shoulder and stopped, thankful that I hadn't smashed into an oncoming car when the psychometric echo had taken me by surprise. It wasn't elegant, but I used my sleeve to wipe my forehead. My hands shook too badly to bother with a handkerchief, and it was always such a nuisance getting to a back pocket when a seat belt is secured.

I leaned forward and rested my head on the cold plastic steering wheel. In a few minutes, I had returned to normal—or as normal as I was likely to get. Leaning back, I put my hands on the sides of the wheel, wondering if I was really able to drive yet.

Where the sudden rush of emotion had come from bothered me. I've come to expect almost anything when I am in a trance and wandering the astral plane. When my senses are twisted and perceptions askew anything is possible. But I hadn't been in my psychometric trance. I had just been driving, paying no special attention to anything and just reacting to the turns in the road.

I needed a vacation, and it had nothing to do with overwork. I needed the respite from psychometry and the flood of emotions that came with it. I had tried to tell Worthington before the last session that I couldn't do any more for him. I had relented because he had information about Katrina I'd needed—or thought I had needed. Now I questioned the wisdom of risking my sanity, even if the suicidal woman's husband had been freed.

I powered down the window and let the cold wind and

salt spray wash the fever from my flesh. It wasn't hard to understand why Katrina had been interested in acquiring property here. The solitude, even along one of only two roads into San Tomás, was soothing. It was possible to believe escape from civilization was a reality rather than a momentary fiction.

The few miles remaining until I reached San Tomás were taken slowly, hardly more than twenty miles per hour. I was glad no one had sped up behind me, because much of the winding road carried double yellow lines and there were few places to pull off and let another car pass. This "let's go for a Sunday drive" speed was all I could handle.

San Tomás hadn't changed since I was here a few days earlier, and I doubted it would change in the next ten years. The twenty-first century would find the community struggling along, content enough but with a feeling that there might be more. The younger citizens would insist on going to the big city for school, to find a better life, restlessly seeking what they could never get here, but those remaining behind would know this slower pace was closer to paradise.

Closer to paradise and maybe closer to the grave.

I shook myself as the thought flashed through my mind. That wasn't the way I envisioned San Tomás, or any small town. They were a dying breed, but that was a sorry casualty of modern life. I had wanted to buy property here to get way from the pace I kept.

"And the damned psychometry," I muttered, glad the window was still down. The freezing wind kept a fever from burning me up inside. I didn't know if it was possible to run away from my talent, but this might be the place to find out.

Anxious because the psychometric flash might return when I least expected it, I slowed even more as I made my way through town. I pulled into the parking lot of the motel where Charlie had been staying, wondering if he was still here. It was with a mixture of relief and apprehension that I saw his car parked in front of his room. I'd wanted to talk to him, but the brooch and box in my pocket made it more difficult.

Giving the two items to him would resurrect old feelings. And I wasn't sure I wanted to go through another channeling, even to find out if Nyushka actually was able to reach beyond the grave. The one tenet I had operated by consistently over the years was in danger of being smashed, and I was halfway seeking a cowardly way out to keep myself from being made uncomfortable again.

I got out and went to the door. Charlie answered after the second knock. From the way his hair went in all directions in a classic case of bed head, I knew he had been taking a nap. I almost envied him the ability to sleep. What little I'd had lately wasn't giving me any rest.

"Peter, come in. I just tried to call you." He blinked and looked at his wristwatch. A sheepish grin crossed his face, turning him back into the Charlie I had known for years. "Well, I tried to call about three hours ago. I guess I fell asleep."

"I was on my way up the coast," I said, entering the too-hot hotel room. I didn't know if Charlie preferred it this way or if the thermostat was on the fritz. I have bad luck in getting rooms; mine either freeze or boil. He might have the same luck.

"Great, great," Charlie said, closing the door. "Sit down. I really need to talk with you."

From his enthusiasm I guessed he had seen Nyushka— and Katrina—again.

"It's uncanny. I never thought it was possible, but Katrina is so, how do I put it?"

"She's dead, Charlie," I said bluntly.

"Well, yes, of course," he went on, unflustered. I saw that he hadn't accepted his wife's death. Had I? "But I can still talk with her."

"Another channeling?"

"Last night. Nyushka called and said that the storm had died enough for us to get through."

He made it sound as easy as picking up London on the shortwave. If weather conditions were right, no problem.

Let a little storm out over the Atlantic or on the astral plane interfere and forget it.

"I spoke with her again, Peter. I *know* it's Katrina. You're having trouble coping with that, but it's her."

"How much did Nyushka charge for the séance?" I asked. It's not always true that there's no such thing as a free lunch, but it comes closer than any other description of modern life I've found so far. The cost might be minuscule and one we're not aware we're paying, but it is always there. I knew a fake medium always waited until the hook was securely planted before reeling in the sucker. Charlie was definitely hooked, but the reeling might not have started yet.

"I've given her twenty dollars to cover transportation. That's all."

I nodded. He was telling the truth. I could tell by the disgust in his voice. This proved, at least to him, that Nyushka was legitimate. Who wouldn't be willing to reimburse carfare to the person putting you in touch with your dead wife? There had to be another demand placed on Charlie's finances, but he might not see it when it came, thinking it was natural.

"What did Katrina say when you spoke to her?"

Charlie swallowed hard. "It was just as if she was alive, Peter. We talked about old times, when we'd met, how it was before she . . . before she died. She told me about the last thing she remembered. She still loves me, Peter."

"I'm sure she does," I said, not knowing what else to say.

"I want you to come along again tonight. I'm sure it'll be all right with Katrina, and Nyushka doesn't care. She said as much. I need to make notes and get everything straight." His voice trailed off, as if he was already thinking about the séance.

"Take notes on what?"

"The land deal. The winery. She was close to finishing it but hadn't told me much about it. There wasn't any need, really. She had a good head for business, and I was always tied up at the plant. We'd been having some design problems on a new megachip."

"Katrina is giving you the information to close the deal on the Alsace Winery tonight?" I smelled the scam closing in like a vise on Charlie's checkbook.

"What? Oh, yeah, that's right. How'd you know the name of the place?" Charlie stared at me for a moment, then laughed. "Part of the magic, isn't it? You know a few things and make it seem like you know everything. Look, Peter, this isn't some con job, or if it is it's the damnedest thing I ever saw. When I talk with Katrina, it's *her*. It's not some fraud impersonating her." He straightened his shoulders and shifted on the bed. A tightness came to his throat. "I just wish I could reach out and touch her again. Just once more."

"What about the land deal?"

"She'll give it all to me tonight, if we can make contact. This was in the works before she died. I feel I owe it to her memory to finish it off."

"Might be expensive."

"I don't know yet, but Katrina's hinted that there might be a considerable profit. There's some development planned for around here the locals don't know about. I might get in and out of the property and make a big profit."

So much for Katrina's memory, I thought. Still, it made sense in a cockeyed way. If Katrina hadn't planned to live here as I'd thought but to speculate in land, Charlie's completion of the project would be a fitting tribute to her.

"I'll be glad to come with you," I said, pulled in different directions. Nyushka had to be a fraud, yet I couldn't see how she was pulling off such an elaborate trick. Even if Charlie wanted desperately to believe he was talking to Katrina, some small item would have surfaced by now to plant a seed of doubt. The content of my brief talk during the channeling had been startling, but the more I thought on it the more certain I was that it had been a hoax. I just didn't know how it had been accomplished.

"I stopped off where Katrina went off the road," I said

lamely, fumbling for words that wouldn't unnecessarily hurt Charlie. "On the beach, at the bottom of the cliff, I found these."

Handing him the brooch and gift box was harder than I'd thought it would be. My hand was shaking, and I saw a tear forming in the corner of Charlie's eyes. How could I have doubted his sincerity or grief after seeing his reaction?

"That was hers," he said, taking the brooch. "We got it a year or two ago in a flea market down in Santa Clara. We were just out for a drive and happened to see it at a fairground. Katrina went on like it was part of the queen's crown jewels and I bought it for her." He clutched it so tight, I knew the pin was sticking into his flesh.

"Thank you, Peter. I hadn't known she was wearing it when she died."

He looked at the gold foil-wrapped box, then at me. "What's this?"

I shook my head. I had no idea.

"You found it with the brooch?"

"It must have been for you. I read the card."

Charlie smiled weakly as he read the simple message over and over. "Let's see what we've got." He ripped off the foil and worked down to a simple cardboard box. He fumbled it open to reveal a Piaget watch. I'm not into ultra-expensive jewelry but knew this timepiece had to run in the tens of thousands of dollars. Everything about it bespoke wealth.

"This is strange," Charlie said, his voice neutral. "It's just like the one Katrina gave me for my birthday a couple months ago." He pointed to the stand beside his bed. A duplicate of the watch rested there on its side. He bounced it in his hand, as if weighing it before pitching it through the window.

"It might be a coincidence," I said, wondering what to say and do. "There have been any number of accidents that ended up on the same beach. I just assumed this was meant for you." But there was no denying the card had been written by Katrina. I'd have recognized her distinctive printing anywhere.

"I don't understand," Charlie said.

"Let me look at it, will you?" I knew better than to psychometrize but felt I had to. What had started as an act of charity on my part had brought pain to a friend. There had to be an explanation, and using my talent, just for a few seconds, was the only way I could see to find out for sure what the right answer was.

I clutched the watch in my hand and closed my eyes. Chaotic swirls surrounded me instantly. The hatred boiled deep within, but it was a fading echo doppler-shifted from the front of my mind. More troubling images sprang up in the senses-twisting fashion of a full psychometry session, the tanklike vehicle pounding toward me screaming reds and acrid burned flesh-scents as it came. Dropping the watch would avail me little. I held on, hoping for more distinct and relevant information from the resonances trapped within its metal-and-crystal structure.

I saw voices but could not get them straight because I was also hearing the flavor of champagne and letting light rip at my flesh. Concentrating on the most pleasant part, I flowed down the straits going to the champagne and heard the texture of cork and laughed at the touch of bubbles on my nose.

Soon, I made out, *soon there will be all we could want!*

As if a giant hand swatted me, the force of my psychometric reading slammed me backward and toppled me backward from the chair. I lay on my back staring up at the cracked plaster in the ceiling for several seconds, not knowing what was going on.

"Peter, are you all right? Peter!" I felt a sharp pain in my cheek and knew my head turned away from the blow.

"Peter, do you need a doctor? Should I call 911?"

"Charlie, wait, don't," I croaked out in a voice that sounded as if it came from the bowels of the earth. It was all heavy sodded over and cracked and inhuman. "I'm fine. It just . . . startled me."

"Here, let me help you up." Charlie's hands under my

arms were what I needed to get my feet under me. I stood on rubbery legs for a moment but strength flowed back quickly. My shirt was drenched with sweat. In a way, this surprised me. I'd thought it would be blood, and I didn't remember why. Something I had touched for a brief instant in the psychometry had convinced me I would die. But what? All that I remembered was the crushing burden of anger and an almost carnal need that devoured all before it.

"Sorry," I said. "I didn't think there would be much imprint on the watch." I stared at the expensive watch laying on the floor, not wanting to touch it. But I did. As if it might spring at me like a cobra, I picked it up gingerly. Through my disordered thoughts it came to me that the watch had only triggered the onslaught of emotions and hadn't been the source.

Like some 1960s acid head, I was having vicious flashbacks.

Then my stomach turned into an acid swamp. I saw the initials etched into the back of the watch.

QG.

CHAPTER 13

"It's just like mine," Charlie said in a stunned voice, "but why did she have it with her? It wasn't for me. Who the hell is QG?" He sounded stricken.

"There might be an explanation for it," I said, putting the watch into my pocket. I hoped that the adage about out of sight, out of mind might work. It seemed to, though Charlie struggled with his brief glimpse at the initials. Not wanting to go into it any further, I diverted his attention a bit more.

"I haven't had anything to eat all day. When is the channeling scheduled? I'd like to get something before we go."

"A couple hours," he said, his eyes fixed on the coat pocket where I'd put the watch for safekeeping. I removed my hand from the pocket, dropping a few coins. I'm not sure if I own any clothing that doesn't have some remnant of a trick in it. The coins were special interlocking shells that can be used in a rapid-fire shell game. The flash of silver as they left the pocket distracted him a little more, and then he was busy worrying about other things.

"We'd better get on over to the diner, since it closes in an hour. Everything in San Tomás closes early."

"Is the food any good? That might make up for it."

"They make a passable meat loaf, but I swear everything else has been run over out on the highway. They ought to rename it Rudy's Road Kill Restaurant."

We went to the diner and ate, Charlie picking at the meat loaf while I devoured a chicken sandwich. The suggestion to eat had come at the spur of the moment. A quick bowl of cereal was all I'd eaten all day, and that was too many hours ago for my liking. The entire day had been spent driving up the winding coast highway—and examining the beach where Katrina's car had crashed.

"Is Nyushka in the same house? I'd like to get there early to look the place over."

"Do you think you'll find how she materializes Katrina?" Charlie pushed his plate away and used the paper napkin on his lips to capture a small spot of grease. "I'm an engineer, Peter, and I tell you there's no way she is faking this. It's Katrina I'm talking to. We're channeling." He said it as if he had just converted to a new religion. And in a way, he had. Belief was paramount in any séance.

"I don't know." I told him about my ambivalence, my rational mind sure that Katrina was dead and could never be reached from this side of the grave, and the other part, the side of me that wanted to believe it had been real.

"You loved her, didn't you?" he asked. I tried to keep my expression neutral. I'm not sure I did too well because Charlie said, "I may be a dumb engineer but I knew that Katrina had been around. She was a wild one before she settled down."

"I loved her," I said, "but it wasn't mutual. Oh, she liked me. I think she looked on me as a brother." The words came out more bitter than I'd intended. Charlie's eyebrows rose.

"I'd always wondered how it was."

"What was in your prenuptial agreement?" I asked.

"Your mind does jump around, doesn't it? Why are you asking, especially since it's none of your damned business?"

"You don't have to tell me. I heard some gossip and just wondered, that's all."

"Mrs. Keenan," Charlie said unexpectedly. "She's had a crush on me for years. What a busybody. What'd she say to you?"

"Nothing about the prenup."

Charlie drained his coffee and motioned to the waitress for more. After she poured it he didn't bother adding the

cream and sugar as he had before. He gulped it black and
hot. It seemed to steady him.

"My lawyer thought it was a good idea. I didn't like it
all that much and neither did Katrina, but she went along
with it. The terms were easy enough. If I divorced her, she
got half of everything. If she divorced me, there was a sizable settlement, but that hardly matters."

"You mean now that she's dead it doesn't matter?"

"No, I mean the agreement was drawn up before we hit
hard times. I've had to put more and more into the business, and it's not doing too well. If she'd divorced me, she
would have gotten ten percent of the company's earnings."

"And there aren't any," I said, wishing I'd spent more
time going over the company's balance sheet.

"We've been running a hefty deficit for a couple years
now. Things will turn around in another year or so. The
company can weather the storm, but it's hard going right
now. Most of my cash has been plowed back into the company to keep us afloat."

I felt sorry for Charlie all over. His company was foun-
dering and his wife had been killed in a senseless accident.
And he was being taken by a clever scam artist.

"Let's look over Nyushka's house," I said. "We can
both use the fresh air if we walk. It's not that far."

It took less than fifteen minutes for us to get to the
house. We cut across country, went through some heavily
wooded spots and emerged not fifty yards away. The night
air was cold and damp, almost like a razor against my
nose in its crystalline purity. The clouds had blown away,
leaving so many stars in the sky I was tempted to stop and
try to count them. I'd heard somewhere that the most stars
you can see without a telescope is six thousand. I knew
there were that many in any given square inch of this sky.
The radiance was enough to make any skeptic believe in
God.

"I don't feel right about barging in like this," Charlie
said. "It must be breaking and entering."

"Is it her house?"

"I don't know."

"I don't, either," I said, "but there's a For Sale sign in the front yard. See it over by the road?"

"No, where?"

"Never mind," I said, not wanting him to get too technical on this. I thought I'd seen a sign earlier. The dark rectangle might be a sign telling me about apple maggot quarantines or something else equally esoteric. "If the place is on the market, maybe we're buyers."

"I am looking for property up here," he said dubiously, "but the deal Katrina was working on is a better one. I don't know what comes with this house."

He had lost sight of the forest for the trees. I could forgive him a little. Checking the front door showed a secure dead bolt. The side door had an equally impressive lock— and it was new, just like the one on the front. But this was a misdirection, the kind that always impresses audiences far out of proportion to its importance. The lock might be secure but that didn't mean anything else was. I ran my fingers between the frame and the wall and jiggled a bit. Turning and twisting, using my strength to its greatest benefit, I got the doorjamb pulled away enough for me to lift the dead bolt out of its slot. The door slid open on well-oiled hinges.

"How'd you do that?" Charlie asked, frowning.

"The door wasn't locked properly," I said, more intent on what might lie inside the house. The first time I'd seen the place, it was supposedly deserted. Nyushka had fixed it up with curtains, veils and other hindrances to seeing what she really did. Dropping to hands and knees, I checked the threadbare carpeting for impressions. It was a lost cause. I went a bit farther and pressed my ear against the floor, listening for movement anywhere in the house. The usual settling creaks and moans were all that came to me.

"Which way did the wagon train go, Tonto?" Charlie was getting some sense of humor back.

"That way," I said, pointing toward a sitting room. I made a quick circuit and confirmed what I had guessed from the layout of the dining room and entry hall. Whatever gadgets Nyushka had used were probably run from this room. I found several places where nails had been driven recently, as if holding slender wires or threads now gone. Nothing I found would hold up in court, though, and certainly none of this would convince Charlie he hadn't channeled into the spirit world and gotten in touch with Katrina.

I wasn't even sure I'd convinced myself how Nyushka had faked the séance I'd participated in.

"I want to check the ceiling." I wandered around near the table, then gave up and did some serious thinking. I turned around and around, then smiled to myself. The table had been moved. Figuring out where it had been gave me a clue about how the mist had been sprayed through the dangling curtains. A small garden hose nozzle was fastened to the ceiling. Against the cracked plaster, in dim light and swaddled with curtains, it was all but invisible.

"So?" Charlie said. "That doesn't prove a hose was ever hooked up to it."

"But it is odd. People don't usually water their dining room from the ceiling fixtures."

"It's odd, but I know people who do things that would get them locked up in the giggling academy if anyone found out—and they're perfectly sane."

I wasn't up to arguing the point, especially since he was right. Why do people who aren't drug dealers keep pit bulls?

"Let's go outside and look around," I suggested, wanting to get out of the house before Nyushka and her accomplices showed up. If I saw what they unloaded, I might be able to point out the trickery. And I wanted to be sure that we weren't getting ourselves into a trap. When con artists are trapped, they sometimes turn nasty. It isn't often a burglar or a bunco artist resorts to violence, but if enough money is at stake, people can be pushed to killing without any thought to the consequences.

We scouted the exterior until I felt like I ought to get a merit badge. Motioning to Charlie, I indicated we ought to retreat to a small stand of trees some distance from the house.

"You taking up tree climbing now, Peter?"

"It looks that way," I said, scaling the rough-barked tree. In the dark I couldn't tell what kind it was. Even in the daylight I probably wouldn't have been able to tell, but I did know I got sap all over my hands and clothing. Settling down on the limb, I craned my neck around until I got a decent view of both the house and the road running alongside it. We didn't have to wait more than ten minutes, for which I was glad. It was cramped on the branch, and if any more sticky sap oozed out it might permanently glue me in place.

"There," I said, rearranging myself and trying not to fall to the ground. My sense of balance is good and my fingers are especially strong, but combining balance, strength and vision was a bit more than I could manage after all I'd been through recently. "Do you see how many are getting out of the car?"

"Yeah," he said dryly, "I can count all the way up to one."

My heart sank. He was right. Only a woman, in a huge flowing cape that made her look like some ominous bat fluttering in the night, got out of the car. She stood beside the car for a moment, then swirled off, the cape floating like a dark nimbus around her. I waited, hoping to see her assistants getting out of the car with their equipment. There was only the one woman.

"Let's go," Charlie urged.

"Wait a few more minutes. No sense appearing too eager." I wanted to see if anyone else would arrive. We were still almost forty-five minutes early.

"Why wait?" he said. "You might think you have something to prove, but I don't. I just want to talk to Katrina again." The plaintive quality in his voice convinced me—that and simple logic. If we barged in now, Nyushka might never be able to set up her equipment. This would serve as much a purpose as watching her cohorts enter the old house with tons of equipment.

Still, if we didn't "contact" Katrina, that proved nothing. Mediums are always willing to admit defeat to make
their "successes" seem even more triumphant. Logic got
twisted when it came to fleecing a mark. Not talking to
Katrina might make Charlie even more certain that he had
before and could again, maybe without me present.

We knocked on the door. To my surprise, Nyushka answered immediately. Going in, I kept an eye peeled for
any changes she might have made in the room. The hangings that had been there before seemed untouched. She
hadn't had time to do more than shuck off her voluminous
cape, which hung over an old chair at the far end of the
dining room. Glancing up I saw that the table hadn't been
moved, either. We weren't likely to get sprayed with cold
salt water during this channeling, if it even occurred. From
the lack of setup time, I suspected Nyushka would fail to
find the proper spirit guide and be unable to reach anyone
tonight.

"You are early. That is good," she said, standing quietly
at the far side of the oval table. "The atmosphere is
charged this evening. A storm comes, and we must work
quickly if we are to avoid its electrical contamination of
the ether."

"No crystal ball tonight?" I asked.

"There is no need. I have the channel open, I know the
guide, I can reach Katrina Hayes without recourse to the
crystal ball. It is only a focusing device." Nyushka leaned
forward, hands on the table. She closed her eyes and began a soft toneless chanting that reminded me of a tune I'd
heard once—almost.

The rest of the channeling went the same way. It was as
if a feather touched the edges of my body and mind, tick-
ling quickly and leaving without ever quite revealing itself
fully. Charlie and I leaned on the table. He closed his eyes
and tried to match the tune Nyushka hummed. I kept a
sharp lookout for trickery. Other than the low hum from
the medium, I heard nothing else in the house I hadn't
heard before.

Wind. Settling. A soft scurrying sound that meant mice

had entered. There might have been a heavier sound, a hunting house cat, but I wasn't sure. Whatever produced the sound, it seemed to fit into the matrix of the environment.

Everything fit until Katrina spoke again.

"You have come back. I miss you so, Charlie. I am lonesome."

"Katrina!" Charlie's eye shot open, but there was nothing to see in the darkness. Nyushka continued to sway and hum. I waited for Katrina to speak again, to see how Nyushka was somehow duping us.

I don't know any way for a human to hum loudly and still speak as plainly as Katrina did. There might have been hidden recordings I had missed, speakers built into the walls or ceiling, equipment that required nothing more than for Nyushka to flip a switch with her foot. But I didn't think so.

"Katrina, it's you," Charlie said, trying not to sob.

"There is so little time, my darling," Katrina's voice came. "You have done what you can on the real estate dealing?"

"Yes, yes, but it's so much money."

"It will make you rich. You will never have to work again. The wine in the cellar is worth more than the land under the winery. You must seize this chance, now that I have . . . gone." The catch in her voice added just enough pathos to cause me to straighten. Everything was as it should be—*too* right.

"Katrina," I said, cutting in before Nyushka had a chance to call the channeling to an end. "What do I have in my pocket?"

"Really, Peter, such a naughty question."

"It's a watch. I found it near where your car crashed. Whose initials are engraved on the watch case?"

There was a long pause. Nyushka chanted louder and swayed more. I took my hands off the table, only to be glared at by Charlie. I didn't think this would break the so-called energy chain, but I relented and leaned back on the table.

"The initials are those of Quincy Graham," came the startling answer. "I had purchased the watch as a present for his part in the land purchase. The winery."

"Katrina," I said, my voice almost breaking.

"You want to ask more, Peter. I understand but time is so limited. In life I never had enough. In death, there ought to be eternity, but there is so little contact with those I love. It is so unfair."

"Where did we go on my last birthday?" I had to ask the questions, though Charlie felt I was crowding him out. There had to be a niche in the information Nyushka had obtained to give such a full picture of a dead woman.

"Nowhere," came the answer. "We were not together on your last birthday."

"The one before?"

"There was a small restaurant in Sausalito. I don't remember the name. You got sick from the fish and broke out in a rash." There was small chuckle so characteristic of Katrina. "I had scallops that were terrible. Afterward, you wanted to go to Fort Point, such a dreary, cold, foreboding place. I didn't like it."

I didn't even remember why I'd wanted to go to the Civil War era fort hidden in the Golden Gate Bridge's shadow. Something about a proposed escape for my act.

"You wanted to see if you could dangle off the bridge while you performed an escape. Bungee cords. Something like that. I was never sure exactly what you were looking for."

"That's right," I said, remembering now. I'd thought of doing a bungee cord jump off the bridge while chained and strapped into a straightjacket. As memory flooded over me, a coldness gripped my heart and squeezed until I almost choked.

Katrina would have known. Even I had forgotten the exact details of a day more than a year and a half earlier. There was no way even the best private detective could have furnished this information since I have never acted on it—and had even forgotten much of it.

But not Katrina Hayes's spirit.

"Katrina, darling, tell me more. What's it like? What can I do for you?" Charlie had pushed me to the side once more, and I didn't mind. I was too stunned by the implication that Nyushka might have reached beyond the grave. Houdini had sought an honest medium for years, trying to contact his dead mother. He had left coded messages to be delivered to his wife after his death, and no spiritualist had ever given the proper statement.

Houdini had never found Nyushka.

"The land deal," Charlie pressed. "Where are your notes on it? Did you have them when you went over the cliff?"

"In my desk at home," Katrina said, as if dredging up some hard-to-remember fact. "Not in the file drawers. Look in a special file folder marked Prospects."

"I'll do it for you, Katrina. I'll contact—"

"Charlie, no!" she said suddenly. "There is nothing you can do for me. Do it for yourself. For yourself. For yourself."

The words began to fade, and eventually they were drowned out by Nyushka's low chanting. The medium suddenly fell forward onto the table; her head hit with a loud clunk. I just stood and stared for a moment, not sure what to do. Charlie rushed around the table and rolled Nyushka over to see if she had injured herself.

"Are you all right?" he asked.

"The spirits, they, there is disturbance. I don't know what is going on." Nyushka pulled herself up and pushed free of Charlie. "I am so dizzy. Did the channeling go well? I cannot seem to remember what happened."

"We got through. We spoke to Katrina again. She's fine. I need to ask her so much, but all she wants to talk about is this land deal."

"I sense in her an urgency. She loved you very much, Mr. Hayes. This is why she channels so strongly through my spirit guide."

"If you can't remember what went on," I asked, "how do you know what Katrina is feeling?"

"You do not understand," Nyushka said, contempt in her voice. She dismissed me completely. "Mr. Hayes, I wish you would leave the unbeliever at home next time. He only takes up valuable seconds when channeling is successful."

"Answer the question," I demanded. "Help turn me into a believer."

"Nothing can do that," she said. The web of scars on her face lightened and turned her into something not quite human. Without the marks, she might have been an attractive woman. "I cannot explain. I do not hear but I feel, I sense, I get the emotional tone of those whose spirits move through me. I do not speak their words. That is done by other means, but I provide the anchor with the world of the living. For only a brief time."

There was more I wanted to ask her, but Charlie crowded close and asked, "What am I to do? When can I talk with her again?"

"I do not know, Mr. Hayes," Nyushka said. "Channeling is not like a telephone. There is more to it than simply picking up the phone and dialing. If there is some news to give her, then the channeling might be easier. The strain this time was so great . . ." Nyushka's voice trailed off, as if a great weariness had descended on her.

"What can ease your pain?" I asked, waiting for the payoff. If Nyushka wanted to collect big from Charlie, now was the time. She had her hooks firmly planted.

"The only thing that can ease my pain is for your Katrina to rest easily, to be content, to accept her fate. Then she will not force her presence on me as she does now."

"Money?" I asked.

Nyushka glared at me. She accepted Charlie's help to stand. To him she said, "I want nothing from you, now, ever. He insults me. I must go."

"Nyushka, wait, he didn't mean it," Charlie pleaded. Nyushka swirled her heavy cape around her shoulders and made as theatrical an exit as any I'd ever seen.

I heard the car door slam and the engine cough to life. A grating of tires and the whine of an engine echoed through the night and she was gone. Charlie spun angrily on me, his face a storm cloud of anger.

"I hope you're satisfied, Peter. She might never agree to channeling again. I *need* her talents. Nyushka is reaching Katrina. Do you deny that?"

I just shook my head. I couldn't deny anything. Katrina's shade had given answers even I had forgotten. And the honesty about the engraved watch put a different slant on everything I'd been thinking, however unworthy of Katrina's memory it had been.

"Don't bother coming with me, Peter," he said. "I have to walk this off." Charlie stomped from the house, leaving me in silence.

I made a quick survey of the house, hunting more thoroughly this time for wires, speakers or other gimmicks. And I didn't find any sign of electronic equipment, wires or other gear used by most dishonest mediums. That didn't make me feel any better.

I had to come to grips with Katrina communicating from the other side of death's dark veil.

CHAPTER 14

Worthless! You are worthless! I could kill you! I could, but I won't. I'll make you suffer, suffer, suffer. I'll kill myself! The screams inside my head died when my eyes flew open. I sat in bed, staring wild-eyed at the far wall of my bedroom. My heart raced and sweat soaked the bedclothes. This was different from the psychometric readings because of the severe bodily changes I experienced. When I walk the astral plane where psychometry takes me, my physical body stays in a trance. Whatever happens occurs only to my astral body, a fact Barbara Chan had shown repeatedly when trying to figure out exactly how my talent worked.

But this was different. Too different for my liking.

Echoes from my psychometry entered dreams and stalked me like a hunter on the trail of a young doe. No matter how I turned and twisted in my dreams—nightmares—the memories always caught up. The only point to be thankful over was that the resonance from the hit-and-run driver had faded. All that remained was the woman suicide.

I wiped the sweat off my face with the corner of a sheet and lay back. The bed had turned cold and clammy, prompting me to roll over and get my feet under me. The heat hadn't come on and the room was freezing. Shivering, I went to the closet to find my robe.

You owe me, you scum. You owe me, you owe meeee!

I staggered and supported myself with one hand against the wall. Having the dream was bad enough. The echoes were reaching into my waking hours now, and this frightened me. There had to be some way to exorcise all I had felt and learned and experienced, but I didn't know how to do it. Simple meditation wasn't the answer; I had tried that. It worked to put me into a light trance to practice the psychometry but did nothing to erase the mental ripples formed by what I'd learned. The notion of seeing a psychiatrist had crossed my mind several times, but what shrink knows the first thing about my unique problem? I had heard of others who could psychometrize but had never come across them.

Whatever they did to stay sane and keep a grip on their thoughts and lives was likely to remain unknown to me. And no psychiatrist was likely to believe me when I said I could get vibrations off items held by another person. That simple declaration might see me carried off to the whackateria for the rest of my life. How can you ever prove you are sane?

Deep breaths helped still the runaway hammering of my heart. I closed my eyes and tried to imagine myself in some tranquil setting. This didn't work; the suicide's thoughts kept creeping back to haunt me. It worked better to have the radio turned on full blast, listening to something that irritated me. I twisted the dial past a jazz station and finally came to the nasal twangs of a country and western singer. It was like a knife through the eardrum, and it pushed away the disturbing thoughts that weren't mine.

I sat and listened to the annoying music with the improbable titles and even more improbable singers. I swear the announcer said one song had been done by a mother and daughter group called the Jugs. This incongruity made me laugh, and with that hearty chuckle the last vestige of the estranged thought vanished.

Dressing, I finally decided I could find something else on the radio. A quick twist of the dial got me to a rock station. I waited a few minutes, decided this wasn't what I needed right now and turned to a more melodic and less decibel-driven station.

It had been a couple days since I had seen Charlie Hayes, and having my attention divided between working on my new act and wondering if I should somehow try to mend differences with him, I had let the suicidal thoughts sneak in. But were they suicidal? I tried to recapture just a hint of what I had felt, and I wondered. The anger astounded me, a seething subterranean rage that might not have surfaced if I'd spoken directly with the woman. What had generated such loathing of her husband?

I cursed Willie Worthington for ever getting me involved in the case, though I was glad that all charges had been dropped against the husband. But what was his life like now, knowing his wife had cheated on him repeatedly to injure him and had even gone so far as to frame him for her suicide? In a way, I wanted to meet the man and find out if he had somehow driven his wife to her desperate act or if it had been some internal cancer of her spirit that had destroyed the woman's self-esteem so totally.

Better off not worrying over this, I said to myself. What about Charlie?

I considered the matter from as many different directions as I could and decided it was better to let him go off on his own. The land deal didn't sound too far afield for him, though real estate wasn't his area of expertise. If Katrina had scoped out the winery and had been convinced it was a good deal, then it probably was. She had talents that seldom came to the forefront, and this might have been one of them. The entire area around Mendocino was lovely and peaceful and just the place for a summer home. As to the soundness of investing in the defunct winery, I didn't have any idea about that.

My gut told me it was a bad deal for Charlie, but that was his business. The only sticking point seemed to be Nyushka and her channeling. How had she done it? Or was it for real? To reach beyond the grave and contact the dead was an age-old dream of millions who could not bear to lose a loved one. And I had to admit there didn't seem to be any way Nyushka could have known the answers to questions I had posed.

Still, a certain stubbornness made me just a small bit skeptical. Why was Nyushka the first real medium to deliver as she had promised? And why Katrina?

My head began to hurt, and I stopped trying to work out the woes of the world. Charlie could wait. Time would heal whatever breach there was between us, though I was more than a little curious as to how things had progressed with him. And my curiosity ran wild thinking about Katrina.

And, I had to admit, it was something more than curiosity. I had always hoped there would be more between Katrina and me than there had been. She was happy and bright on the outside, but I had occasionally seen this as a shield against revealing her real self. There had been a darkness inside I had never touched. The times we'd had together had been those shared by good friends and nothing more.

I had to amend even this. In retrospect, I had been more her friend than she had mine. My sexual desires and thwarted hopes had kept me closer to her than I would have been under other circumstances.

I looked at the telephone, willing it to ring. I wanted to talk with Barbara right now, maybe not about Katrina or the channeling, but certainly about the specters haunting my mind. I almost jumped out of my skin when the phone did ring. Scooping it up before the answering machine could click on, I almost yelled, "Hello!"

"Hey, Peter, I'm not deaf. Or is this some new way of keeping the phone peddlers at bay?"

"Hello, Willie," I said, my spirits sagging and a lethargy flowing over me like a wave of warm molasses. Every movement now became a chore. I'd have gone back to bed except I didn't want to face my dreams again. Not yet, not without a few hours of wakefulness to act as a barricade.

"You don't have to sound so happy to see me," the detective said. "I just wanted to call and see how you were doing."

"You don't want anything?" My question was more paranoid than I had anticipated. It did Worthington a disservice, since he was a friend and often called without putting any demands on me or my talent.

"If I caught you at a bad time, let me know."

"Sorry. I've been jumpy the past couple days." I quickly explained how the second channeling session had gone and my lingering doubts that Nyushka had really reached Katrina Hayes.

"You're apologizing for not being convinced. There's no burden on you to believe, Peter," he said. "I've never seen a séance that wasn't gimmicked some way, and so why think this one isn't?"

"I have to admit Nyushka's act is convincing. Damned convincing. I asked questions only Katrina and I could have known—not the kind of things that ever got written down in diaries or even told to a friend."

"Hayes couldn't have known?"

"I doubt it. I went over the scene of the wreck and found a fancy watch in a gift-wrapped box. The watch had Quincy Graham's initials on it. Katrina—her spirit, at least—said it had been intended as a gift for Graham, thanking him for his work on a land deal."

"A fancy watch, I'll bet," said Worthington. "Sort of like a lover would give?"

"That was something I had considered. This explanation is as good, though, and fits what I'd uncovered about them. There doesn't seem to have been any connection between Katrina and Graham, other than business."

"Did you check? I mean, did you do a real canvass of neighbors and motel registries and restaurants and bars?"

"No."

"So there might have been." Worthington sounded pleased. "You could always ask the ghost. You think she's square with you, so why shouldn't she answer?"

My mind began slipping away on a tangent, odd bits of past and present mingling, swirling around and forming a totally confusing picture.

"Charlie's mad at me for being such a skeptic, and you're sounding angry because I'm not more of one," I said. "No matter what I do, I'm trapped between a rock and a hard spot."

"I hope I'm the rock," said Worthington. "There's not any part of my body that qualifies as a hard spot. The doc told me to go on a diet, lose fifty pounds, lower my blood pressure and cholesterol and everything else."

"So, are you going to?" Worthington had been in serious need of dieting for all the years I'd known him. About the only vice he didn't embrace joyously was smoking.

"I'm taking a few days leave to get my nerves settled down," he said. "I was thinking maybe you and me could take in the Giants game Saturday."

"Who are they playing?" I hadn't known Worthington was a baseball fan. I certainly am not.

"Who the hell knows? The doc suggested it. Get outside, go to a game, relax. Hell, I'm so uptight trying to figure how to relax I feel my blood pressure rising. The next thing you know, he's going to tell me to go fishing. My blood ought to really boil at that. Enforced boredom, that's what fishing is."

"Don't you have a cabin down around Ben Lomand?"

"Used to. Mary needed that operation a couple years back, so we sold it. Nice place, except the loggers were moving in. Huge strips cut through the forest. Whole place is going to hell. So?"

"So?" I didn't know what he wanted from me.

"What are we going to do? I'm depending on you to help me relax. I've got a whole goddamn week to relax in, and I don't know how."

I had never heard Worthington mention any hobbies. From the almost wretched way he spoke about this week, he didn't want to spend it with his wife. I'd never figured out the precise relationship between Willie and Mary Worthington. He seemed to love her as much as he hated her cooking, but there was a friction between them that belied affection. I suppose it's possible to love someone without much liking them, but such a relationship seems alien to me.

"I need a vacation myself," I told him, "but I've got a new act to get together. I know what I want to do, but there are rough spots that require practice. My assistant will be back in a few days, and I want to have the act blocked so we can practice it."

"Yeah, Michelle," Worthington said almost wistfully. "She's a hot one."

"I don't mix business and pleasure, Willie."

"I don't either. That's the problem. I don't have any pleasure to mix with homicide."

"Think of it as preparation for when you retire." I bit my tongue the instant I said it. Worthington was the type who died a week after forced retirement, unable to find anything else to fill his life. "Look, we'll get together in a day or two. Why don't you just go over a file or two from work?"

"Got a clean desk. That's why I decided to take the time off." He sounded as if his dog had died. Again, I marveled at how little I really knew of Worthington. Did he even have a dog? There had never been evidence of one the times I'd been over at his house. And he didn't seem the cat-lover type.

"We'll get together, I promise."

"Great, Peter. I'll keep my eyes open for more stuff on this Hayes business. Maybe something will come up on a background check. Or Nyushka might slip up. I've asked the guys over in bunco to slip me any paperwork they come across."

Worthington wasn't going to use his vacation to get away from work. In a way, though, I appreciated him nosing around. Katrina's death still didn't feel right to me. And the channeling, for all its verity, didn't either. I just wished I knew why.

CHAPTER 15

It had been a mistake asking Worthington to help me put together a few of the gadgets for my act. He was all thumbs, and he spent most of his time pressing me for details about other tricks. I didn't mind if he figured out how I was doing one or two of the more obvious stunts, but the magician in me made it a sacred trust to prevent the "audience" from learning how I did the more arcane ones. Penn and Teller notwithstanding, it never pays to let the audience see how a trick is done. They pay good money to attend a performance and want to be mystified and entertained; there's no reason a good stage magician cannot do both simultaneously. After a great performance you can overhear the audience as it leaves arguing over the way a trick might have been done—and getting it completely wrong.

I finally chased Worthington out and spent two solid days putting the finishing touches on my equipment. I would start with some flashy antic, lots of fire and smoke and Michelle coming onstage in a rush, to lift everyone's expectations. A big stunt, then a couple minor ones to let me rest and gather momentum, then another big one with more complex apparatus, an escape that would keep them buzzing through a second drink order. It was all coming together nicely in my head. I wanted to do an escape with great dramatic appeal, though probably not the milk can escape that had been so dangerous for me previously. The bayonet fittings inside the can ought to work properly but they hadn't before and I was leery of trying it again, even after eight years. There were plenty of other interesting escapes that would awe even a jaded Vegas crowd intent on little more than ogling naked women and losing a few more dollars at a gaming table.

Most of the equipment assembled in my apartment had to be moved to a warehouse across town down by Franklin Square. I needed a staging area close to both rail and sea transportation for my equipment, and this afforded me the best of both worlds. The storage area was less than a half mile from a railhead and hardly more than a mile from a dock, in case I wanted to tour the Orient again. The thought of leaving the country for any length of time right now, though, didn't excite me. I wanted to stay closer to home and work out the problems popping like corn on a hot griddle inside my head.

The nightmares had diminished, but I hadn't been sleeping much, either. Work drove out the annoying echoes I had experienced so powerfully and had also given me the adrenaline rush to keep going. If a project interests me, I can keep at it for days on end, hardly sleeping or eating. I had to keep reminding myself to exercise. I try to jog three miles a day and work out several times a week with free weights to keep up both strength and stamina. Houdini's secret had been his marvelous muscle tone and power in his fingers. I wasn't in his league but that didn't keep me from trying.

I heaved a big sigh of relief as I looked at a clone of Thurston's spirit cabinet. I'd need two more assistants, but they were plentiful in a town like Las Vegas. The hinges allowed the rear doors to work both directions, affording a small platform on the corners where a small, black-clad assistant could crouch, moving in and out of the cabinet as necessary when the cabinet was spun around to show the exterior. Pairs of phosphorescent gloves over the black made it appear as if hands floated freely—or without the gloves, simple implements like tambourines and cymbals would rattle and bang and create a ghostly havoc that always pleased.

Satisfied that the cabinet had a few of my own touches incorporated, I began dismantling it for transport to the warehouse. From there everything would be sent by rail to

Las Vegas. Michelle and I could block out the show; she was a quick study and had a natural presence about her rare in one with her background.

I was on the point of calling her to see if she had returned from her vacation when the phone rang. I picked it up, thinking it might be her calling me. There was a woman's voice, but one I didn't immediately recognize.

"Peter Thorne?"

"Speaking," I said, moving around to move some tools off the sofa. It didn't sound as if the woman was selling encyclopedias. I have a away of getting rid of even the most aggressive of telephone salesmen. If they want to take my picture, I have been hideously disfigured in a fire. Dance lessons? I'm a paraplegic. Stocks? I'm under indictment for insider trading. It sometimes seems cruel to do this to people trying to make a living, but I didn't ask them to call and waste my time. As far as I can tell, none who have gotten such an answer have ever called back, saving me more time.

I had the gut level feeling this call wasn't in that category of time dissipator.

"This is—you know me as Nyushka."

Recognition came on me then as I did recognize the voice. This wasn't the confident channeler, though. And neither was it the slick con artist scamming a mark. Nyushka was upset.

"What can I do for you?"

"Mr. Thorne, this—I can't go into it over the phone. It's too important."

"My phone's not tapped," I said. As far as I knew, it wasn't. I didn't see what difference this might make, unless Nyushka wanted to come clean and tell all. I found myself intrigued by the professionalism of her séances, and more than a little curious how she had gotten the information the spirit Katrina had passed along. A large part of me was almost convinced that Nyushka had successfully channeled, simply because I couldn't figure out how she had gained such intimate data. But a tiny core of me held on to a lifetime of skepticism. I had to *know,* and channeling wasn't a good explanation, in spite of Occam's Razor. There had never been good evidence for it before. Why now?

"Do you want to meet somewhere? I'm in San Francisco. It'd be tomorrow before I could drive up to San Tomás."

"I have a house in Mendocino," she said, almost absently, as if talking to herself.

"What's your real name?" I asked.

"Carol," came the answer. I heard a small exhalation, as if she damned herself for telling me. If anything, it assured I would meet her. This might be the first truthful utterance she'd made since we'd met. I wanted to know more and considered this a decent start.

"Well, Carol, if it is important, maybe we can meet halfway."

"That's fine. I have to talk to you right away. Where would you suggest?"

"I'm open to suggestions. Sausalito is just across the bridge for me. If you're in Mendocino, it'd be a couple hours for you. There might be somewhere closer to in between. Petaluma?"

"Sausalito is fine, but I don't know it very well. Is there a restaurant where we could meet?"

I found myself nodding, though she couldn't see me. Eating was something I had been doing only occasionally the past week or so. Between driving back and forth to San Tomás for Katrina's funeral, the channeling sessions, general information gathering and working on my act, eating had taken a back seat. Glancing at my clock, I made a few quick calculations.

"Six o'clock ought to give you time to get to Sausalito," I said. "There's a small bar and restaurant just off the highway. Bucky's Place is the name. It's easy to find."

"I think I know it," Nyushka said. With more confidence she said, "I'll be there. Six."

I didn't get a chance to say anything else. She hung up and I found myself listening to the irritating dial tone. Dropping the phone back to the cradle gave me a moment's satisfaction. I had been right about Nyushka being a fake. Why else call but to confess?

What was different now? Charlie had seemed to have the hook sunk deep enough to be reeled in, and we hadn't parted on great terms. He *wanted* to believe Katrina was still available to him. I walked to the balcony and stared across the bay, over darkly foreboding Alcatraz toward Sausalito. Nyushka—Carol—would do better confessing her sins to Charlie rather than to me, but maybe she thought of me as another professional. That might make it easier for her.

But why confess at all? Why?

The restaurant wasn't top quality but did serve about the best hamburger to be found in the Bay Area. I waited a half hour for Nyushka. When she didn't come, my growling stomach got the better of me. I hadn't thought she would back out, not from the way she sounded, so she might just be late in driving down from Mendocino.

I finished the hamburger and my second bottle of Grölsch before looking at the rotating clock on the wall behind the bar. It spun slowly, making a rotation every thirty seconds. The face came into view. A little after seven. I continued to stare until I got a forest scene so far removed from reality even the drawn squirrels in the picture looked unhappy at the lie. I considered a third bottle of beer, but there had to be a limit to how long I'd wait.

In college such things are fairly mechanical. If a teaching assistant doesn't show up for class in fifteen minutes, you're free. A professor gets twenty minutes. How long for a medium who wanted to talk about duping a friend?

I pursed my lips and thought harder. Nyushka hadn't really said what was bothering her. In her mind, she might have a talent and reaching Katrina was part of it. Hell, for all I knew, she may have really channeled. Considerable evidence pointed that way. If I'd been called into court as an expert witness, all I'd be able to say truthfully was that I didn't know how she did it.

An hour? Ninety minutes? How long was long enough before I got in my car and drove back to the city?

I paid the bill and stood outside. The fog had crept in and a small breeze blowing from the ocean swept enough forest scent from Muir Woods to convince me I wasn't going back to San Francisco. By the time I keyed the Bimmer to life, I knew I was going back to San Tomás, just one more time.

Yeah, like hell, one more time.

I opted for the faster route inland rather than taking 1 up the coast. The gravel road jolted and shook and caused the beer and burger to become radioactive in my stomach. I found a roll of antacid tablets and munched two as I took the turns in the darkness. It was almost nine before I found the branch in the road. To the north lay Mendocino. South promised San Tomás. Nyushka had said she had a place in Mendocino, but other than her first name I had no idea how to find her. That left the house outside San Tomás where she had conducted her channelings.

Ten minutes was all it took to gun down the road, slide through a couple curves and come to a halt in front of the place. I stifled a cheer when I saw Nyushka's car parked in the driveway, almost exactly where it had been when I'd spied on her before. I killed the engine and coasted to a halt behind her. She'd wanted to talk to me. Parking this way made it a bit harder for her to get away without answering some of *my* questions.

I got out and paused for a moment. In the distance a wolf howled. I hadn't realized there were any left in the area. Between the foresting and the dope growers, most medium-sized wildlife had been killed off. The wolves destroyed the dope growers' crops—and also made them nervous. Too many of the drug dealers put in sophisticated electronic surveillance gear that picked up anything larger than a house cat trying to sneak up on them.

Since the DEA used dogs to sniff out the marijuana fields, this was about the right size to calibrate on. I'd read reports of more than one wolf or coyote shot to ribbons by an automatic weapon.

The night breeze was stiffer than it had been in Sausalito, and far colder. The few miles north along the coast worked wonders. Farther south, down in Bodega Bay, the water was cold enough year-round for the great whites to breed. I pulled my collar up and shivered a bit as the chilly fingers of air sought my throat. It was small enough penalty to pay for the silence, the magnificent stars above and the sweet scent of forest.

I looked into Nyushka's car. She had been in a hurry. The keys dangled from the ignition, and she hadn't bothered locking the car. I walked slowly to the dark house, wondering why there wasn't even the flicker of a single candle from inside. Pausing, I strained to hear anything other than the horny wolf still yowling his heart out in the distance. The wind whispered through treetops and across the eaves of the house. There were no unusual sounds.

Curious, I circled the house. No light shone from any window. Remembering the heavy hangings, I decided Nyushka could have blacked out the light. She might be in the middle of another séance, though it didn't seem right that she would come here with her customer. Unless Charlie—or someone else—had walked here, as we had done before, she ought to be alone inside the house. Why drive the mark to the site of the séance? It's more mysterious to make a decent entrance, flaring capes and swirling about theatrically.

The front door was securely locked. I went to the side door Charlie and I had used before. Prying loose the jamb was easier this time. The nails didn't hold it nearly as well as they had before I'd pried the strip of wood loose. Getting the door open took less than five seconds. Keeping the door closed as much as I could, I slid inside. Again I listened. Chittering from mice told me the place needed a good house cat to keep down the pests.

But there was a stillness to the house that troubled me. It was more than silence. It was as if I had walked into a space filled with dead air, air not touched by movement in a hundred years.

Walking softly, keeping from placing my full weight until I was sure I wasn't going to cause a floorboard to creak, I made my way across the entryway, through the kitchen and into the dining room. The large oval table where Nyushka conducted her séances had been moved back under the garden nozzle.

On the table lay a dark lump. I bit my lower lip as I moved closer. It didn't take second sight or psychometry or even much imagination to know what it was.

Nyushka had been bludgeoned with something very, very heavy. There wasn't a chance in hell she could have survived such a massive head wound.

CHAPTER 16

Worthington had taught me more than I wanted to know about dead bodies. Edging away, I looked at the floor to be sure I hadn't walked in a puddle of blood. Whatever blood there was from the wound at the back of Nyushka's head, it had all accumulated on the table or had been soaked up by her voluminous cape. It was difficult to take my eyes from the still body. The presence of death was hypnotic.

Questions. Answers. The veil pulled closed for a final time. Nyushka had both asked questions and given answers and now only she knew if her channeling had been real. Death was the final arbiter of all such questions—but I wasn't the one who had learned. I got to the door and slipped through it. The cold night air hit me like a hammer blow, staggering me a little. I closed my eyes and tried to settle my mind. In the distance the lonely wolf continued to howl. Just under the eaves of the covered porch poked the object of the wolf's love songs. A gibbous moon crept slowly out of the forest and into the diamond-clear sky. It hardly seemed the night for anyone to die.

I drove into San Tomás but couldn't find the sheriff's office. There might not be much in the way of law enforcement in the community; it was hardly large enough to support more than a part-time sheriff and a deputy. And maybe even this would strain the town's budget. Finding a telephone in an honest-to-God telephone booth out of the old Superman comics, I pawed through the blue pages until I saw that I'd have to call Mendocino. A sheriff from the larger town might be interested. It also might be better to call the California Highway Patrol, but no district office was listed. That seemed odd until I saw that the page had been ripped out. Even out in the country people are too lazy either to remember or write down numbers.

The sheriff answered with a bored, "Evening, Mendocino Sheriff's Office, Sheriff Culhane speaking."

It took a few minutes to convince the man I wasn't making a prank call.

"Lemme get this straight. This woman, who called herself Nyushka but whose name was really Carol and who lived in Mendocino, has been bashed to death down in San Tomás?"

"That's right," I said, wondering if I'd have to find the California Highway Patrol number. The sheriff wasn't buying anything he'd heard. It had been a mistake to add too many details, especially about Nyushka's channeling and the house being where séances had been conducted.

"And you're Peter Thorne?"

"That's right," I said in exasperation.

"Not the guy who does the magic stuff?"

"Yes."

"You must be calling from the corner of Oak and Main down in San Tomás."

The way he said it wasn't so much a question as a statement. I peered out and saw a battered black and white sign missing a few vowels. It might have been Oak Street. Or maybe it was just K Street, using the unimaginative system like the one over in Sacramento around the statehouse.

"It might be. I can't tell."

"It reads K, doesn't it?"

"Are you going to investigate or do I have to call the California Highway Patrol?"

I held up my hand to fend off the glare from headlights suddenly shining on me. Through the brightness I saw a light bar on top of the car. Both doors opened and the men came toward me. From both the telephone and through my other ear I heard, "You can go on and hang up now. We're here."

Sheriff Culhane held a cellular phone in one hand. His other rested on the butt of his service revolver. His deputy stood to one side to catch me in a crossfire if the need arose. I dropped the phone back into the cradle and stepped out, being sure to keep my hands in plain sight. Reporting a homicide was bad enough. Getting cut down by a hick sheriff for doing my civic duty was about as bad as it could get.

"You talking about the place across town that's been for sale for months?" Culhane slid his telephone into a belt pouch where it hung like a modern walkie-talkie.

"It's for sale. I don't know how long it's been on the market."

"Let's take a little ride on over and check the place out," Culhane said. He motioned me around the car. I hesitated, wondering if the deputy was going to frisk me. He looked to his superior for approval but didn't get it. He opened the rear door of the cruiser and almost shoved me in. The door slammed with the finality of the switch on an electric chair closing. A heavy wire mesh screen separated me from the two officers in front. The pungent smell of stale vomit almost made me gag. I didn't even try rolling down the windows; I knew they wouldn't budge. And there were no door handles inside for me to use in getting out. Settling back, I studied the arrangement and tried to remain calm.

The car accelerated smoothly. We came to a halt behind Nyushka's car in less than a minute. Both officers got out—and so did I. The deputy went for his pistol but Culhane just stood and stared.

"How'd you get out of there?" he asked.

"You knew I was a stage magician. Part of my act is escape." Getting out was easier than I'd thought it might be. A few prods and pokes here and there on the door panel told me where the wire connecting the outer handle lay. A steel needle and a strong twist was all it took to pull the wire and open the door.

"Don't go doing that again, Thorne," the sheriff said. He motioned to the deputy to put away his pistol. It was with some reluctance the deputy obeyed. I'd seen his kind before. He was a coward who liked the power a gun in his hand gave. Killing, whether he called it sport or self-defense, was possibly his only real pleasure. I moved closer to Culhane, who seemed to understand my appraisal of his assistant.

"Johnny, you go circle this place and see if you can flush anything," he said to the deputy. "Thorne and I'll check inside and see if there's a stiff like he said."

"But Ben, I—"

"Do it." Culhane's voice had turned to carbon steel and cut through the night with more authority than the distant wolf's howls. When Johnny moved to obey, Culhane said in a low voice, "Takes a while to train 'em properly."

"You shouldn't give him a firearm until he's house-broken," I said.

Culhane laughed. "Now that's a good one. I'll have to tell Johnny."

He'd made his point. I wasn't to badmouth his deputy or there'd be hell to pay.

"Up there," I said. "Through the side door. The others were locked."

"Now why's that a problem with you?" he asked. "You ought to move through them just like you got out of our car."

"I already got in the side way." I had to stand back while he ran his flashlight beam over the doorjamb I had pulled away. It was apparent this door had been locked, too.

"You figure the murderer's got keys to this place?"

I just shook my head. It wasn't necessary, but I didn't say so. The murderer might have arrived with Nyushka, then used her keys to lock the doors after leaving. Or more likely, the main doors had snap locks that didn't require a key to lock. The killer need only have been inside and thrown the lock before closing the door.

Culhane hung back until his deputy joined him.

"What'd you find, Johnny?"

"Didn't see anything worth mentioning, Ben. Need more light. There's tire tracks in the drive—"

"Mine," I cut in, "from before. When I found the body."

"Any other tire marks?"

"Didn't see any." Johnny's hot yellow eyes focused on me as if he were a hunting lion and I were dinner. In his mind he had found the killer, and he hadn't even examined the body yet. Given another few minutes, he'd work himself up into judge, jury and executioner.

"Let's go in," said Culhane. He moved faster than I thought possible for a human. He swung inside, pistol drawn. He moved quickly, swaying to and fro to cover any possible hiding spot where a gunman might try to cut him down. Culhane made it through the entryway and the kitchen in large steps, stopping only when he got to the dining room.

For a moment I was afraid the body had been moved. I couldn't see past the sheriff, and the set of his body told me nothing. Then he moved enough for me to see the corpse on the table. I felt a curious combination of relief that my report had been accurate and apprehension over what it might mean to the officers who would interrogate me.

"Yep, Thorne's right on this one. She's deader than a doornail." Culhane swung through the room, then quickly searched the rest of the house. He didn't find any prowler lurking. He returned to the dining room in less than five minutes, his pistol safely tucked back into his holster. I wished Johnny would copy his superior. The bore of his revolver was less than an inch from my spine. I could almost hear him grunt as his finger tightened on the trigger.

"You just step away and don't go muddying the waters," Culhane said. I wasn't sure if he spoke to me or his deputy. We both moved as he pulled out his telephone and dialed a long number.

I heard the ringing across the stillness of the room. "Hey, Doc, you still up? Sorry about this. We got a homicide. Doesn't look to be a sexually motivated one, but you'll have to tell. I'll get Johnny working with the camera so you'll have a clear field when you get here."

I didn't hear the doctor's answer, but it wasn't polite. Culhane held the phone away from his ear, then said, "Make it a half hour, then. But you're going to get your ass over here. The county's not paying you to sleep, dammit." He savagely thumbed the switch on the front of the phone and stuck it back into the belt pouch.

I glanced over my shoulder and saw that the deputy had already left to get a camera from the cruiser. They apparently didn't have a full-time forensics team.

"You ever see a dead body before, Thorne?"

I nodded. My mouth had turned to cotton as waves of memory flooded my mind. There had been so many, too many. Worthington was responsible for introducing me to the dark world of homicide, and my psychometry led me into even murkier depths.

"Not too pretty." Culhane shone the flashlight on Nyushka's face. "Rigor mortis is setting in. Starts high and works down, you know. She's been dead a couple hours. Why'd you barge in here?"

I related as much of the story as I could, but every word I said made me feel just a little sicker to my stomach. There was no evidence that I had killed Nyushka. I didn't have a motive, and there wasn't any obvious weapon. That might work against me; I didn't know. But every word from Culhane's mouth hinted that he had his perpetrator and there wasn't much need to look further. As Johnny began snapping flash photos, I stepped out of the way. They might be taking my mug shot before too much longer.

"It'd be real dumb for you to kill her, then report it, wouldn't it?" Culhane asked suddenly.

"I didn't kill her. I didn't even know her that well. We'd met twice before."

"And yet she calls you up, long distance and all, and wants to have dinner with you."

"She wanted to tell me something. All I really know is that she lives in Mendocino and her first name was Carol."

"These séance things you and Charles Hayes engaged in. Were they satanic?"

"What?" This off-the-wall question stopped me completely. I turned and stared at him in disbelief. "You mean did we take our clothes off and sacrifice farm animals and dance around in the moonlight? No, Sheriff, we did not."

"That's what all this New Age crap is about, isn't it? Satanic worship and pentagrams and blood smeared all over the place? She might have been a witch and you sacrificed her."

I had no answer to this. It had come as a total surprise, though I suppose some people can't separate the harmless New Age philosophy from more perverse devil worship. The only thing cops enjoy prattling on more about than drug busts are satanic arrests.

"Naw, as I said before, you'd be dumb to report the death, and you don't strike me as the dumb sort."

He motioned and I was the subject of a series of photographs. Johnny grunted when he ran out of film and had to reload. They wouldn't find any trace of blood on my clothing, or shoes for that matter. I had approached the body carefully and hadn't disturbed anything that might be evidence.

"Lemme get going on the report," Culhane said. He sent Johnny back for a clipboard and a three-page report form. He started with the standard information: name, description and so on. I answered mechanically, distracted by the echoes beginning to reverberate in my skull. Something was out of place—or wasn't. I couldn't put my finger on it, but a few minutes with some possession of Nyushka's might provide the answer.

Maybe. It might also bring back the nightmares and the visions—hallucinations—that had plagued me so long after the double crimes I'd psychometrized for Worthington.

"So this Charlie Hayes might have a motive," Culhane rumbled on.

"What motive?" I asked.

"What if you were right and this Nyushka couldn't reach the dead? What if it was a fraud and he found out he was being taken?"

"She hadn't asked for any money."

"Maybe she liked practical jokes. I've heard of women doing stupider things than faking a séance. Or maybe she was getting revenge on him. Men like this Hayes don't

grow a big business worth millions without making ene-
mies."

I hadn't considered that. My train of thought was de-
railed when a cursing homunculus of a man entered.

"You could have waited, Sheriff," the man complained
without preamble. "I haven't had a good night's sleep in a
week. Damn insomnia. And you wake me up to look at a
goddamn stiff."

"Quit bitching, Doc. Get to it. I'll want prints, teeth, the
works. This might be a real murder to solve."

"She sure as hell didn't commit suicide," the doctor
grumbled. "Not unless she figured out a way of bashing
herself in the back of the head. Must have been nearly instantaneous. Incredible power in the blow to shatter the
skull. Perp was taller, maybe his height." The doctor
waved vaguely in my direction. "Find the murder weapon?"

"We're looking around," Culhane said, watching me
carefully. "What should we be looking for?"

"Steel rod. Rebar, maybe." The doctor was examining
the fingernails and hands. I took still another step back.
Culhane followed.

"We got most of what we need, Thorne. Why don't you
find a place to stay out of trouble for, oh, call it a half
hour. I want to talk some more with you, but we're a tad
shorthanded. You know how it is. All the time with budget
cuts."

"And auditors," I said, remembering Worthington's has-
sles.

"You got it."

"Mind if I look in the cellar?"

"Why'd you want to go and do that?" Culhane asked,
curious. "You thinking to find some gizmo that she used?"

"Something like that. I won't disturb anything if it looks
like it might be important."

"You just let me look around first," Culhane said, leaving the doctor and his deputy to the work of examining the
body and making notes. I wasn't sure where the door leading down into the cellar might be—or if there even was

one. We found it just off the kitchen. Culhane examined the door carefully, then led the way down, using his flashlight to make sure we weren't destroying any evidence. I found a switch and the place filled with a dim light.

"Now fancy that," Culhane said. "The electricity's still on." He wandered over and stared at the bulb, then chuckled. "Reckon this place has been the hangout for some transients. Looks as if they hot-wired this bulb. See what I mean?"

My eyes darted along the indicated wire, which vanished through the cinder block wall. Someone had tapped into the light pole outside and was draining just enough electricity to light the dirty bulb. I hadn't thought there was any power upstairs, except whatever Nyushka had used for her speakers and amps.

It took only an instant to appreciate the crudeness of the wiring. Nyushka might have done it, or one of her assistants, to give them enough power to run their equipment. I walked to the center of the cellar and looked up. A trapdoor opened easily when I thumbed back the catch. Just above was the frosted glass screen I had noticed several times before, just off the main entry.

"Looks old," Culhane said, studying the trap. "Can't even guess what it was used for."

I didn't have any idea why the owners of the house would install the trapdoor, either. It certainly suited Nyushka's purposes, though. Anyone agile enough could come and go through the trap, hide behind the frosted screen and pretend to be Katrina. I had completely missed an easy answer to the channeling. The how of the illusion was answered simply enough, but the source of the details still eluded me. How had the imposter known, in such detail, items of my own life I had forgotten?

"What are you looking for, Thorne?"

"Mechanisms, electronics, a place where her assistants operated the show." I explained about the garden nozzle and the cold spray. Culhane wrote furiously. I wandered the cellar and found scrapes on the wall where someone might have wiggled out a window facing the driveway.

Other than these faint marks, there wasn't anything of interest in the cellar.

Scratching my head, I wondered what else of importance I'd missed. A medium needs gimmicks to support the illusion, just as I need for my tricks to be carefully thought out and the proper equipment installed. There wasn't much evidence that Nyushka had used the basement. And there weren't small items obviously dropped by her or her accomplices for me to use my talents on. Psychometry wouldn't be good for me, but it would put to rest the curiosity eating away at my guts.

"You thinking you might use her gimmicks in your own act?" asked Culhane.

"Something like that," I said, the idea never having entered my head. I devote a great deal of time to debunking mediums and their séances. A new turn that I couldn't explain was something more than a lost opportunity for a stage act: it was a personal affront. To admit defeat in figuring out how Nyushka had operated amounted to an intellectual Waterloo.

"Let's go on up, Thorne," the sheriff said. "There's nothing to speak of here, is there?"

"No," I said, preceding the officer up the steep wooden stairs. He had come with me to see what I was up to. That meant he still considered me a prime suspect.

"Good. We can go back to Mendocino. I got a raft of new questions to ask about this, Thorne. You don't have any objections, do you?" The way Sheriff Culhane spoke told me it didn't matter if I protested or not. He was going to ask his questions at his office, and I was going to answer.

Nyushka had done more than thwart my curiosity by dying. She had left me on the hot seat, and I didn't appreciate that.

CHAPTER 17

"You gotta be kidding," Culhane said. He rocked back in his battered chair and leaned it against the wall. A dark line going down into the wallboard showed where the chair had rubbed across the paint a thousand times before. The sheriff's eyes bored into mine until I felt we were in a staring contest. I didn't flinch. Everything I'd told him was the truth.

"You mean you just *touch* stuff and you can tell me something about the owner?" He shook his head and broke eye contact. I didn't feel that I'd won any victory.

"It's more complicated than that," I said wearily. The lengthy interrogation had taken strange twists and turns, as if Culhane wanted to pin every crime that had ever been committed in Mendocino County on me.

"It's always more complicated," he said, not believing me. I wasn't going to argue with him. I was more interested in what he was going to do about Nyushka's murder. Until he told me I was under arrest, I wasn't allowed a phone call—and who did I call then, since I didn't have a lawyer? My agent? Michelle might not be at home, and calling Willie Worthington struck me as wrong. Worthington was a cop and inclined to think anyone the police arrested had to be guilty, just as most juries believe everyone standing trial is guilty because the state has gone to all the trouble of trying them.

I'd never been arrested before and didn't know the proper responses, or if I was telling Culhane too much. I might be incriminating myself.

"We got a small problem with jurisdiction, you know," he said. "Ukiah is the county seat. Mendocino isn't the county seat of Mendocino County. Go figure, huh? Me, I call myself sheriff but I'm more a deputy."

"And that makes Johnny a deputy deputy?" I asked.

Culhane's eyes turned to chips of ice. "Don't go ragging on the poor boy. He's had a hard upbringing."

I heaved a sigh. Another sob story. If Johnny hadn't been wearing a badge, he'd as likely have been out sticking up convenience stores and killing the night clerk for ten dollars and change. All personality flaws were being excused because of child abuse or broken marriages. Although it was deplorable, I think there is more to a human being than reacting to environment. Rising above misfortune to overcome such obstacles is what distinguishes us from the animals. Some of us.

"I could just toss you in a cell and let him watch you."

"I'm sure he does a good job," I said, knowing what to expect if the sheriff carried out the threat. Johnny might not kill me, but it wouldn't be for lack of trying. He had the look of the coward and bully to him, only going after prey he thought was weaker.

"That was mighty sarcastic, Thorne. You trying my patience?"

"No," I said, tired of this. "You have my statement. I knew Nyushka from two prior meetings. I don't know what she wanted to tell me tonight." Glancing out the chicken-wire covered window at the dawn, I amended that. "Last night. I found her. I called you. I did what any law-abiding citizen is supposed to do. What else do you want from me?"

"Something more than this cockeyed story," Culhane snapped.

"I've given you what I know, and it's all the truth."

He almost sneered. "Sure it is. Even the part about that trick with touching an object."

He had a heavy metal paperweight on his desk. It seemed the only item out of place on the cluttered desk. Other than this twisted blob, he had no personal effects such as pictures or knicknacks. I pointed to it silently.

Culhane moved slightly so his hand was closer to the butt of his pistol, then motioned for me to go ahead.

I closed my eyes and composed myself. Going too deep into a trance wasn't a good idea. The hallucinations from prior psychometries sneaked up on me again like a bad acid trip. When I had settled my thoughts, I reached out and cupped my hand over the metal blob.

A rush of air sailed past me, as if I had stepped into a wind tunnel going full blast. The senses-twisting occurred and I saw butterscotch and smelled a roar and heard pain ripping out my insides.

I jerked back and looked at him. Outwardly I knew I had shown no emotion. My heart hadn't even accelerated. Inside I was wrenched about until I wanted to scream. There had been only a flash of what caused the metal to melt, and I had experienced it all.

"She died," I said softly. "Your daughter died and you didn't know it was her until you arrived." Staring at the lump of metal, I tried to decide what part of the car it had once been. Maybe something from inside the passenger compartment since it had been imprinted so strongly with the dying girl's last instant of life.

"You're one lying bastard," Culhane snarled. "You must have asked around. You knew."

My hands began to shake and reaction set in with a vengeance. Sweat popped out all over my body, and I sagged in the chair. The assault wasn't physical; it came from within. Again I saw the huge bore of the pistol pointing at my face and felt the ice against my feet and knew the woman's self-loathing as she killed herself. My brain had put straight all the sensations from the suicide, or perhaps I had lived them so many times I had unconsciously edited them to keep from being overwhelmed. And mixed with it was the feeling that the earlier psychometry mixed in with the present.

My head threatened to explode like a melon with a cherry bomb stuffed inside it.

"I never even heard of you before tonight. But what do I care?" I stared at him, my eyes matching his now. We were both at the breaking point. "You might have saved her, but you didn't. What took you so long to get there?" I hadn't thought out what I was saying. The words rushed up from inside, from hints and feelings generated during the brief touch with the metal.

"You know, damn you. I ought to . . ." Culhane was reaching for his pistol when the doctor came into the office. The man looked as if he needed more than a good night's sleep.

"Got it, Ben. Here's the whole goddamned report. Figure she was killed between five and seven tonight."

"You sure, Doc?"

"I'm not even sure the sun's going to come up tomorrow." He turned and looked out the same window I had, then coughed. "See what I mean? Sun's already up and I might have bet against it. Hell, yes, I'm sure enough about it. Read the fucking report. Believe it or not, as you see fit. And if you don't, get another sucker to do your dirty work." The doctor stalked from the room, stifling a wide yawn.

"So?" I asked.

"So you don't look like a good choice right now," Culhane said. "We called that bar where you claimed to have eaten dinner."

"Where I *did* eat dinner," I said.

"Yeah. The barkeep and waitress both remember you. Something about you putting on a little show with coins. Pretty convenient how you made such a good alibi for yourself, isn't it?"

"I wasn't trying to build an alibi," I said. "These things just happen." My eyes dropped back to the metal from the car crash that had killed his daughter. Tiny details kept popping up until the picture became clearer. His daughter had found him with a woman, not her mother, not his wife. The rest of the story refused to come, but I interpolated enough to know why Culhane was touchy. His daughter must have raced away, heedless of speed and smashed her car. He hadn't been reached until much later after the wreck was discovered because he had been with his mistress.

The lack of pictures on his desk might mean his wife had divorced him because of it. Everyone's got a story. How we overcome adversity is the mark of personal achievement. I wasn't thinking very highly of Culhane's victories at the moment.

Culhane scanned the doctor's autopsy report and snorted. "Her name was Carol Nyquist. You don't need to know where she lived."

Unless Mendocino was different from most small coastal towns, finding out wouldn't be difficult, if I wanted. She was probably listed in the phone book, and if she wasn't, if she was living with a boyfriend or roommate, a few discreet inquiries would be all it took to find out what I wanted.

"She wasn't a professional medium. Hell, she worked as a clerk in one of the curio stores." Culhane looked over the top of the page, as if I had lied to him. "Clean record, nothing to connect her with any bunco scheme like you intimated, except maybe being a drama major in college. So what are we going to do, Thorne?"

"You're either going to charge me or release me."

"Shouldn't let you out of my jurisdiction."

"Sergeant Worthington of SFPD will vouch for me," I said.

"And what does this reputed cop do?"

"Detective in homicide."

Culhane spent the next twenty minutes on the phone while he let me stew. Finally, he dropped the phone and said, "He just happened to be in the office. Seems he's in the middle of a vacation."

I had forgotten. I thanked my lucky stars that Worthington was a workaholic and couldn't leave the cop shop for more than a few days without getting anxious.

"He says you're all right. I don't believe that, but I'm not holding you in this matter."

Saying something sarcastic might land me in jail. Holding back the impulse took all my self-control. "Thank you," was all I said.

"I'll be on you like a shark on a drowning bloody carcass if you're lying, Thorne."

"Thanks for the vote of confidence in me." I left quickly, not wanting to cross verbal swords again with a man capable of such a vivid simile. The sheriff might just unleash his abused pet hound Johnny for a little savage sport. Landing in jail on some trumped-up charge after the harrowing time I'd already spent didn't seem like a good idea.

I drove a few miles per hour under the speed limit, letting the morning traffic pass me. Let the sheriff stop them. I took the road over to Ukiah and then down into the city. As I drove, my thoughts tumbled and turned like rocks in a lapidary's drum. Usually the rough edges get knocked off and some polished gem emerges. Not this time. No matter which way I looked at the facts, they just didn't fit together into a coherent picture. Why had Nyushka—Carol Nyquist—been killed and what was it she was going to tell me? The two might be connected, but how? What was the thread of logic I wasn't following?

By the time I crossed the Golden Gate Bridge my head pounded from a raging headache. Going back to my apartment was the most logical thing I could do. It was only a minute or two off Lombard after I turned east off the bridge. Rest was good for you; I had heard that often, and after everything that had happened, it sounded like incredibly good advice.

I kept driving, heading down 1 toward South San Francisco to see Charlie Hayes. He might have already been notified about Nyushka's death, but maybe not. Culhane had been adamant about wanting to pin the crime on me. I needed some support, and mending fences with Charlie was a good way to start. Besides that, I wanted to see how he reacted to the news. He was my only real link with Nyushka.

I didn't want to think that he was the killer, but the facts leaned in that direction. If she had been shaking him down and he'd found out about the cruel hoax, Charlie was capable of exploding and killing her.

But how had Nyushka done the channeling? It was a great gimmick and, as Culhane had implied, would make a good addition to my act if I figured it out. Whatever the mechanism had been, it was something new, one I'd never even considered. Still, I *had* missed the trapdoor in the floor. That had been careless on my part.

I pulled into the parking lot of RadChipTech and just stared at the simple block building. So much had happened that a few minutes wasn't out of the question. As I got out of the car, hardly ready to face Charlie but knowing it had to be done, I saw him talking with Anna Keenan. Whatever they were discussing, it was a hot topic. Charlie waved his arms wildly, and the woman closed in on herself more and more. First she just crossed her arms, then she began leaning away from Charlie. By the time he angrily spun and stalked off, she had even crossed her ankles and stood looking like some weird modern sculpture.

This wasn't a good time to talk to him, not considering the way we'd parted company before, but it had to be done. I was too tired to want to try at some other time.

"Charlie!" I called.

He stopped and glared. Seeing it was me changed his expression subtly. He was still angry, but it was a different anger than he'd shared with Anna Keenan.

"What do you want, Peter? I'm busy."

"I saw you with your financial officer and didn't want to intrude." This simple statement caused the man's face to redden. I thought he might burst a blood vessel. Whatever they had spoken about, it had not been pleasant for him.

"Aren't you ever going to stop meddling?"

"Carol Nyquist is dead," I said, choosing my words carefully. If there had been even a flicker of recognition at the name I missed it.

"Who's that?"

"Nyushka. That's her real name. I thought you might like to know." This time he looked stricken and swayed.

Before I could reach out to support him, he turned away and bowed his head. A tiny sob escaped his lips.

"No, it can't be. Not now!"

"She was murdered last night," I said, noting the sun had crept to a halfway point in the sky. It had been a long and tedious night and sleep was stalking me. This had to end soon, but I needed to see a bit more of his reaction. I put my hand on his shoulder. It quaked with emotion.

"Who did it?"

"The police think I did."

He swung around. His fist cocked back, and he looked as if he was ready to punch out my lights. Moving slightly, I pushed him and got him off balance. From that position he couldn't possibly get in a good shot at my face.

"You killed her?"

"No, Charlie, that's not what I said. I discovered her body, so the sheriff thinks I'm the prime suspect. But I was in Sausalito, a good three hours away. When was the last time you saw her?"

"Yesterday," he said, the shock settling in to leave him numb. "We did another channeling. Katrina told me what had to be done on the real estate deal. God, it's better than I thought."

"How much better?" I asked quietly, hoping for an answer. This had to be the payoff to Nyushka's fakery.

"Six million five," he said. "But the winery, the land, the equipment and a cellar with over eight million in wine comes with it. There's no way to lose on it."

"Where are you getting six and a half million dollars?" I asked. Charlie had been going through rough times financially and couldn't raise that kind of money.

"None of your damned business," he snapped. Charlie glanced back toward the building but Mrs. Keenan had gone inside. He didn't have to tell me he had been doing some financial legerdemain with the company to raise the money.

"What did Katrina say when you talked with her?"

"The money's committed," he said, his mood shifting suddenly. "I don't know about these things. What am I going to do? I need to get in touch with her again." He looked at me, pain and even fear in his eyes. "Peter, do you know another medium? One who could reach Katrina like Nyushka?"

I shook my head. The skeptic in me refused to admit one hundred percent that Nyushka had been channeling. Just because I wasn't able to figure out her methods didn't mean she had been on the up-and-up.

"We're so near to closing the deal."

"What about the other investors?" I remembered what Quincy Graham had said when I'd inquired about the winery.

"There aren't any other investors. What makes you think that?"

"Nothing. I just assumed there might be since this is such a big sum." There was more to this than he was telling me, but that was Charlie's business.

"Not that big, considering the payoff. The land and equipment are worth a million, maybe, but the real value is in the inventory. I need to know how to market it." He looked back toward RadChipTech, as if the answer might be painted on the side of a building. "Anna doesn't think the company can go into the winery business, or distribute the wine that's already bottled. Something about the company charter. God, I need to talk to Katrina again!"

"You're in over your head on the deal, aren't you?"

"Peter, I've optioned my entire share in RadChipTech to get the money."

"There's more, isn't there? Your share wouldn't come close to six million." His face turned gray with strain.

"I'm doing this for Katrina. God, I neglected her so when she was alive. What else can I do?"

"What else *have* you done, Charlie?" I asked as gently as I could.

"I've optioned off stock that doesn't exist." He swallowed hard. "I've optioned off my stock four times over to get the cash for the deal, but it'll all come back. I can pay it all off when the wine is sold, and when the winery is running again, it'll be a cash cow."

I wasn't exactly sure how Charlie had gotten together his stake for the winery, but it had to be fraudulent. A ghost had talked him into buying a nonworking winery and now his only contact with her was dead, murdered. It wasn't worthy of me but I found myself glad I wasn't in Charlie Hayes's shoes.

CHAPTER 18

Eighteen hours out of your life might not seem much, but I spent it sleeping and it put me back into the pink. When I awoke it was almost nine o'clock the morning following my talk with Charlie Hayes. What amazed me most was that I had actually slept without any of the psychometric echoes haunting my dreams. Exhaustion can do that, I suppose, driving out all nightmares, though it usually lets them sneak in more easily. Whatever the cause, I had rested soundly and felt a world better for it.

I'd just stepped out of the shower when the phone rang. I don't like the sound of a ringing phone, even the electronic beeping ones. The phone company has undoubtedly spent years and untold millions of dollars to develop the most insistent sound imaginable, one that simply cannot be ignored unless you are stone deaf. If they'd turned the ring into a 25-hertz cat's purr no one would ever answer.

"Hello."

"Peter, I'm glad I got hold of you. The greatest thing happened. It must be a miracle."

I didn't have to ask who had called while I was still dripping wet. Charlie's excited voice came over the wires as more vibrantly alive than I'd heard him since the first séance. He must have found another medium promising to reach Katrina.

"I've got a lot to do," I said. Work was piling up. I needed to move the spirit cabinet to the warehouse and then practice the act a few times without Michelle. When she got back from her vacation—any time now—we would go through it again and again. It hardly seemed possible but I was due to go onstage in Vegas in a little more

than a week. I didn't feel ready for a really good performance, but my bank account could certainly use the infusion
of cash to keep it alive and struggling while I got into the
swing of the act.

"I just wanted to tell you everything's going to be all
right. I got a note and—"

"What note?"

"From Nyushka. She must have sent it before she was
killed."

"So what's in it?" My suspicions flared. Charlie didn't
sound as if he had a clue to the woman's killer. Instead it
sounded as if the note contained the answer to his financial
troubles. That meant more trouble in the long run.

"She must have learned to do, what do you call it when
a spirit inhabits your body and you can write like the spirit
did when they were alive?"

He jumbled everything in his rush to tell me. "Automatic writing," I said, mind racing. "Are you telling me
you got a letter from Nyushka in Katrina's handwriting?"

"It tells me all I need to complete the deal. I've talked
with the general partner and—"

"General partner?"

"Peter, I'm sorry. This is making me crazy. You were
right yesterday when you said there were others in the
deal. I just didn't want to go into details, not after fighting
with Anna. It's a limited partnership. You know how they
work."

I did, but only in vague terms. "Your share is six and a
half million? This must be one hell of a vulnerable winery."

"The general partner puts up management expertise,
something I don't have, and the day-to-day operations
costs. The limited partners put up the equity. I know it
sounds strange, what with the winery and land and stock
worth only a fraction of what I'm paying, but it'll work
out. When the wine is sold, I get all the money and can
buy back the options on my stock. Then it'll be easy
street."

This scam took on new and different turns. Usually

greed alone is enough to hook a mark. Nyushka had set a doubly baited hook out when she went trolling for Charlie. He wanted his wife back and was following her instructions blindly. Nyushka—or those putting her up to this— couldn't have asked for a better sucker. The more I heard, the less I believed I had spoken with Katrina's spirit during the channeling. Something had gone wrong in the swindle and Nyushka had died over it. That still left someone out there actively working Charlie like a marlin on a hundred-pound test line.

"She sent you a letter? What does it say?"

"It gives all the details, all the things to look for, how to negotiate with the general partner, everything!"

"And you are sure it's Katrina's handwriting?"

"I'm no expert but I ought to know my own wife's writing."

Possibilities came to me. These might be notes Katrina had made for her own benefit, and Nyushka had somehow come across them. Whatever the medium's source of information on the dead woman, it was damned good. There wasn't any reason to think that she couldn't have found and stolen Katrina's notebook or photocopied something left laying around where anyone could find it. The theft of a notebook off the seat of an unlocked car takes only a few seconds. If Katrina had been involved with other matters, copies could have been made and the notebook returned and no one would be the wiser.

Another thought entered my head. This might be an original, in Katrina's hand. If so, that meant she hadn't had the note with her when she died. The accident that had taken her life might not have been an accident after all. Whoever had backed Nyushka might have plotted out the elaborate hoax to sucker Charlie out of the money, leaving him a complete loser. Both his wife and money would be history.

"Charlie, who's your lawyer? Has he checked out the details?"

"There's no need for a shyster on this one, Peter. Katrina was more thorough than I'd ever seen her."

"Did *she* have a lawyer to go over the papers?"

"I don't know," he said.

I glanced at the digital clock on my nightstand and cursed myself for being such a fool, but Charlie needed help—and I might, too, if Sheriff Culhane didn't want to do any work in solving Nyushka's murder. Even a public defender lawyer fresh out of school could handle my case and win. My alibi was solid and, more important than all the circumstantial evidence in the world, I hadn't killed the medium. But Charlie needed to wiggle free of this land deal, or at least get someone to go over the papers who understood limited partnerships, real estate and the value of wine and wineries.

"You still have the letter?" I asked.

"Of course I do," he said indignantly. He might frame it and hang it on the wall over his fireplace to remind him of Katrina.

"I want to see it."

There was a long pause, then he asked, "Can you reach her? With your psychometry?"

There was no way to tell without trying. I doubted it was possible because paper carries so little of the resonance that gives the emotions, the feel, the essence of the person handling it. Metal is far better, and then metal in the person's possession for a long time is best of all. If too many people handle an object, the vibrations locked in the crystal lattice are muddled and worthless unless exceptionally strong emotions have been released.

"Let's meet for breakfast." The decision was made mutually, for entirely different reasons on each of our parts. Charlie needed a new link to Katrina and thought I might provide it, in spite of my skepticism.

I quickly toweled off and dressed, then cursed the slowness of the elevator as it seemed to stop on every floor to pick up people on their way to work. I enjoy the view from high up in the apartment but there are disadvantages. This was one of them. Fuming, in a hurry, I hiked the two blocks to where I garaged the car. The drive to café where I'd agreed to meet Charlie for breakfast seemed to take forever, though it was just down Columbus near Washington Square. To go along with my impatience, finding a parking spot took almost as long as the drive over.

When I entered the café, Charlie was at a table, his elbows holding down a single sheet paper menu in the breeze from the open front door. I sat with my back to the wind, but this did little to stop the flapping of the menu.

"You got here fast," I said.

"I was in town. I thought I told you. That's why this seemed like a good place. I was a couple blocks over and down Kearny and just walked." He reached into his pocket and pulled out the letter. It snapped in the wind coming through the door. I turned and motioned to the waitress to close it.

"You sure?" she called. "The fan's out in the kitchen. This place will get real stuffy if we don't leave it open."

"For just a few minutes, please," I said. The wind was cold and I wasn't going to take off my jacket. Unless the café filled with smoke from the kitchen, I thought the few patrons would prefer it without the wind blowing off the Bay. When she closed the door, leaving it propped open just a few inches in way of compromise, I took the envelope and examined it.

For a few seconds I couldn't figure out what was wrong. Then I said, "The postmark is yesterday evening." The good old days, if there were such, had a more efficient post office, or at least one willing to let you know to the minute when a letter was canceled. All that came through on this was PM. Afternoon, early evening. I doubted it could have been later, since Nyushka was dead by then. But what finally registered was the city.

"It was postmarked from here in San Francisco," I said.

"What?" Charlie took it and peered at the smeared cancellation. "I hadn't noticed. So?"

"Maybe nothing." If Nyushka had been in the city and had dropped it off yesterday morning, it would have taken till the afternoon or evening to get it canceled. That fit into what I knew of the time of her death, but when she'd called me, it had been from Mendocino or maybe San

Tomás. Of that I was sure. No matter the clarity of a fiber optic line, there is a distinctive quality about long distance. That put her in town yesterday morning—and if so, why hadn't she called me then?

What had happened between mailing the letter and that afternoon that prompted her to call me after returning to Mendocino?

Anything more from the envelope would require a forensics expert, and I wasn't sure there was anything more to be discovered. The envelope was cheap, the kind sold in bulk at any of a hundred drugstores. The stamp was the ridiculous F flower, showing Nyushka had either hoarded a desk drawer filled with them or just didn't mail much. The standard twenty-nine cent stamps had been available for a year or two.

"You ready to order?" The waitress stood, hip cocked and her pad in hand, as if daring us to try anything. She hadn't liked having to close the door and it showed. A nose-curling odor was sneaking in from the kitchen, strong enough to kill any appetite I might have had. This place is usually good for an omelette or a few pancakes, but this morning I wasn't up to it.

"Just a glass of orange juice," I said.

"Coffee?"

"Don't drink it." I turned to the envelope and ran my fingers over it, as if I had become a phrenologist and the slightest bump might reveal hidden character flaws. Charlie ordered and I barely heard. There wasn't anything more I could tell from the outside. As if handling a religious relic, I slipped the letter out and carefully pinned it to the table to keep the slackened breeze from blowing it away.

"See? That's Katrina's handwriting."

I nodded, absorbed by the edges of the letter. There was a slight fuzziness, as if this had been run out on a computer and the tractor feed holes had been ripped off. The paper matched the envelope: cheap. There was no sign that this had been in a notebook and ripped out. And even my untrained eye could tell the writing was original, not a photocopy. Whoever had written had done so quickly, with powerful strokes, sometimes almost cutting through the paper.

And I recognized the handwriting, too. It was Katrina's.

"So?" urged Charlie. "What can you do with this?"

I moved back enough to let the waitress put the orange juice in front of me. Charlie had coffee and a gooey-looking sweet roll sure to rot his teeth and give him diabetes. I tried not to shudder at his tastes.

"I don't know," I said when the waitress had left. She was giving us strange looks, as it was. "The resonance from the writer isn't going to be strong unless the letter was in her possession for some time. This looks recently written." I held it up to the light and saw that tiny drops of ink in the heavy periods and dots over the *i*'s were still damp enough to run. This wasn't a forgotten sheet taken from Katrina's desk. It was done recently, within a few days.

"Go on, Peter. Do whatever it is you do. I've got to reach Katrina again."

From the way he said it I knew he wasn't needing more advice on real estate. He just wanted to contact his lost wife once more.

"How do you know Nyushka did this with automatic writing?" I asked, the idea blossoming on me. "Was there another note with this one?"

"No, but who else could have sent it?"

"Good point," I said. This bothered me, but no other answer suggested itself. I took a deep, cleansing breath and felt my insides begin to settle softly. I was both more aware and less aware of everything surrounding me. The wind coming in the front door helped wipe out the ugly vapors from the kitchen, but my easy breathing pulled in little of this distraction. I envisioned myself floating along, dancing from cloud to cloud, lighter than air, floating, drifting, settling down so that my mind was receptive to the faintest vibrations trapped within the fibers of the paper.

I never got into a full trance. The feeble resonance wasn't enough to give me any clue about the paper or the person writing it. I had a feeling of distance, of anger, of wanting revenge.

I shook myself. This was an echo from the woman who had killed herself. Worthington would have to pay for polluting my mind with that viciousness, I vowed. Returning to the letter, I got subtle hints of Katrina, but the resentment kept rising to blot out any true message.

"I'm sorry, Charlie, there's nothing I can do." For the first time I pressed the letter to the table and quickly scanned the contents. I wasn't a forensics expert, I know little about graphoanalysis and my psychometric skills had failed. What had been written was all that remained to satisfy my curiosity.

"This is awfully explicit, isn't it?" I asked, scanning the page. "Was Katrina facing the same problems you are?"

"This has to be automatic writing. There might not have been time for another channeling," Charlie said with great earnestness. "Katrina must have forced herself on Nyushka to give me this."

I couldn't argue with his interpretation. It didn't seem to be a scrap left over and found to add verisimilitude to the channeling. That séance routine didn't need any bolstering. It was a crowd pleaser by itself, but what if it was no longer possible? What if the method was no longer available to Nyushka? Or with her dead, to whoever had killed her? The deal smelled to high heaven and this letter kept Charlie charging straight ahead with it.

"Have the note examined by a professional," I suggested, sliding it back to him. "Let someone who is unbiased compare this with something Katrina wrote months and months ago."

"I don't need to," he said. "This is from Katrina, and it spells out what I have to do. It's all falling into place." He carefully folded the letter and put it back into his pocket. He looked up and asked, "You can't reach Katrina?"

"Not like Nyushka," I said.

He looked crestfallen. There was so much advice I wanted to give him, but he would ignore it all. He was focusing on the wrong thing. He ought to be figuring out the trouble he'd find himself in if the real estate deal turned sour on him. However he had raised the millions for this deal, it wasn't legal, no matter what he thought. As a businessman, Charlie Hayes was a fine electronics engineer. But what could I do to help him—other than pretend I could reach his wife beyond the cold grip of the grave?

CHAPTER 19

The next two days went by in a rush after my stage assistant returned from her vacation. Michelle looked better than ever—tanned, trimmer, more confident and a perfect distraction for the audience. After we had worked twelve hours straight both those two days, I called a day off for a much-needed rest. I needed to think through some rough spots in the act. And it was then that I remembered Charlie and the letter and my intention to do something about it.

I had considered faking a séance for him to warn him away from the land development deal. I've been to enough channeling sessions to know the best ways to make them solidly credible—at least to those inclined to believe in the first place. It wouldn't match Nyushka's marvelously convincing technique, whatever it had been, but Charlie was desperate enough to believe just about anything. Michelle's voice and Katrina's might be a close enough match if I had her speak through an electronic gadget I had bought years ago for my act. No matter the person's natural timbre, twisting dials and resetting meters can make the voice squeak like a mouse or boom in a deep basso profundo. It might take some tinkering but I could match it close enough to fool him. The only problem lay in the questions Charlie might ask and that Michelle couldn't answer in a million years.

The usual way a medium got around that was simply garbling the communication, misinterpreting, misdirecting, claiming that the ether was too turbulent for easy reception. There were a thousand excuses. But I didn't think they would fly with Charlie because he had the damned letter that proved Katrina's spirit was strong enough to force itself onto Nyushka's body and make her write.

Torn between concocting a fully faked séance and preparing for Vegas, I found myself drifting toward letting Charlie work through his problems by himself. The only thing keeping me from cutting him entirely free was the memory of Katrina Hayes. She had meant something to me, and I resented anyone fleecing Charlie by using her this way.

I hunched over my desk and went back to work. After the first three tricks, there was a spot that needed punching up. The audience would start to drift when the stagehands set up the next big trick, an escape while suspended above the stage. A crane and hook had to be positioned and the rope prepared. I didn't trust anyone other than Michelle to do that. This left me alone on stage and the few card tricks I'd chosen weren't flashy enough. A bigger attention-grabber was needed. As I mentally went through the tricks that might work, the phone began its insistent jangling.

I grabbed it, hoping to be done with whomever was calling.

"Peter, this is Charlie. I've got good news."

"What's that?" My mind was still onstage and performing. I had to shift gears and remember everything he might be happy about.

"The deal. It closed this morning, and it went smooth as silk."

"Six and a half million?" The amount was staggering to me. I had no idea what I would do if someone just walked up and handed me that much. I certainly wouldn't have to knock myself out working up new ways to keep an audience amused, though I didn't think I could ever give up performing. Not entirely. There were rewards other than the money.

I shook myself free of the tangent I'd drifted along and returned my attention to Charlie.

He didn't answer directly. I heard him catch his breath, as if he was realizing how much this was, too. "Yeah," he said in a low voice. "It went just like Katrina had written.

I got an ironclad clause put into the partnership agreement giving me complete rights to the wine as it's sold off."

"So you pay back the money you, uh, borrowed," I said. "Where's the profit?"

"We're subdividing the land. Each parcel will go for a hundred grand or better, and with quarter acre plots, I stand to make a profit of better than ten million."

"Sounds as if the land is pricey, Charlie. Are you sure it'll sell fast? And the wine?"

"It's all guaranteed," he said. "Quincy balked a little, but I followed the line of reasoning Katrina had outlined and he finally relented."

"Quincy Graham? He's the general partner?"

"He's a nice guy. I understand why Katrina liked him. He did everything he could to keep me in the deal."

I shook my head. I bet he did. If this wasn't on the up-and-up, Graham might stand to make a hell of a lot of money fast.

"Isn't it usual to do these real estate transactions through a bank and an escrow department?" This bothered me, but I don't know much about real estate. My landlord at the warehouse had been a fine source of information on what constituted normal business dealings. Everything was done by instantaneous computer entries and no tangible money ever changed hands.

"The owner insisted we do things quick, and there was, well—" Charlie's voice drifted off, then came back stronger. "There was also the, uh, way I borrowed the money. I thought it would be better dealing directly."

"You do have a clear title to the land?" I didn't know much but I did know that title searches protect against claims made later. Guaranty companies make a pile of money in this business.

"We not only have a clear title to the land, we're not selling the mineral or water rights," Charlie gloated. "If anything turns up, that's ours. Pure gravy."

"When were you ever this interested in making a quick buck?" I asked.

"This isn't for me, Peter. It's for Katrina. Her memory."

"Ever think that now that the deal is completed, you won't be able to contact her?"

"Why not?"

"If you follow the line of thinking, ghosts hang around because something is left undone in their lives. Katrina's mission might be over now that you've sunk six and a half million dollars into this winery." I heard myself repeating the amount over and over, and I couldn't stop it. That was more than enough money to kill someone over. Nyushka had been murdered? Had Katrina? It looked that way, and the only likely winner in this deal was Graham.

"Then she ought to rest easy," Charlie said, a touch of grief in his voice. "I did everything just like she wrote."

"Has Sheriff Culhane contacted you?"

"I dodged him while this was going on. I don't have time for some hick's investigation."

"This isn't just some street person hitting you up for spare change, Charlie," I said, startled at how unlike him this was. He usually had a modicum of compassion. He was completely involved in this land transaction. "This is the woman who put you in touch with your wife."

"Death isn't as frightening as it used to be," he said. "Katrina has shown me that there is more than the obvious physical world. I had just never seen it before."

The twists and turns of his thinking left me light-headed. The world around us meant little but he had embezzled millions to finish the deal for his dead wife. What happened to him was of no consequence compared with assuaging her ghostly desires.

"Did Culhane say anything about me?"

"I don't know. As I said, I put him off. There'll be plenty of time to talk to him and get everything straightened out. Look, Peter, I just wanted to thank you for all you've done. Got to run. See you."

He hung up, and I didn't utter a word trying to stop him. I leaned back, working on all the pieces to Charlie Hayes's puzzle rather than trying to fit together the elements for my act. In a way, it was better for me to concentrate on the problems surrounding Nyushka's death—I had the feeling that I hadn't seen the last of Sheriff Culhane or his bully boy Johnny. I was an outsider and perfect to hang that crime on. Who knew how this would play when he came up for reelection—or was it election? Culhane had said he was more a deputy than a full-fledged sheriff. Whoever held the official position might keep his feet hiked up to a desktop in Ukiah. Taking that job might look to be a promotion to Ben Culhane.

My thoughts turned to Quincy Graham. He hadn't been interested in new partners for the winery when I went to his office. He couldn't have known if I had a million in hundreds stashed in the trunk of my car from a successful drug deal or if I were worth billions legitimately. If anything, he had worked hard to dissuade me from asking about the property. If it was a done deal, why hadn't he just said so and let the refusal lead into a pitch for some other property? Mendocino County was in the throes of a land recession, just like the rest of the country. Business wasn't good enough for Graham simply to blow off a possible deal.

Or had I spooked him asking about the Alsace Winery?

Grumbling to myself, I went to the closet and pulled out a heavy coat. It was colder up in San Tomás than it was down in San Francisco, and I might be spending a day or two up there this time. I wasn't coming back until I'd worked everything through to my satisfaction.

My attention on the drive was split between worry over Charlie's involvement in the land deal and the nearness of my opening in Las Vegas. The act had too many rough edges. I've been in the business long enough to be able to gloss over them, but Michelle needed the practice. She'd only been working with me a few months, and I wondered how much longer I'd keep her. Her aunt owned an art gallery and was hinting that she needed extra help with it— and a partner to take over in a few years when she retired. That was a profession for Michelle; all I offered was a job.

I swung left and headed toward San Tomás, wanting to leave my inquiries with Sheriff Culhane in Mendocino for last. First I wanted to talk with Quincy Graham and find out the names of the other partners in the limited partnership. Charlie hadn't been too explicit about who they were, or even if there were more. Not once had he said anything about discussing the deal with any of them. I wasn't even sure if he could name the other parties to this fabulous subdevelopment scheme.

My foot almost smashed down on the gas pedal when I saw the police cruisers parked around Quincy Graham's realty office. People milled about outside the door, talking to themselves in the way most conducive to spreading rumors. Some held their hands over their mouths to keep from being heard by more than half the town. Others made no bones about voicing their speculations to any who would listen.

I drove to the rear of the building and saw a familiar car. The doctor who had done the autopsy on Nyushka had parked here. I cut the engine and coasted to a halt beside his battered auto. He obviously didn't spend the money he made as doctor or from his job as coroner on fancy wheels. Rust ate through the body of the 1984 Plymouth in a dozen spots. The car might collapse under him if he pushed it too much.

"You just hold it right there," came the cold command. I knew the voice and obeyed instantly. It wouldn't matter to the deputy how I died, surrendering or running, but it did to me. There might be some questions raised by the coroner if Johnny killed me with my empty hands raised over my head.

"I want to see Culhane. What's happening here?" I turned slightly and looked over my shoulder. A chill ran up my spine that had nothing to do with the harsh wind blowing off the ocean or the icy water I was standing ankle-deep in. The deputy had his heavy revolver cocked and pointed squarely at me.

"I just bet he wants to see you. Inside. Now!"

I obeyed, trying not to feel too foolish and he herded me around the building and I went past the gathered crowd. A hush fell on the spectators, then a ripple carried to the back as some people recognized me. After this fiasco I'd be forever branded as a criminal.

"What you got there, Johnny? Oh, it's Thorne. Glad to see you showed up," said Culhane, not bothering to get up from where he knelt on the floor. "Saves us the time of fetching you back up here."

"What's happened?" I asked, keeping my hands up. Johnny hadn't bothered to lower his pistol, and I wasn't going to give him any excuse for murdering me.

"Seems since you started poking around San Tomás there's been a rash of deaths. Can't rightly say you had anything to do with the Hayes case, but you were real handy for the Nyquist murder and for him." Culhane moved and I saw what I had already guessed.

Quincy Graham lay on the floor. I didn't need to note the jaundice or the way his sphincters had opened to tell me he was dead. No living human can have an expression of such pain etched on his face and still live.

"You knew him, I bet," Culhane said.

"I talked to him a week back," I admitted. Wanting to say more but knowing how deep a grave I might be digging for myself, I remained silent. It was best to let Culhane ask the questions. Details would come out from what he wanted to know.

"Now he's dead. What do you think the cause is, Doc?"

The coroner looked even more harassed than before. "Hard to say without a complete drug screen. From the pallor and the look of the body, I'd say he swallowed enough carbon tetrachloride to do himself in."

"That's some guess, Doc," Culhane said in disgust. "Johnny found a half-used can of carbon tet in the back room."

"No fooling," the doctor said. "Hit it right on the money, then. Figure we can save the county the cost of the lab work?"

"Don't get smart," Culhane snapped. He jerked around to me. I still had my hands up in the air; they were beginning to turn cool from lack of circulation. "Put those damn hands down. What do you think this is, some goddamn Western movie?"

I didn't obey immediately. I glanced at Johnny. He hadn't moved an inch and his service revolver still pointed at me. Only slowly did I lower my hands, and even then I wasn't sure if he would cut me down.

"Yeah, he swallowed an unhealthy dose of carbon tet. Bet that's damned near half of what's in his drink." The coroner pointed to a drinking glass on the edge of Graham's desk. A clear amber liquor had been diluted by the ice in the drink.

"Bourbon?" asked Culhane.

"That's what everyone says he drank. Most of 'em say he drank too much of it, too. The taste of a third or fourth drink could have covered the carbon tet. With enough alcohol in him, the poison would have acted fast. Wouldn't have taken ten minutes to put him down."

"What was it like for him?" asked Culhane.

"Not too pleasant," the coroner said. "Pain in the guts, might have tried to vomit, breathing all screwed up and his heart would have turned irregular. Might have become so confused he didn't know what was going on until he passed out. I'd say, with the alcohol, every organ in him is suspect for proximate cause of death."

"I'm putting it down as murder. You have any trouble with that, Doc?"

"None. Can't see how anyone could mistake a clearly marked tin of carbon tet for branch water. I'd say someone fixed him a doozy of a cocktail." He began stripping off the rubber gloves he'd worn examining the body. He dropped them into his jacket pocket and closed his equipment case. "Transport him up to Mendocino where I can do the autopsy. This might take a week or so to get complete results. Why couldn't this one have just been bashed in the head like your other one?"

The coroner left before Culhane could answer. The sheriff spun on me, glaring. He wanted to strike out at someone and I was close, but so was the morbid crowd pressing against the front window and peering in. Culhane could no more torture a confession out of me than his deputy could get away with gunning me down in plain sight.

"What's your story?"

"When did he die?" I countered.

"Doc says he's been dead about three hours. Where have you been?"

"Driving up here," I said.

"What kind of alibi you got?"

The time frame was harder this time for me to zero in on. "Before I left San Francisco I filled up my car. I used a credit card. The attendant might remember me."

"More coin tricks?" Culhane said sarcastically.

"My card took forever to get an authorization. I've been sitting on it while driving up here too much and put a bend in it. That does something to the magnetic strip on the back."

"And I suppose the receipt's got the time on it?"

"Maybe," I said, not knowing. The cash registers used in most stations now furnish such a complete history that I don't pay much attention. For all I know, they put not only the card number and amount of purchase but my blood type and DNA pattern onto the receipt. "I talked with Charlie Hayes just before I left, too."

"Convenient. He's up to his ears in this, just like you, and I can't get through to talk to him. Damned convenient you supplying each other an alibi."

"Where were you when he called?" chimed in Johnny.

"At my apartment. I didn't record the call, if that's what you mean. But he called me, so that puts me in my apartment."

"Not really," Culhane said, glaring at his deputy. "The gadgets the phone company provide now might let you forward calls through your apartment to your car or some other phone. Maybe this was the signal for you to poison Graham."

I didn't even acknowledge such a wild notion. Telephone company records would show that I didn't have a car-phone or use a portable cellular, and I don't pay for call forwarding. It might be a part of my telephone service, but I don't know how to use it if it is, and even more important I'm not paying for it. That had to mean I didn't have anything but a bare bones system.

Looking past Culhane, I tried to get some sense of what had happened here. If the coroner was right. Quincy Graham had been poisoned about the time I left San Francisco. There didn't seem to be any sign of struggle; he must have drunk the poison willingly enough. I doubted if it was suicide. That meant someone he knew well enough to fix him a drink had killed him.

"Who were his friends?" I asked.

"We're looking into this, Thorne. We don't need your help."

"No sign of forced entry."

"The damned company was open for business. Of course there wouldn't be any forced entry." Culhane was fuming. I knew that silence was golden but couldn't keep from thinking out loud.

"No forced entry, someone he knew fixed him a drink, or several maybe," I went on. "Wasn't it early in the day for him to be drinking so heavily?"

"He was an alcoholic," Culhane said. "We got that from a dozen people. He just about kept the liquor store down the street in business all by his lonesome."

"Any papers on his desk?" I stood on tiptoe and peered around Culhane. The sheriff moved to block my view.

"You're not the one asking questions. I am. Johnny's going to take you back to Mendocino for a full report. Get him out of here," Culhane ordered. Johnny took my elbow in the grip cops everywhere enjoy so. He lifted enough to get my weight onto my toes so I couldn't move easily, dodge or make a break for it. At least he didn't whip out the handcuffs or make me walk with my hands in the air again.

"Hey, Sheriff," called a man from the door. "I got these from down the street at the drug store. Quincy had left the files there to be copied. Said his copier was busted."

The man waved a sheaf of papers. Culhane went to take them and Johnny relaxed. As he did, I noticed an expensive fountain pen on the floor just at my feet. It might have rolled off the desk as Graham thrashed about, the poison beginning to work its way into his vitals. I shrugged off Johnny's grip long enough to stoop and pick up the pen. It was ridiculous of me to do so. My prints would now be on the barrel.

Culhane leafed through the copies the man had brought to him. I used this to take a deep, settling breath. There wouldn't be time for me to do a deep psychometric reading on the pen. It might not get me anything, but I wanted to try. Anything this expensive had to be used by Graham on a daily basis and might never have left his possession. It was the kind of writing instrument a real estate man might whip out to sign documents to impress a client.

Eyes closed, mind in a light trance, I let the vibrations from the pen well up and wash over me. I staggered just a little as the murky impressions began to make sense. Johnny grabbed me again and hustled me toward the door when Culhane demanded to know why we were still here.

As we passed, I bumped into him. The pen left my hand and slid easily into his shirt pocket. With any luck I had managed to wipe the gold barrel clean of my fingerprints. Culhane might never connect the expensive pen with the murder and wonder how he came by it, or he might place it instantly. Whatever happened, it was out of my possession and into his.

And I had a quick psychometric reading of it.

Katrina Hayes's image had been so prominent in the reading it was impossible to miss.

CHAPTER 20

The interrogation ended more abruptly than before. Culhane had lost his interest in me quickly, even if his deputy hadn't. I wondered if there might be something to the notion that everyone walks around generating an invisible aura. Taking an instant dislike to someone you've just met, no matter how fleetingly, is a fact of life. It happens to me several times a year for no good reason, but seldom does my initial opinion change too much. I had seen Culhane and knew he wasn't the kind of guy I'd want to invite to my next party, and his deputy was even worse. If they had auras, both would be black with ghostly maggots chewing up their ectoplasm.

Johnny had taken an obvious dislike to me. He kept hitting his left palm with a long nightstick, as if wondering what it would be like planting that squarely on top of my head. The expression on his face was more than a little frightening. He showed no hatred. Rather it was a mask of complete indifference, the expression a sociopath might have as he beat his child to death for not finishing the vegetables on his plate.

"That what you used on Carol Nyquist?" I asked, to keep him off balance. The question brought him out of his private mental hell enough to react like a human being. His face turned florid and I thought he was going to hit me.

"You son of a bitch. You don't know a damned thing about what goes on up here. We hate your kind."

"What kind is that?"

"You city folks think you know it all. You breeze on into our territory and buy it, and that nothing else counts."

"What else does matter?" As long as he kept talking he wasn't beating on me. That had to be an improvement over needing plastic surgery before going onstage again—or pushing up daisies out in some unmarked field, no matter how lovely the view of the ocean might be.

"Friends, that's what counts. You got to have friends what back you up, no matter what."

"Ben does that, huh?"

"Yeah, Ben's a good man. Nobody'd give me the time of day, but he took a chance on me and made me his deputy."

"But you're not really a deputy," I said, remembering what Culhane had said before. The sheriff of Mendocino county was over in the county seat of Ukiah, not out here. The way the law was run here was more than a little lax if Johnny was any indication of the way Culhane operated.

"Maybe not, but I do what I'm told."

Asking what Culhane told him to do wasn't going to get me anywhere. Johnny might think with his biceps and enjoy a good gang-bang now and then to relieve the tension, but he wasn't going to spill his guts to me. If he did, I'd be found dead somewhere along the road. How many others had crossed the law and ended up that way?

"Do you need anything more from me? I've told you what I can about Graham. I only met him once."

"We got ways of finding these things out. You're not buying your way out of this with some fat-ass, fancy San Francisco lawyer."

"I asked after the Alsace Winery when I talked with Graham." A shot in the dark never hurt. Johnny's face didn't show so much as a flicker of emotion at the name. This kind of interrogation, me asking leading questions and him promising to bash my brains out, just wasn't working. It wouldn't be much longer before I ran out of questions and Johnny got his hardwood nightstick swinging in the proper arc to turn my head to bloody jelly.

"We'll find out everything we need to know. Sheriff Culhane's good at that."

"What's the coroner's name?" I asked suddenly. It occurred to me I hadn't heard it mentioned.

"Dr. Weiss? What you want with him?"

"That's the name," I said, as if I'd merely forgotten it for a moment. It struck me that Culhane, Weiss and Johnny were all cut from the same cloth, each inept in different ways. The order of danger from them was obvious. Johnny was the muscle, Culhane the brains and the doctor? He didn't take enough of an interest in his job to count as a power in the area, but he fit in well with the sheriff. From the way they spoke to each other, they were comfortable and had a longstanding relationship.

The phone rang on the sheriff's desk. Johnny whirled around smartly, scooped it up and glowered as he listened. He finally grunted and then dropped the receiver back into the cradle. The news didn't please him. That could only mean that I might live to dance in the streets another day.

"You can go. The sheriff's gonna be busy for a while, and he don't want you around sticking your nose in everything. We ain't done with you, though. He's likely to call you up in a day or two to finish answering questions."

"I'm history," I said, getting out of the office as fast as I could. Behind me, Johnny growled deep in his throat, sounding more like a rabid dog than a human being. Outside in the cool, sweet breeze of freedom I remembered I'd been dragged back to Mendocino and my car was down in San Tomás. Several miles isn't too much of a walk to avoid disagreeable people like Culhane and his barely housebroken deputy, but I did want to get out of this place. Hitchhiking was the quickest way, since I doubted Mendocino had much in the way of taxi service, but first I wanted to contact Charlie. He deserved to know his land deal had fallen apart in a big way.

Finding a telephone dangling precariously on the side of a convenience store and pulling out my calling card, I began punching in the interminable code numbers needed for making a credit call from a machine not equipped with a magnetic strip reader. After what seemed like enough digits to encompass even the national debt, I heard the phone ringing as if at the bottom of a deep well. When Charlie answered, his voice was much clearer than I'd expected from the tinny ring and distant hum on the line.

"Charlie, this is Peter."

"I'm pretty busy right now. Got a meeting coming up in ten minutes to talk over some consumer electronics gadgets the guys have come up with. We have to move that way since the government contracts are drying up, though heaven knows why we need to put a radiation-resistant chip into a dishwasher. Nobody eats off uranium plates these days."

"This won't take but a second," I said, wondering if I should sugarcoat it for him. I decided it wouldn't do any good. He was rambling on and on, his mind already focused on his meeting and nothing else. I had to shake him free and get him thinking in other directions. "Quincy Graham was just found murdered."

"Peter, this—" He started to accuse me of a practical joke, then bit it off, knowing I didn't like practical jokes. The few people who had ever played them on me found their lives turned into a living hell even they couldn't dismiss as simply having a good time.

"He was found poisoned in his office," I went on. "The sheriff thinks it was done with an industrial cleaner found in the back room of the real estate office."

"He's dead?" Charlie's voice was cracked and barely audible, and it wasn't because of the poor quality of the long distance line. "This is awful!"

"You haven't paid him for the land yet, have you?"

"It's all done, as of yesterday afternoon. I sent a bank wire. You know, an electronic transfer from here to his Mendocino bank. It didn't take ten seconds to get confirmation."

Wire transfers are virtually instantaneous. Checks flash back and forth at the speed of light and business goes on, not caring if the transfer is ten cents or ten billion dollars. It wasn't anything more than zeroes and ones to a modem. Charlie's money was long since digested in Quincy Graham's account.

"You'd better get a lawyer on this right away. See if you can squelch the deal and freeze the money."

"But Katrina wanted . . ."

"Katrina's dead," I said harshly. "And I'm not so sure you haven't stepped into a pile of something you're not going to scrape off your shoe very easily."

"The deal's good, Peter. It might not matter if Graham's dead. This was a limited partnership, like a corporation. It's a legal entity unto itself and ought to go on, no matter what happens to any of the investors. Just because something happens to the general partner doesn't mean the limited partners lose everything."

"Who gets Graham's share?"

"I don't know," Charlie said, distraught enough now to mumble under his breath. I caught only every few words, but he wasn't taking the news very well.

"I'll do some asking around since I'm up in Mendocino," I said. Pausing for a moment to think, I added, "By the way, did Katrina ever mention giving Graham a pen?"

"A pen? You mean like a ballpoint? I doubt it. Why do you ask?"

"Nothing. You get your lawyer into this right away."

"I don't know. Katrina wanted the deal to sail, and Graham's death might be coincidental to the partnership. If I do too much poking and prodding, it . . . Never mind." He seemed to understand that confessing to securities fraud on the telephone wasn't the best thing in the world to do at any time, no matter how safe he felt making the admission of guilt to me.

"Maybe," I said, "but the cops are going to be asking you hard questions. First Nyushka and then Graham, and you had dealings with both of them."

"Thanks, Peter. I'll see what I can do." Charles Hayes hung up, but it didn't sound as if he was going to immediately call his lawyer. He might not even make his meeting. I just hoped that whatever he decided to do wasn't going to dig him any deeper. Any SEC investigation of how he had gotten the money for Graham's winery partnership would land him in jail for twenty years—and this might be the least of his troubles. I didn't think Charlie was capable of murder, but it's hard to tell about people, even those you've known for twenty years. Pushed far enough, given the right emotional trigger, everyone is capable of incredibly heroic or hideously venal acts.

I hung up and looked around. There weren't too many choices for Graham to use for his banking, even in a town the size of Mendocino. It wouldn't take me too long to find which he used. Maybe a little razzle-dazzle could get me information. I checked my pockets to see what little tricks were hidden there and then started off to see.

I sat in the chair facing the president's desk. The other bank officers gathered in a tight knot just a few feet away, all discussing the matter. I had dropped a small bombshell in their laps. How long it would be until someone came up with the proper way of checking out my spurious claim to the Alsace Winery depended on how closely Graham had worked with his bankers. From the panic on one young officer's face, I knew who was on the hot seat.

My fingers dipped into my side pocket to a small roll of flash paper. This and a few fake coins were all I had in the way of equipment. How it could be used was beyond me, but even a quick glimpse of the computer screen, facing the other direction, would give me some idea as to the balance in Quincy Graham's account. If the money had come to rest here, Charlie might freeze the assets until everything clarified itself. From all I could see, the best that might happen was him getting his money. He could repurchase the options he had sold on his stock in RadChip-Tech, maybe losing a few thousand dollars in transaction fees but not ending up for a long vacation at Club Fed for securities fraud. The worst that could happen lay beyond my ability to guess. Culhane wanted to solve the dual murders fast. No cop likes having an open charge of murder one on the books, especially since the big city clearance rate is only around sixty-five percent now. Two in a single week in a small town had to send ripples all the way up the line and might attract unwanted political attention. A quick solution, no matter who got burned, might even start Ben Culhane's political star rising.

I cursed the day I had ever agreed to attend the séance with Charlie. Going a bit further, it hadn't helped me any to attend Katrina's funeral. The feelings of loss had intensified as I had gone through Nyushka's channeling sessions.

I closed my eyes and tried to calm myself. If I felt bent out of shape over Katrina's death, was it any wonder Charlie had done the incredibly stupid things he had? He wanted to believe in her continued existence, even beyond the grave, and he had hung on the slimmest of evidence.

"Damn," I muttered aloud. I clamped my mouth shut. How had Nyushka done the channeling? It was too good a show to go with her to the grave.

"Mr. Thorne," called the bank president. "This is Joseph Lowenthal, our vice president and loan officer in charge of the Alsace property. Perhaps you can go over with him what you told me. I'm at a complete loss to understand this."

"I represent an investment group in San Francisco," I lied, "that had put up earnest money with Mr. Graham to purchase the winery. I discovered that he had formed a limited partnership intent on buying the property, establishing himself as general partner. It seems to me he is selling the same land twice."

Lowenthal cleared his throat and looked even paler. "There must be some mistake, sir."

"The Alsace Winery, out on the highway? The one with a cellar full of vintage wine?"

"That property was repossessed by us almost two years ago. Since then, we've had it up for sale but there haven't been any interested buyers."

"Absurd," I said. "Graham had the listing."

"Quincy Graham did *not*," the loan officer said forcefully, looking almost apologetic after he exploded. His washed-out eyes darted from me to the bank president and back. He was on firm ground, but he worried that a fault might lie underneath that would crack and send him to the fiery pits of hell.

"Repeat that," I asked, frowning. "You're saying his realty company didn't have an exclusive on it?"

"We had it listed for almost a year with a major national realty company. It was decided to keep the property on our books as a nonperforming loan after that contract expired and attempt to sell it ourselves and save the eight-percent commission. And what wine cellar do you mean?"

"The Alsace has a million dollars worth of bottled wine in its cellars, that's what wine. That is part of the reason—"

"There is no wine. The former owners had been selling bits and pieces of the winery for almost a year prior to declaring Chapter Seven."

I blinked. The owners hadn't even tried for a court-ordered debt restructuring. They had simply thrown in the financial towel and walked away from the property.

"Their equity," I started.

Lowenthal got an even more pained expression. This was his albatross, and he didn't like people reminding him in front of his boss how he had been taken.

"There was a complex loan structure on the Alsace," he explained. "The amount of equity was quite small. This isn't too unusual, as you probably know."

I didn't but nodded as if I did. This was taking on the air of heavy motive for murder for Charlie Hayes. Nyushka had duped him with a fake channeling and he killed her, but not before he had invested heavily in the winery which Quincy Graham wasn't even legally empowered to sell. Any title search, any guaranty of ownership, had to be faked. What had Charlie received in way of surety on the title? I doubted it was anything a lawyer would have allowed.

All for Katrina, he had done it all for Katrina.

"Naturally, since we are the owners of record, we'd be happy to discuss selling the property. . . ." Lowenthal's voice trailed off when I scowled harshly at him.

"We have already given Graham a sizable sum. He said he deposited it with your escrow department."

"Here? No, I'd know of that," the president said.

"Can you check his account and see if a deposit of two hundred fifty thousand was made last week." The amount was large and it was close enough to yesterday's date that Charlie's transfer ought to show up if they ran Graham's entire account onto the VDT screen.

"There was a large sum that transferred yesterday," Lowenthal said, "but it had nothing to do with the Alsace property. Mr. Graham was only holding the money temporarily for another party who wished to make a purchase elsewhere."

"You were parking funds for him? Isn't that illegal?"

"No, not at all, Mr. Thorne," said Lowenthal. "We do it all—"

The president shook his head curtly and Lowenthal shut up. I wanted to hear the frantic young man continue running off at the mouth. As far as the bank was concerned, the money Charlie had transferred wasn't Graham's but someone else's. The president punched at the keyboard and finally got an account up, but I couldn't see it. Sometimes, if the light is just right, reflections on glass behind a person will give a hint as to what they're looking at. The large plate glass window facing out on the ocean reflected only a dim green rectangle, not enough to ever read the details.

"This is—"

I turned and sent the flash paper out into the lobby. The sudden eruption of flame startled two customers and brought a guard running. I yelped, as if I'd had nothing to do with it. My cries only added fuel to the panic to find out where the gout of fire had come from.

"A gas leak!" I cried. "The floor!"

The president and Lowenthal shot to their feet and hurried to see what was happening. I bumped into Lowenthal, recoiled and staggered behind the president's desk. My foot stuck out just enough to trip the vice president and send him flailing facedown into the lobby. The addition of the last of my flash paper added to the budding chaos.

I had only seconds, but it was enough for me to verify what had been said. The last transaction in Graham's business account was six and a half million dollars, but it had resided in the bank for less than five seconds. The computer had coughed, accepted the entire amount from Charlie's bank in San Francisco, then shipped it electronically to an offshore bank.

The World Bank of the Grand Cayman Islands sounded like the kind of place money laundering was done.

"What happened?" I asked, stalling for a few more seconds when I saw the president returning to his desk. I glanced down the list and saw other amounts sent to the same bank, but to different account numbers. Whatever Graham had been up to had been going on for some time.

"Nothing we can find." The man waved his hand to get me out from behind his desk. I moved around the desk, my fingers working quickly to erase the screen display. When the man sat, he glanced up at me, then grunted. He worked another few seconds to get the information back, thinking I had seen only blank screen.

"You find any evidence of Graham depositing our escrow money?" I demanded, shifting to attack.

"That must be between you and Mr. Graham. We have no record of it. And Mr. Lowenthal assures me Quincy Graham did not represent us in the Alsace Winery matter. If you are interested—"

"I'll be in touch after I've discussed this with my principals," I said, standing and leaving quickly. A small singed spot was the only evidence remaining that I had used the flash paper, but I felt all eyes on me until the heavy metal door had closed with the finality of a jail cell clanking shut. Outside the sun was setting over the ocean. It would have been a pleasant sight if it hadn't turned the sky bloody red. I couldn't help wondering how long it would take Culhane to link Nyushka and Graham in the scam to bilk Charlie out of millions.

When he did, Charlie Hayes was in a world of trouble. And for all that, I might be, too. Guilt by association looked to be the way Culhane operated.

CHAPTER 21

I had just put in a hard day's practice with Michelle getting the act into gear. There were still a few rough spots, but the mark of a good entertainer isn't so much having a perfect act as it is glossing over the mistakes when they happen—as they always do. I had been on stage with "flawless" equipment, only to have it glitch up in the middle of the trick. A line of patter helps, joking with the audience does also, but most of all it's a presence. It took years to develop. I'd worked a fair amount as a street performer where patter means the difference between going hungry and having enough to eat. This might be the hardest way in the world to make a few dollars, but I'd done all right at it. I have nothing but admiration for anyone trying to make a living working crowds of passersby intent on their own lives, not wanting a song or a trick or a clever bit of mime. In this respect San Francisco was better than many cities since there is such a huge flow of tourists through the city, all looking to be entertained at every turn and most of them willing to pay when they were.

I wasn't worried about the act anymore, though it would take a week or so to get into full swing with it once we got to Las Vegas. The blocking still bothered me, but the problems would come out as we worked, and the large pool of assistants I could draw on in Vegas might make up for minor problems.

But what did worry me was Charlie Hayes and the murders in San Tomás. I hadn't heard from him since I'd told him about Quincy Graham's death. After my brief foray into the Mendocino bank, I had tried to call him with what

I'd discovered, but Charlie had headed for parts unknown. His secretary only said that he was unavailable. That was better than being in a continual meeting or always being tied up on another line, but it went beyond that. I had reached his answering machine at home a half dozen times. Loath to leave too much information on a recording anyone could hear—or subpoena—I had only asked that he call me back.

He hadn't.

I wasn't sure what that meant. I wasn't sure what anything meant anymore. Graham had been funneling a lot of money through his bank to the Cayman Islands. From the look of the real estate market in San Tomás, he wasn't getting the money legally. And it would take federal hound dogs to sniff out where the money went after leaving the U.S.

The knock at the door startled me. Usually callers buzz up on the intercom next to the electrically locked front door. I hurried to the door and peered through the peephole. Willie Worthington shifted weight from one foot to the other as he stood impatiently. I had barely opened the door when Worthington barreled past.

"Glad you're in, Peter. Been doing some of your work for you."

"I'm always happy to see a new trick," I said, "but everything's worked out for Vegas. Maybe if it's—"

"Not that," he cut me off. "Here." He thrust a manila envelope at me. I took it more by reflex than intent.

"What is it?"

"If you'd open it and look you wouldn't have to ask silly questions like that."

I'd seldom seen Worthington so testy. He's usually a mellow enough fellow, even when dealing with his Neanderthal partner's hatred of anything that wasn't named Burnside. More than testy, Worthington was nervous. He walked to the window, peered out, swung around and started pacing.

"What's wrong?" I asked. "You look like a caged tiger."

"The damned vacation. I'm going nuts. I *want* to work.

And Mary's trying to kill me. God, I had forgotten how awful it was when I had to eat three of her meals a day."

"Considering what you eat when you're on duty . . ." I knew' his wife was a terrible cook, but there had to be more to it than choking down unpalatable food. Worthington had been having marital troubles; that was one reason he had taken the vacation time. Things must not be working out too well.

"I *enjoy* work," he rambled on. "There are millions of perps out there thumbing their noses at the law. What's wrong with wanting to put a few of them away where they belong?"

"Nothing," I said, knowing his problems went deeper than any civic duty. If he'd put as much time into his personal life as he did to thinking about how to nail felons, there might not be the strife in his marriage. Or maybe there would. Who was I to know what Worthington's personal affairs were like?

"Read the damned files. It took a while for me to get them. Damned shoddy work going on up there. This Ben Culhane isn't going to amount to a pile of dog shit. Piss poor work." Worthington continued to rant as he went to the kitchen and rummaged through my refrigerator. I doubted if there was much he would enjoy in it, but he was free to help himself. It gave me a chance to glance through the envelope without being distracted by his grumbling.

I thumbed through the thin set of papers he had given me. The additions to the death certificate he had given me before weren't enough to make Worthington gripe like this.

"Look at that coroner's statement," Worthington said, waving a sandwich he had made from odds and ends in my refrigerator. Some of the things sticking out from the sides of the whole wheat bread weren't easily identified. I wondered how long the sandwich's interior had been resting in my refrigerator turning into exotic biology experiments.

"So?"

"So, dammit, *look.*"

I finally saw what he meant. The technical jargon wasn't so esoteric that I couldn't follow it easily.

"He didn't really do an autopsy on Katrina, did he?"

"I'm not even sure he saw the body. Look at the description. It could have been a street person from Union Square for all the description he gave. Female, Caucasian, that's about it. He didn't even do a height and weight, much less sensible things like blood workups or drug screens. He just plopped a cadaver on his table and wrote this up."

"I met Dr. Weiss a couple times," I said, thinking hard. "He didn't look to be the soul of caring."

"Worse," Worthington said firmly. "This guy might have written that coroner's report because of what he was told. He might never have even seen the body."

"There are other things missing in the sheriff's report," I said. "There's nothing to show what was done with the body once it was removed from the car. He doesn't say it was sent to the morgue. He doesn't say it was sent to a mortuary. He doesn't report any disposition."

"Neither does the coroner. It's as if this body sorta slipped through their fingers and nobody noticed or cared."

I leaned back and laced my fingers behind my head. Putting into words what was running through my head wasn't easy. "Graham was up to something illegal in San Tomás," I said. "Don't ask too many questions, but I got a quick look at his bank account. Lots of money flowed through to a bank in the Grand Cayman Islands."

"He was a money-laundering spigot," Worthington said. "You know that?"

"Makes sense." Worthington was getting excited now. He gobbled his sandwich and didn't even know he was doing so. "He's fallen on hard times. Everyone up north has since the recession hit, the drought is forcing people to cut back, you fill in the reason. So Graham decides that the number one local crop deserves some of his attention."

"Crop? You mean grapes?"

"I mean dope," Worthington said in disgust, irked at my

naiveté. "There's more marijuana grown in Northern California than any other crop. Millions to be had."

"Millions in cash, and what do you do with cash in such a small community," I said, getting the idea. "Graham put through phony real estate deals—"

"Maybe not phony. He might have been selling property back and forth for big bucks. He sells it to his left hand and his right hand deposits the money."

"Then it goes through to the offshore bank, filters into a dozen corporations and comes back to him."

"He might just take a percentage," Worthington said. "But he knew the fake companies doing the buying and selling to each other since he was the agent of record. Who's to know? It's a little like masturbation."

Worthington was looking smug, satisfied that he had solved this portion of the puzzle for me. But there was more and it just didn't fit in, no matter how I squeezed and poked and tried to pry the pieces into place.

"That might explain why he was killed. A dope deal gone sour."

"He might have taken too big a cut," agreed Worthington.

"But I don't think so. There's more to this than Graham dipping into the local illegal economy." I thought even more while Worthington went to fix himself another sandwich.

Graham had the connections to handle a vast sum of money—such as the six and a half million Charlie Hayes had handed over for the property. I doubted there were any other partners in the Alsace Winery deal, just as there didn't seem to be any vast wine cellar of vintage wines waiting to be sold off for a quick buck.

"Nyushka was a local hire," I said. "She might have been good enough an actress to pull off the rigmarole required for a fake channeling." I tried to remember if Culhane had mentioned that she was a college drama major. I thought he had.

"Why do you say that?"

"She wasn't in your bunco files. She was a new player

in the game, maybe hired for the one performance. She might have been killed because she figured out what was really happening."

"So what was happening?" Worthington munched contentedly on his second sandwich. From the depths of a hidden cabinet he had found three large dill pickles and even some fancy crackers left over from a party I'd thrown a month ago. He didn't seem to notice or care that the crackers bent when he chewed them rather than going crunch. This flew in the face of Ralph Nader's assertion that Americans will eat anything as long as it looks good, tastes good and goes crunch.

"The reason her channeling was so damned good was that Katrina was supplying the information herself." I tapped the papers. "There's nothing identifying Katrina positively as the one who died in the wreck. It could have been any woman."

"I did notice that," said Worthington. "The only ID they got was the car and personal belongings."

I remembered the melted gold of her wedding ring. It had been in the wreck, and it had been Katrina's. She must have removed it and placed it on the finger of the woman who had gone over the cliff in the car.

"So what's the motive?" asked Worthington.

I didn't answer right away. I remembered the confusing mix of mental echoes after I had worked over the scene of the crime for Worthington where the woman had killed herself. It troubled me greatly, but what had really been in the middle of the muddle was a recognition of Katrina's feelings for Charlie. The suicide had hated her husband enough to frame him for murder. Katrina had hated him enough to set up this plot to make him think she was dead.

"Money. The six and a half million Charlie funneled through Graham's account. If Graham and Katrina were in this together, and I'll bet they were—"

"The wristwatch with his initials engraved on it," Worthington cut in. "Why was it still in the car? Or rather, how'd it come to get thrown out?"

"An oversight. But Katrina covered well during the

channeling. She knew I had detected her resonance in the watch and that lying wouldn't get her anywhere. She always was quick on the uptake. She invented the story about it being a thank you for Graham's work."

"Why is it more?" Worthington asked, becoming the devil's advocate.

"She had given him other expensive gifts. A fountain pen, for instance," I said remembering the vibrations I had gotten off the pen in the dead man's office. "She might have seduced him. It wouldn't have been hard," I said with some bitterness.

"Do you think she offed Graham?"

"She might have," I said. "And I think I know how she got to the second channeling session. I was watching carefully and Charlie and I had already searched the house. Nyushka wore a voluminous cape. It wouldn't have been hard for Katrina to sneak in under its cover, then leave while we were both inside the house."

"So she set her husband up to take a big fall."

"Katrina and Graham would have waltzed away with six and a half million dollars, everyone thinking she was dead and buried. She may have gotten greedy and killed Graham, once the money had sifted through the various accounts. It might be in Switzerland, in a numbered account only she can reach, or it might have been shuffled around a half dozen more times in the Bahamas. Anyway, I think she knows how to get the money and there's nobody left who knows she is alive."

"Sounds farfetched," said Worthington, "but there's one way of telling if this is a pipe dream or reality."

"Weiss could be bought. Culhane might have been. Or maybe they were just doing Quincy Graham a favor and expediting the accident report and death certificate. We might never know, and I don't think either of them will confess." The more I considered it, the weak link in the chain had to be Dr. Weiss. The alcoholic coroner might crack if enough pressure was applied.

"That's not the way I meant, Peter."

I swallowed hard, knowing what he'd meant. "I'd rather try to get Weiss to confess," I said. I didn't have much stomach for getting an exhumation order and opening the coffin I had watched being buried.

CHAPTER 22

It had all come together perfectly in my head, and I didn't like it. Charlie had been a dupe, and Katrina was responsible for stealing six and a half million from him—and possibly for killing three people who got in her way.

Who the woman was in the car was beyond my ability to find out, especially since she had been buried in Katrina's grave, but an exhumation might give her identity if dental records could be compared to anyone listed as missing. If she was a street person Katrina had simply killed, there might be no chance at all of ever identifying her. I doubted there would be any artifact buried with her that might identify her. Katrina would have replaced everything that might give a clue to the woman's real identity with rings and other possessions. Her only mistake had been leaving Quincy Graham's present in the car, and that was a minor oversight for such a plan.

I had held her wedding ring and had felt the heat and death. The woman in the car had died when it plunged over the cliff and had caught fire.

Katrina being a cold-blooded murderer was hard for me to accept, yet that was the only possibility I saw. She had killed Nyushka—Carol Nyquist—when the woman had either balked or outlived her usefulness as a medium. And Graham? That was even easier to understand. She knew where the money had gone and had a way of accessing it through the offshore bank. Graham simply was an unwanted partner at this point, probably nothing more than a fool kept in line by the lure of money and sex. Dropping the carbon tetrachloride into his liquor would be an easy and fast way of handling the problem of removing this spot on her plans. She was probably long gone, but I had to get the police on her trail. Ben Culhane wasn't the one to do it. If she had fled across state lines, the FBI was the logical agency to contact.

But proof. I needed proof and a way of keeping Charlie and me out of the investigation as much as possible. His financial dealings wouldn't stand up to scrutiny, not that he was going to get away scot-free on this. The people he had optioned his stock to would want to be paid off, either in RadChipTech stock or money, and he simply couldn't do it.

No one commits a crime like this without leaving some evidence behind, though what evidence there was pointed squarely at Charlie. Where had their marriage gone wrong? Why had Katrina hated him so? Katrina had always been used to money, and when she'd married Charlie there had been more than she'd ever seen in her life from his company. But the past two years had been hard. This might have been her way of getting out of a marriage she considered a dead end—and getting money she never would have any other way. A divorce settlement of even half of RadChipTech wouldn't have brought her six and a half million.

But such hatred was almost more than I could believe and left me grasping for some other explanation, any other explanation. I tried to sort out everything from the suicide Worthington had brought my way to the vague psychometry and the similar resonances. I had confused them, mistaking feelings I'd received from the channeling as a residue from the suicide.

"Evidence," I muttered, knowing where it was most likely to be found. If the coroner wasn't paid off, he had to be a complete fool. The times I'd seen Dr. Weiss didn't give me much hope of worming anything worthwhile from him, no matter what the reason for his sloppy work.

I wheeled north, wondering if I might convince the auto club to give me a discount for the thousands of miles of driving I had done. Tires, gasoline, wear and tear, I was using it all in just the past ten days. I entered Mendocino slowly, looking this way and that for any sign of Culhane or his deputy. I didn't want to cross them, and I certainly didn't want to be seen by any of the bank officers. Culhane would have talked to them by now about Graham's death. The realtor's checking account would be impounded, and Lowenthal would have gratefully spun the sheriff a good yarn about my interest in the records. It might not get the young vice president off the hook entirely for the discrepancies in the account, but it might help.

I turned down a side street, heading toward the ocean and a tiny knot of wood buildings containing restaurants, curio stores and other businesses aimed solely at the tourist trade. It took almost ten minutes for me to find a pay phone with an intact telephone book.

Leafing through the pages revealed only a handful of doctors and a single entry for Dr. Conrad Weiss. There wasn't any indication that he doubled as the coroner, but I hadn't expected it to. Coroners don't need to advertise. I read the address twice and committed it to memory, then replaced the phone book in its sheltered niche. What the telephone's patrons hadn't done to the book, wind and salt-water had.

I bought a map of the town and surrounding area for two dollars from a vendor and set off on foot, not seeing any reason to drive when my destination was only a quarter mile up a steep hill. But from the coast everything is uphill. I trudged past two-story frame houses, some well-tended but most needing paint and repairs. These places did little to bolster the image of Mendocino, but then again they were off the beaten path. Only a local was likely to see them, and every town has its slum section.

A simple shingle swung in the wind. The paint was peeling and made reading it difficult, but the sign did say this was the office of Conrad Weiss. I pushed through the gate, fighting against rusted hinges and swollen wood. Either Weiss didn't see many patients or they were all in good shape. I had to dodge through loose flagstones in the walk, and making it up the steps was akin to braving a mine field. More than one board slipped under my foot and threatened to send my leg down into the dank hell beneath the front porch.

I punched the doorbell but heard nothing inside. A second try didn't get me any more response, so I knocked. This time I heard movement inside, mostly grumbling and grousing at being disturbed. The house's walls weren't thick enough to cover the complaints.

"What's it?" Weiss blinked at the sunlight pouring onto the porch from the east. His hair hadn't been combed and stood up in thick spikes in mockery of a punk hairdo, and the smell of his liquor breath came at me like a charging bull.

"Dr. Weiss, my name's Peter Thorne. I need to talk to you about the autopsy you did on Katrina Hayes."

"Whatsamatter?" He rubbed his eyes with shaking hands but didn't produce anything approaching clarity. Weiss shook his head and looked as if he regretted this minor mistake. He groped around at a table near the door, for what I couldn't guess. It surprised me that he found a bottle of scotch with enough liquor still in it for a stiff drink. The doctor knocked it back, made a face and finally said, "Didn't do an autopsy. Wasn't necessary. Obvious why she died."

"May I come in and discuss this a little more?" Peering past him I knew he didn't get many patients. The interior of the house was a mess. I'm not the most orderly housekeeper in the world, but there is a vast difference between clutter and outright filth. For a doctor, Weiss had no conception of what sepsis meant.

"Suppose so. Don't get up this early." He motioned for me to enter. I wondered at how early he did rise. He was fully dressed, but the wrinkles told me he had probably slept in the clothes. That's one way to always be ready if the sheriff calls you out to look at still another corpse. Weiss didn't do it to be prepared, though. This was his usual mode of living.

The empty bottles sitting around the living room attested to that. He dropped heavily in an overstuffed wingback chair. I had to move a straight-backed wooden chair around to speak to him face to face. This was only one of the clues that told me Weiss didn't entertain often.

"A friend of mine in the SFPD went over your report on Katrina Hayes's death and pointed out a few missing items," I said, choosing my words carefully. "There wasn't any blood test for alcohol level, no drug screen, nothing to explain why she went over the cliff."

"She went over because that's a damned poor stretch of road. Been trying to get the county to fix it, put in a bank at the right angle, but there's never any money. Killed a bunch there, but the county says that's okay, they're mostly tourists and what's the difference?"

Weiss looked as if he could use more than the slug of scotch he'd already taken. His eyes began darting around the room, checking each bottle for even a trace of dampness left in the bottom. I'd already counted eight 750ml bottles, all completely drained. Unless he had a fresh bottle in some other room, he was out of luck.

"You just assumed it was the road?"

"The others have been."

"Not a single prior death had alcohol as a contributory factor?"

"What are you, some kinda lawyer? Hell, I don't know. Dead's dead. As long as they don't take anybody with 'em, why not give 'em a break? The family doesn't want to hear more bad news."

"What if Mrs. Hayes was murdered?"

"That's for the sheriff to decide," Weiss said. He ran his hands through his greasy hair in a crude combing that did nothing to get the cowlick in back to lie in place. "I don't remember the Hayes case too well, but I do know he told me that he didn't suspect any foul play."

"That's the way the report reads," I said. "But how do you know it was Katrina Hayes in the car?"

"Who else would have her driver's license, jewelry and keys to her car?" He rose suddenly and left, in search of more scotch. I heard a grunt from the next room, then a contented sigh. Weiss returned a few seconds later, looking more alert. His hands had steadied and there was clarity to his eyes that only a quick ounce of liquor could restore to an alcoholic.

"I consider the matter closed. If there's anything you need to know, take it up with Sheriff Culhane," he said in a firm voice. If I hadn't seen him a few seconds earlier, I'd never have known he was in the pits of a deep hangover.

"You didn't specify the disposition of the body. Why not?"

"Didn't know what the sheriff wanted done with it," he said. "I think it was sent to the San Tomás mortuary."

"It was, but isn't it your job to check before releasing the body?"

"This isn't the big city, Mr. Thorne. We do things in a more laid-back way. Now if you'll excuse me, I've got work to do."

"How long have you been coroner?"

"Can't remember exactly. Two years, maybe three. Now . . ." He rose and pointed toward the door. I heaved to my feet, knowing there wasn't any more I could get from him. He'd never be able to testify in court that the body he had examined was definitely Katrina Hayes. He might not have even looked at the body. Any mixup—or payoff—could have been Ben Culhane's doing.

I walked away from the tumbledown house, my hands shaking as badly as Weiss's had been when he came to the door. I knew what I had to do to get information that would interest the FBI, and it didn't please me at all. Of the many things I've been in my life, grave robber was never one. Until now.

Waiting until dark proved the longest few hours I'd ever spent. My mind kept coming up with all sorts of reasons I shouldn't do this, other than it was illegal. To go through the authorities I needed more evidence than I had. They would laugh at any psychometric reading, dismissing it as pure nonsense. I wasn't sure if even Willie Worthington believed my talent was for real. He used it, and me, because he had hard facts that it worked. But he might not have truly believed in the process since other logical routes might take me to the same answers.

I had accumulated what I'd need for my foray into grave robbing. Any number of movies had shown me the usual grave robber was a hunchback intent on stealing a body for his evil master to strip for parts. More than this, I knew I'd need a torch for light—I bought a Coleman gas lantern since this was the modern equivalent. A shovel with a short handle was always part of the grave robber's impedimenta; I opted for a longer-handled version since I was more than a foot taller than the hunchback seemed to be. Other twentieth century equipment I added for my benefit consisted of a pair of rubber gloves and a handkerchief to tie over my nose and mouth to block the inevitable grave odor. I had experience enough accompanying Worthington to the city morgue to understand the need for the latter. A short pry bar completed the heavy equipment. The only other item I was taking along was a small Kodak S-Series with a built-in flash. Pictures of a corpse in the ground for almost two weeks wasn't going to be much proof, but it would help get the court order for a proper exhumation.

The closed casket funeral hadn't been held because of extreme disfigurement, I didn't think. But if that had been the reason and the appearance of the body would not prove it wasn't Katrina, that left the distasteful process of psychometry. Finding out who actually was in the grave would let me backtrack and get the exhumation order from another direction. Either way it showed that Katrina was not dead.

Fretting and fussing, I spent the early evening hours just driving around, circling the graveyard like a vulture waiting for dinner to die. I had no sense of exhilaration as a vulture might, though. The dread growing inside made me want to chuck it all and see what Worthington might offer as an alternative.

By ten o'clock San Tomás was sound asleep or waiting for the news to be over so they could watch Jay Leno on the *Tonight Show*. I drove directly to the cemetery once I had it in my head that there wouldn't be a parade of people to disturb me. As I pulled into the small parking lot, I momentarily worried about teenagers coming here to park. Then I breathed a little easier. There must be a hundred better places deeper in the woods or along the coast. It was creepy thinking that anyone would want to make out at a cemetery, though I've heard of stranger things.

I felt as if I were moving all my belongings as I heaved my implements of excavation from the trunk of the car. Camera in pocket, rubber gloves under my belt, pry bar, lantern and shovel in hand, I made my way gingerly through the tombstones. I thought I knew exactly where Katrina's grave was. The darkness foiled me, and I ended up having to start over, then retrace my route from the day of the funeral.

Eventually I found the grave. The dirt hadn't yet begun to slump into a concave depression as wind and rain compacted the earth. A tentative poke or two with the shovel showed the dirt to be loose, which ought to make for easy digging. I laid my equipment down, got the lantern fired up with a propane hiss and put it close to the tombstone to keep the light from getting away from me and alerting someone in the parking lot that something was amiss. Paranoia runs deep among grave robbers.

I started digging, finding it harder work than I'd thought, not because of the physical exertion but because of my distaste for the task. If anything, the dirt was as loose as if it had been dumped in only a day or two earlier. Almost twenty minutes later I reached the top of the ornate casket. For the first time in my life I appreciated backhoes and other earth movers. Dropping onto the casket top, I began wiping the dirt off. It took another ten minutes to dig deeper around the perimeter so I could use the pry bar. A good twist, a loud screech of sealant breaking free, and the lid popped open.

Taking this as my cue to get out of the grave, I put the handkerchief over my nose and mouth and donned the rubber gloves. I checked the camera, opened the shutter cover and got the flash charging. Only then did I go back into the grave. I wanted to make this corpse viewing as quick as possible.

The pry bar lifted the coffin lid to expose the occupant. In a way I had hoped it would be empty. That would have cinched it. Katrina had faked her own death and had bribed the sheriff to just say someone had been in her car.

But there was a body in the coffin. Even wearing the filtering handkerchief, I found myself holding my breath until I turned woozy. I rose up out of the grave and moved the lantern closer until it cast its sharp white light directly onto the corpse's face.

My heart almost missed a beat. There was no question about it. Katrina Hayes was dead and in the coffin.

CHAPTER 23

My carefully constructed house of cards collapsed as I stared down at what had been Katrina. Some of the old clichés are completely wrong. There's nothing composed about death. Dead people look ... dead. I turned away, trying to remember her as she had been rather than the puffy, pale corpse she was now. The pain would be too much if this image displaced that of Katrina as vibrant and alive.

It wasn't going to work, and I knew it. I'd always remember her *this* way.

I went around and sat with my back against the stone marker on her grave, staring off into the darkness of the surrounding forest. It was almost a new moon, which suited me fine. Putting the coffin back together was beyond me. I had broken a seal and wouldn't be able to do anything about it. That only meant the decomposition would be faster than usual. I shuddered as images flashed through my mind of the obscene white worms eating away at lovely Katrina's body.

It had been so good, casting Katrina as the villain, of her running off to enjoy the fruits of her murderous crimes. As much as I hated to admit it, Quincy Graham might have been killed by the marijuana growers he did business with, and Nyushka? I could only guess. It might have been Charlie after all, enraged when he found the woman had been scamming him. That still didn't explain how Nyushka had been so uncannily accurate with everything revealed during her channeling session.

Dammit, I wasn't wrong. How could I be? Turning it all around in my head did no good. Conclusions weren't reached, and I was getting a headache from thinking too much. I settled myself and tried to work out other schemes for what had happened.

Charlie as villain. That didn't work. I had seen him at the channelings, and he wasn't that good an actor, even for six and a half million dollars. And how did he really come out ahead? Embezzlement of that much money would send him up the river for a lot of years, even if he was majority stockholder in RadChipTech. If he wanted to embezzle, there wasn't any reason to go to through the charade of channeling his dead wife's ghost.

Nyushka as villain. This worked up to a point. If she and Graham were in cahoots, fine. He could have killed her. But who killed him? I had to assume the drug dealers were in the picture again, a violation of Occam's Razor.

KISS, I told myself. Keep It Simple, Stupid. It might have happened that way, but it seemed to twist facts in a tight ball.

"Weiss never saw her body," I said out loud, talking to fill the eerie silence in the cemetery. "Culhane must have been bought off. That's a given. He's involved up to his ears since he's the law and he's in charge of investigating deaths. What would it take to buy him off?" I didn't have a specific amount in mind but didn't think it would be too much. His ambitions were small ones, and his idea of immense greed would make someone from San Francisco laugh.

"Culhane, Graham, Nyushka," I muttered. They had to be involved, but this didn't explain the expensive fountain pen at Graham's I had touched psychometrically. Katrina's presence had been strong. And the watch. The answer given by the spirit during the channeling was glib, but there had been a slight pause, as if whoever had spoken was considering the consequences. That the answer had been truthful still stunned me. It was an audacious chance, one I doubt Nyushka and Graham would have taken. Better to lie and try to gloss it over with other techniques. The channeling had been *damned* good.

"So who's got the money?" I wondered. "The drug dealers? Did they claim it because Graham was double-crossing them?" I sat and thought hard and long, knowing I was missing something. It only slowly came to me. I had seen but hadn't understood. Getting to my feet, I returned to the grave for another distasteful descent. I put the rubber gloves back on and slipped the handkerchief over my face like an old-time train robber. This time I moved the light so it shone directly on Katrina's battered face, the face I remembered with such longing.

Lovely, bruised face. Not a face ravaged by a car wreck or intense flames. She had not been wearing her wedding ring when the car burned. I hesitantly reached out and touched her flesh. It was rigid. I jerked back, irrationally fearing she might open her eyes and ask what the hell I was doing.

"Rigor mortis," I muttered. She hadn't been dead more than eighteen hours. Too many small facts had accumulated since I'd been working with Willie Worthington. Rigor mortis would have vanished when embalming was done. I swallowed a rising gorge and looked closer. There wasn't any evidence of a mortician's work on her. The contusions on her face were more indicative of a heavy beating with someone's fist than a car crash, even if she had bounced around inside the passenger compartment. And there were no burns, just the ugly blue and black bruises on her face and neck. Katrina Hayes rested in her own grave, but she had come here recently. Very recently.

The bruises on her neck let me make an educated guess how she had really died. Someone had choked the life from her.

I climbed out of the grave. Contacting the local authorities would be like putting the fox in charge of the henhouse. Worse, I might end up in a ditch with a bullet through my head. Johnny wanted to do it, and Culhane would unleash his rabid dog if any of this might tarnish his good name. And it would. I knew it would. Whatever the sheriff had done, even if it wasn't murder, he was in-

volved and would do time. Worthington had regaled me
with horror stories of what life in San Quentin was like for
a convicted lawman. Most didn't live very long—and they
were the lucky ones.

The FBI wouldn't be interested since I still had no proof
that a federal crime had been committed. That didn't leave
me many choices. I went back to my car and drove to a
filling station halfway between San Tomás and Mendocino
and made the long-distance call.

"Willie?" I almost shouted when the phone picked up.
"I need some help."

"What? Who is this?"

"It's me, Peter. I'm in San Tomás and need your help."
I had done too many psychometry sessions for him to help
nail felons who might have gotten away. It was time for
Worthington to help me. I explained as fully and coher-
ently as I could what I had found and what my guesses
were as to motives.

"Sounds flimsy," he said.

"So get out of bed, drive up here and do a better job."

"Can't hardly call the locals in, can you?" He made tiny
nibbling sounds over the phone as he came to a conclusion. Finally he said, "How long does it take to get up
there? I got to be out of my mind, but I'll be up to bail
you out."

"About three hours, but at this time of night there won't
be any traffic. Even though there's a stretch of unpaved
road, it's better to go through Ukiah. The coast road will
kill you with all its turns."

"Don't go doing anything foolish, Peter. I'll be there before you know it."

He must have flown in a jet. It was hardly two hours
later when I heard tires crushing the gravel in the parking
lot. I had turned down the lantern and put the shovel and
pry bar back into the trunk of my car. I began worrying
even more than I had over the last hours that this might be
Culhane rather than Worthington. It's a felony to open a
grave without a court order.

Improperly interfering with a corpse, the charge goes, as if anyone but Van Helsing could properly interfere with the dead.

"That you, Peter?" came the soft voice against the wind. "Where the hell are you?"

"Over here, Willie." I didn't call out as I wanted. I still didn't trust to fate that Culhane and a thousand deputies weren't lurking in the bushes just waiting to get the goods on me. It was a paranoid thought but being alone in a cemetery for hours—and having opened the grave of someone who had once meant a great deal to me—worked to steal my confidence.

"I knew there'd be hell to pay asking you to do all that work for me," he grumbled. "Mary's fit to be tied that you got me out of bed on the last night of my vacation. Last night we'll have together for a long time that'll be free of police business."

He walked around, looking at the grave from every possible viewpoint. Worthington finally bent and turned up the light from the gas lantern. "Better make this fast. Attracts bugs," he said, but I wondered what kind of insects he was talking about.

With an agility that belied his bulk, Worthington dropped into the grave and spent more than ten minutes examining Katrina's body. He finally jumped up, light as a feather, and rolled on the dirt, coming to his feet. He brushed himself off.

"The bruises were there before she died. So she was beaten, then strangled."

"Flesh doesn't bruise after the heart stops," I said, more to myself than Worthington. "And there was no attempt at cosmetics, as there would be at a mortuary."

"Maybe they skipped it," Worthington said, "since it was a closed casket affair. But that's just blowing smoke. She's just come to rest here, and you were right about her not having been dead more than twenty-four hours. The face and neck appear to be putrefying now, but the rest of the body is still in rigor mortis."

"There wasn't much trouble digging down," I said. "It

didn't occur to me that someone had recently buried her. I thought it was usual for the dirt not to have packed down."

"After a week? Naw," said Worthington. "It takes a few months to tamp down properly, but you'd have had a hard shovel getting to her. The grave diggers pack it down pretty well before they go. Otherwise there's a mound of unsightly dirt to deal with."

"What do I do now?"

"First, turn off the lantern, then stow it in your car. I'll go fetch the sheriff. He's the one who's got to see this."

"He had to be involved, Willie," I protested. "Culhane will just—"

"It won't matter what he has done. He's got to report it, because he knows what I'll do if he doesn't follow up on this. He may have shit for brains but he's not going to ignore this. My guess is that he'll bounce it up to his boss over in Ukiah and pretend to be as innocent as a little lamb."

"Culhane's not that good an actor."

"Wait and see." Worthington cleared his throat and, as if talking to himself said, "It'd be a real shame if all the tools vanished from the rear of your car before I got back. You know, just in case Culhane takes it into his head to search your trunk without a warrant." Worthington said nothing more as he turned and started for his car. He stopped and asked, "What time do you have?"

"What? It's just about four in the morning."

Worthington muttered to himself, then said, "Lemme wait awhile. I doubt if this Culhane gets to his office before dawn. Maybe not then. How much action can there be in a place like this?"

I didn't bother telling him that, counting Katrina, there had been three murders in less than two weeks. For a town with a population less than a thousand, this was an unparalleled crime spree. We sat and talked aimlessly, not quite discussing what might have happened, yet never too far from it. We both had theories but weren't up to putting them into words until they took a more factual form.

"Better go," he said after we'd whiled away almost two hours. "Remember what I said about the tools. Just toss 'em in a ditch and cover them with brush. It doesn't have to be too fancy."

Worthington went off, whistling tunelessly through his teeth. His hands were crammed deep in baggy pockets, and he seemed not to have a care in the world. This was a different man from the one who had badgered me while I was trying to put together my new act. Worthington belonged in harness, not on vacation.

He roared off like he'd just lit an afterburner on his car. I hurried to mine and followed him a ways down the road. He went north, toward Mendocino, and I curled around to the south and San Tomás until I found a potholed dirt side road. It took less than ten minutes to wipe the tools clean of my fingerprints and toss everything into a shallow trench. I moved enough dried brush to cover it. If Culhane was on the ball, he could trace the tools to me in a flash. The store owner would remember selling the equipment to me, and I wouldn't have a good explanation why I'd just tossed such new tools into a ditch. If luck held, there might not be any such questions asked. I hurried back to the cemetery and sat listening to an early morning radio talk show. I couldn't begin to concentrate and didn't know what the people were saying. Only their impassioned tones seeped through my heavy thoughts on death and Katrina and life after death.

Culhane came up with his cruiser's red lights flashing as if he expected trouble and big crowds. Seconds behind came Worthington. I got out of my car and waited, more exhausted emotionally than I was physically. The psychometries over the past two weeks had taken a toll on me, but not as much as knowing that Katrina was really dead—and that she had only been killed within the past two days.

"What's been going on here?" demanded Culhane.

Johnny wasn't with him. There just might be a God, after all.

"The grave's open. It's Katrina Hayes in it."

"You damned fool, of course it is. She was buried ten days back." He stormed over and shined his flashlight down into the hole.

Worthington and I stood back and waited.

"How'd this grave come to get dug up?" Culhane asked.

"Mr. Thorne just came by to pay his respects and found it this way," Worthington said.

"You haven't answered my question why you're up here, a big city detective and all."

"Vacation," Worthington said. "I'm due back on duty tomorrow. Well, this afternoon now. Time does fly."

"Everything you said about the condition of the body looks to be right, Sergeant," Culhane said, crouching down but not getting into the grave for a closer examination. "I'll have to get Doc Weiss to make a—"

"This is out of the league of an amateur ME," Worthington said. "This Weiss might be top-notch, but if San Tomás is like most rural places, he's not full-time."

"He's got his own practice, and he's up in Mendocino," said Culhane. "But I know what you mean. This might be better being carried by the county seat."

Culhane shone his flashlight in my eyes, but the beam had turned dimmer in the advancing sunrise. Bright rays sneaked through the limbs of the fir and pine to the east. It was working the way I'd thought. Culhane would try to wiggle out of being charged with filing a false report and gross negligence and probably taking a bribe. There were any number of lies he could tell and people he could blame for not having Katrina Hayes in this grave at the burial service. Weiss might take the blame or even Johnny. Culhane had to keep him around for more than his blind devotion.

I just hoped he wouldn't get away with his part in the crime. I needed to know for certain if Katrina had been the driving force behind this chicanery or if she had, in the end, just been the innocent victim. It was hard to believe the latter.

And then there were Graham and Carol Nyquist. And Charles Hayes. So many questions, and I was just now coming up with the answers.

CHAPTER 24

"How much longer do you think he'll keep us?" It was an hour into a new day, and I wanted to do something other than sit in Culhane's dingy office.

Worthington looked as anxious to be on his way as I was. He scribbled constantly in his spiral notebook and chewed ferociously at his pencil until I thought he was turning into a termite with yellow-flecked lips. He finally flipped the worn notebook cover shut and went to the phone like a homing pigeon finally seeing its roost.

"Wait a minute. What do you think you're doing?"

"Making a courtesy call," Worthington said, puffing himself up to intimidate Johnny. Worthington is a huge man, but I don't find him especially intimidating. The expression on Johnny's face told me others didn't see the jovial side. He hadn't been a cop for eighteen years without picking up some air of authority. Or maybe he'd always had it and I just hadn't been exposed to it.

"No personal calls."

"Then there's no problem. Listen in if you want." Worthington dialed quickly and waited as impatiently as I did. Johnny was wondering if he ought to fetch his boss. He didn't like Worthington using the phone, but the detective hadn't been charged with any crime. For that matter, neither had I, but my chance of bulling through to use the phone was nonexistent.

"Fred, hey, good to hear your voice again. Yeah, this is Willie. I'm over in San Tomás. Mendocino, really. Yeah, right. No, nothing of the sort. I'm working on a hot case. Triple murder, extortion, fraud, a bit of bunco, the works. Yeah, yeah, of course I will. Why do you think I'm calling?"

Worthington listened for several seconds, then said, "You're on top of it, aren't you? The Nyquist-Graham killings. We got one more added to it. Katrina Hayes, the woman who started it all. She wasn't killed in the car wreck a couple weeks back. Murdered within the last twenty-four hours."

He listened awhile longer, then laughed. "Doesn't surprise me. I'm in his office now. Talk to his deputy, will you?" Worthington thrust the phone out for Johnny.

"Who is it?" the befuddled officer asked.

"Captain Palermo, California Highway Patrol. He's got some real interesting things to tell you about Culhane."

Johnny took the phone and held it to his ear as if afraid of getting burned. He turned white as he listened. Worthington motioned to me to leave while the deputy was occupied. Outside, Worthington said, "Let's get the hell down to San Francisco. I don't think we're too late."

"Too late?"

"To finish this off and come out looking like a pair of certified, gen-yoo-wine geniuses. Get in. I'll drive."

"But my car—"

"Culhane won't be impounding it." Worthington chuckled as he grunted and slid behind the wheel. He fastened the seat belt with a dull click and then gunned the engine to a life I hadn't known was in the battered relic. Worthington slid a magnetically held red flasher onto his roof and then floorboarded the accelerator as if he were a Grand Prix racer. The pressure crushed me into the hard cracked vinyl seat as I struggled to get my belt fastened.

"What's going on?" I demanded. "What was it that turned Johnny into a zombie?"

"Captain Palermo is an old friend of mine. We started out together too damned many years back. He moved up fast. Me, I just sort of dawdled along."

I knew what Worthington really meant. His friend had played the political game better and had risen dramatically. Worthington was as sharp as any other detective, either on the SFPD or with the state police. Also, a captain didn't spend much time in the field. For Worthington, that was the only reason to be a policeman. Paperwork always took a backseat to finding the criminal.

"What'd he tell you about Culhane?"

Worthington chuckled again, this time holding back a real laugh. Even so, his belly quivered over the top of his seat belt. He took the curves on the road with dangerous speed, going into a four-wheel drift on many of them. Wherever we were going, it was in a big hurry.

"Culhane's been the object of an ongoing investigation for almost a year. They finally got the goods on him, and this might be the final reason for them to throw away the key to his jail cell. He's been on the take from the local dope growers. A few bucks here, a few there and he looks the other way, makes a phone call if he hears any rumbles from the DEA, that sort of thing."

"So he might have known Graham was laundering money for them." Things fit well, but there wasn't real proof. It must exist though, and the state police would find it. A warm feeling of satisfaction at helping get Culhane off the street, even for relatively petty crimes, rose inside me. This was what civic pride was all about, that and I had never liked the way he operated.

"Probably got the money from Graham. Good old Quincy's name was mentioned once or twice there. His death brought the investigation to a head. Seems the feds are interested, the state's interested, even the Mendocino County Sheriff's Department is, especially since one of their officers is in the dope trade up to his earlobes."

I closed my eyes to keep from watching the road and the way Worthington weaved in and out through the sparse traffic. In no time we hit 101 and were barreling along even faster. How this old bucket of bolts held together without falling apart was beyond me.

"You still with me, Peter? You're mighty quiet."

"Just composing my last thoughts before we die."

"It's not that bad. Hell, I drive faster than this inside the city."

I believed him. As we hurled down the road and got to Sausalito the traffic grew thicker. The morning rush hour traffic was starting in full swing, the commuters in Marin County flooding into San Francisco for another day's work doing who knows what for enormous salaries. Worthington didn't even slow as we hit the Golden Gate Bridge and the traffic there. He kept in the car pool lane and got across without hitting anything. The flashing light got us through the toll house and into the city itself.

"Where are we going?"

"To the airport, of course," Worthington said. "I wondered when you'd get up the nerve to start asking questions. My driving's not that bad. I passed the police course, after all."

"When?"

"Must have been ten years back. Maybe longer. What's the big difference?" Worthington sawed at the wheel, got us through the Presidio and farther south weaving and wobbling, swaying from side to side. I gave up praying for my life. If he hadn't killed us by now, our time wasn't up yet.

"The last hour's been a revelation," I said. "Your life doesn't flash before your eyes before you die."

"Good. Then you'll be able to help me with the collar."

"What do you mean?"

"I did some calling when we were back in San Tomás." He patted his radio. "There's only one flight leaving today going straight to the Bahamas. We might be in time to see it off."

"And keep someone from getting on," I said, suddenly more tired than I was scared. "You could just radio in. There are officers all over the place. We don't have to be there."

"Of course we don't have to be there, but it's more fun this way." Worthington sobered. "I'm sorry, Peter. I know you aren't getting a kick out of any of this. Excuse me my little joys of life."

I said nothing. There was only one way everything fit, and Worthington had pieced it together just as I had. He might have even arrived at the logical conclusion before I did. Score one for being a professional. Score another point for not being personally involved. We got to San Francisco International and did what I'd always wanted to do. We parked in a No Parking zone and hurried inside the terminal.

"You made it, Sarge. Didn't think you'd get down from Mendocino in time." The uniformed officer handed Worthington a sheaf of papers. Worthington barely glanced at them.

"Where is he?"

"About ready to make the bust."

Worthington glanced at me, then said, "Be discreet. I don't think there'll be any trouble, but you never know."

The officer nodded, then pulled out his walkie-talkie. A few seconds later he nodded curtly. "We got him," he said. "Holding room just past the ticket counters."

We almost ran to get there. Worthington went through first, but I crowded close behind. Charlie Hayes sat at a plain table, hands folded in front of him. He looked pale and drawn. This was about all I could expect of someone who had just murdered his wife.

"Hello, Peter. I never thought you'd be here."

"You never thought anyone would," snapped the uniformed officer. Two plainclothes detectives stood behind Charlie. Worthington turned and said something to the uniform, who blanched and backed out of the room. He motioned to the two detectives.

"You sure, Willie?" asked the taller of the pair. "He's guilty as sin. It's a righteous collar."

"I'm sure. Wait outside."

The one shrugged and the other looked as if he'd developed sudden indigestion. But both left. I slipped into the chair across from Charlie and stared at him. His lip quivered slightly and tears ran down his cheeks.

"I did love her, you know," he said. "When I found out she hadn't died in the wreck—"

"Have they read you your rights?" Worthington cut in.

"I don't care," Charlie said. "I killed her, and I admit

it. She and that real estate salesman were having an affair. She told me so." He almost choked. Biting his lower lip for a moment, he found the courage to go on. "They were having an affair, and Katrina cooked up this scheme to get the money."

"We've figured out what happened," I said softly. "She bribed the sheriff to say she was killed. The coroner is such a lush he'd never know if a body was there or not. Graham probably paid him off, too, to get the death certificate signed."

"Everyone was in on this," sobbed Charlie. "Nyushka was someone Katrina met in Mendocino. She thought she was doing little theater or something. She'd been scarred in an accident in college and that ruined her career. This was a chance to perform again, and who knows what all Katrina told her about the channelings."

"Charlie, you don't have to—" He cut me off.

"I wanted to kill her, Peter. It was almost an accident that I saw her, but I knew she had to be there somewhere. The channeling ought to have told me she was still alive. I never believed in that gibberish, not really. But I wanted to when I thought I could reach her after she'd died. God, I loved her. I did. And look at what she tried to do to me!"

"Where did you find her?" asked Worthington, working on his notebook with the stub of his pencil.

"At the real estate office. Isn't that rich? She had just poisoned him. I followed her but lost her in that podunk town. I kept looking. San Tomás isn't that big a place. It wasn't until yesterday morning that I found she was hiding out at that worthless winery. There wasn't any wine in the cellar, there wasn't even much in the way of land. Forged. That Graham forged the papers and I never checked."

The tears vanished and he sat at the table, slumped down, a hollow shell of the man I had known. "I followed her, and she laughed at me. She said she had all the money, that I was going to do time for embezzlement and she was getting away. I didn't mean to hit her, but I did."

"You beat her savagely," Worthington said. "And you

got her to tell you the account number in the bank. Isn't that right?"

Charlie hung his head and nodded.

"You were going to get the money and buy back your options?" I asked half hopefully.

Charlie Hayes looked up, and this time there was defiance in his gaze. "No, Peter, I was going to keep it. What else was there for me to do? Katrina was dead."

The taller of the detectives who'd gone outside stuck his head in, cleared his throat to get our attention, then called out, "Willie, we got the brass coming. You wrapping this up?"

Worthington looked at me and saw how I felt.

"We're done here. Let the circus begin."

And it was. Media ranging from the networks to the tabloids had a field day with the story of swindle, channeling and triple murder.

POLICE THRILLERS by
"THE ACKNOWLEDGED MASTER"
Newsweek

ED McBAIN

CALYPSO	70591-5/$4.50 US/$5.50 Can
DOLL	70082-4/$4.50 US/$5.50 Can
HE WHO HESITATES	70084-0/$4.50 US/$5.50 Can
ICE	67108-5/$4.99 US/$5.99 Can
KILLER'S CHOICE	70083-2/$4.50 US/$5.50 Can
BREAD	70368-8/$4.50 US/$5.50 Can
80 MILLION EYES	70367-X/$4.50 US/$5.50 Can
HAIL TO THE CHIEF	70370-X/$4.50 US/$5.50 Can
LONG TIME NO SEE	70369-6/$4.50 US/$5.50 Can

Don't Miss These Other Exciting Novels

WHERE THERE'S SMOKE	70372-6/$3.50 US/$4.50 Can
GUNS	70373-4/$3.99 US/$4.99 Can
VANISHING LADIES	71121-4/$4.50 US/$5.50 Can
BIG MAN	71123-0/$4.50 US/$5.50 Can
DEATH OF A NURSE	71125-7/$4.50 US/$5.50 Can

TAUT, SUSPENSEFUL THRILLERS BY EDGAR AWARD-WINNING AUTHOR
PATRICIA D. CORNWELL
Featuring Kay Scarpetta, M.E.

BODY OF EVIDENCE
71701-8/$5.99 US/$6.99 Can

"Nerve jangling...verve and brilliance...high drama... Ms. Cornwell fabricates intricate plots and paces the action at an ankle-turning clip."
The New York Times Book Review

POSTMORTEM
71021-8/$4.99 US/$5.99 Can

"Taut, riveting—whatever your favorite strong adjective, you'll use it about this book!"
Sara Paretsky

*Look for the Next Exciting
Kay Scarpetta Mystery
Coming Soon*

ALL THAT REMAINS